THE CASTING AWAY OF MRS.
LECKS AND MRS. ALESHINE

"THESE TWO WORTHY DAMES SPENT THE GREATER
PART OF THEIR TIME ON DECK."

THE *CASTING AWAY* OF
MRS. *LECKS* AND MRS. *ALESHINE*

WITH ITS SEQUEL *THE DUSANTES*

By

FRANK R. STOCKTON

WITH *ILLUSTRATIONS BY*
FREDERIC DORR STEELE

DOVER PUBLICATIONS, INC.
NEW YORK   NEW YORK

Published in the United Kingdom by
Constable and Company Limited, 10 Orange Street,
London, W.C.2

This new Dover edition, first published in 1961, is
an unabridged and unaltered republication of the work
first published by The Century Company in 1886,
1892, and 1898.

The illustrations in this edition are by Frederic
Dorr Steele and are from the original edition.

This edition designed by Geoffrey K. Mawby

Manufactured in the United States of America

Dover Publications, Inc.
180 Varick Street
New York 14, N.Y.

CONTENTS

THE CASTING AWAY OF MRS.
LECKS AND MRS. ALESHINE

PART I

MRS. *LECKS* AND MRS. *ALESHINE* DESERT A *SINKING* STEAMER

I WAS ON my way from San Francisco to Yokohama, when in a very desultory and gradual manner I became acquainted with Mrs. Lecks and Mrs. Aleshine. The steamer, on which I was making a moderately rapid passage toward the land of the legended fan and the lacquered box, carried a fair complement of passengers, most of whom were Americans; and, among these, my attention was attracted from the very first of the voyage to two middle-aged women who appeared to me very unlike the ordinary traveler or tourist. At first sight they might have been taken for farmers' wives who, for some unusual reason, had determined to make a voyage across the Pacific; but, on closer observation, one would have been more apt to suppose that they belonged to the families of prosperous tradesmen in some little country town, where, besides the arts of rural housewifery, there would be opportunities of becoming acquainted in some degree with the ways and manners of the outside world. They were not of that order of persons who generally take first-class passages on steamships, but the stateroom occupied by Mrs. Lecks and Mrs. Aleshine was one of the best in the vessel; and although they kept very much to themselves, and showed no desire for the company or notice of the other passengers, they evidently considered themselves quite as good as any one else, and with as much right to voyage to any part of the world in any manner or style which pleased them.

Mrs. Lecks was a rather tall woman, large-boned and muscular, and her well-browned countenance gave indications of that conviction of superiority which gradually grows up in the minds of those who for a long time have had absolute control of the destinies of a state, or the multifarious affairs of a country household. Mrs. Aleshine was somewhat younger than her friend, somewhat shorter, and a great deal fatter. She had the same air of reliance upon her individual worth that characterized Mrs. Lecks, but there was a certain geniality about her which indicated that she would have a good deal of forbearance for those who never had had the opportunity or the ability of becoming the thoroughly good housewife which she was herself.

These two worthy dames spent the greater part of their time on deck, where they always sat together in a place at the stern of the vessel which was well sheltered from wind and weather. As they sat thus they were generally employed in knitting, although this occupation did not prevent them from keeping up what seemed to me, as I passed them in my walks about the deck, a continuous conversation. From a question which Mrs. Lecks once asked me about a distant sail, our acquaintance began. There was no one on board for whose society I particularly cared, and as there was something quaint and odd about these country-women on the ocean which interested me, I was glad to vary my solitary promenades by an occasional chat with them. They were not at all backward in giving me information about themselves. They were both widows, and Mrs. Aleshine was going out to Japan to visit a son who had a position there in a mercantile house. Mrs. Lecks had no children, and was accompanying her friend because, as she said, she would not allow Mrs. Aleshine to make such a voyage as that by herself, and because, being quite able to do so, she did not know why she should not see the world as well as other people.

These two friends were not educated women. They made frequent mistakes in their grammar, and a good deal of Middle States provincialism showed itself in their pronunciation and expressions. But although they brought many of their rural ideas to sea with them, they possessed a large share of that common sense which is available anywhere, and they frequently made use of it in a manner which was very amusing to me. I think, also, that they found in me a quarry of information concerning nautical matters, foreign countries, and my own affairs, the working of which helped to make us very good ship friends.

Our steamer touched at the Sandwich Islands; and it was a little more than two days after we left Honolulu that, about nine o'clock in the evening, we had the misfortune to come into collision with an eastern-bound vessel. The fault was entirely due to the other ship, the look-out

on which, although the night was rather dark and foggy, could easily
have seen our lights in time to avoid collision, if he had not been
asleep or absent from his post. Be this as it may, this vessel, which appeared to be a small steamer, struck us with great force near our bows,
and then, backing, disappeared into the fog, and we never saw or heard
of her again. The general opinion was that she was injured very much
more than we were, and that she probably sank not very long after the
accident; for when the fog cleared away, about an hour afterward,
nothing could be seen of her lights.

As it usually happens on occasions of accidents at sea, the damage
to our vessel was at first reported to be slight; but it was soon discovered
that our injuries were serious and, indeed, disastrous. The hull of our
steamer had been badly shattered on the port bow, and the water came
in at a most alarming rate. For nearly two hours the crew and many of
the passengers worked at the pumps, and everything possible was done
to stop the enormous leak; but all labor to save the vessel was found to
be utterly unavailing, and a little before midnight the captain an-
nounced that it was impossible to keep the steamer afloat, and that we
must all take to the boats. The night was now clear, the stars were
bright, and, as there was but little wind, the sea was comparatively
smooth. With all these advantages, the captain assured us that there
was no reason to apprehend danger, and he thought that by noon of the
following day we could easily make a small inhabited island, where we
could be sheltered and cared for until we should be taken off by some
passing vessel.

There was plenty of time for all necessary preparations, and these
were made with much order and subordination. Some of the ladies
among the cabin passengers were greatly frightened, and inclined to be
hysterical. There were pale faces also among the gentlemen. But everybody obeyed the captain's orders, and all prepared themselves for the
transfer to the boats. The first officer came among us, and told each of
us what boats we were to take, and where we were to place ourselves on
deck. I was assigned to a large boat which was to be principally
occupied by steerage passengers; and as I came up from my stateroom,
where I had gone to secure my money and some portable valuables, I
met on the companionway Mrs. Lecks and Mrs. Aleshine, who expressed considerable dissatisfaction when they found that I was not
going in the boat with them. They, however, hurried below, and I went
on deck, where in about ten minutes I was joined by Mrs. Lecks, who
apparently had been looking for me. She told me she had something
very particular to say to me, and conducted me toward the stern of the
vessel, where, behind one of the deckhouses, we found Mrs. Aleshine.

"'DO YOU SEE THAT BOAT THERE?'"

"Look here," said Mrs. Lecks, leading me to the rail, and pointing downward; "do you see that boat there? It has been let down, and there is nobody in it. The boat on the other side has just gone off, full to the brim. I never saw so many people crowded into a boat. The other ones will be just as packed, I expect. I don't see why we shouldn't take this empty boat, now we've got a chance, instead of squeezin' our-selves into those crowded ones. If any of the other people come after-ward, why, we shall have our choice of seats, and that's considerable of a p'int, I should say, in a time like this."

"That's so," said Mrs. Aleshine; "and me and Mrs. Lecks would 'a' got right in when we saw the boat was empty, if we hadn't been afraid to be there without any man, for it might have floated off, and neither of us don't know nothin' about rowin'. And then Mrs. Lecks she thought of you, supposin' a young man who knew so much about the sea would know how to row."

"Oh, yes," said I; "but I cannot imagine why this boat should have been left empty. I see a keg of water in it, and the oars, and some tin cans, and so I suppose it has been made ready for somebody. Will you wait here a minute until I run forward and see how things are going on there?"

Amidships and forward I saw that there was some confusion among the people who were not yet in their boats, and I found that there was to be rather more crowding than at first was expected. People who had supposed that they were to go in a certain boat found there no place, and were hurrying to other boats. It now became plain to me that no time should be lost in getting into the small boat which Mrs. Lecks had pointed out, and which was probably reserved for some favored persons, as the officers were keeping the people forward and amidships, the other stern-boat having already departed. But as I acknowledged no reason why any one should be regarded with more favor than myself and the two women who were waiting for me, I slipped quietly aft, and joined Mrs. Lecks and Mrs. Aleshine.

"We must get in as soon as we can," said I, in a low voice, "for this boat may be discovered and then there will be a rush for it. I suspect it may have been reserved for the captain and some of the officers, but we have as much right in it as they."

"And more too," replied Mrs. Lecks; "for we had nothin' to do with the steerin' and smashin'."

"But how are we goin' to get down there?" said Mrs. Aleshine. "There's no steps."

"That is true," said I. "I shouldn't wonder if this boat is to be taken forward when the others are filled. We must scramble down as well as we can by the tackle at the bow and stern. I'll get in first and keep her close to the ship's side."

"That's goin' to be a scratchy business," said Mrs. Lecks, "and I'm of the opinion we ought to wait till the ship has sunk a little more, so we'll be nearer to the boat."

"It won't do to wait," said I, "or we shall not get in it at all."

"And goodness gracious!" exclaimed Mrs. Aleshine, "I can't stand here and feel the ship sinkin' cold-blooded under me till we've got where we can make an easy jump!"

"Very well, then," said Mrs. Lecks, "we won't wait. But the first thing to be done is for each one of us to put on one of these life-preservers. Two of them I brought from Mrs. Aleshine's and my cabin, and the other one I got next door, where the people had gone off and left it on the floor. I thought if anythin' happened on the way to the island, these would give us a chance to look about us; but it seems to me we'll need 'em more gettin' down them ropes than anywhere else. I did intend puttin' on two myself to make up for Mrs. Aleshine's fat; but you must wear one of 'em, sir, now that you are goin' to join the party."

As I knew that two life-preservers would not be needed by Mrs. Lecks, and would greatly inconvenience her, I accepted the one offered me, but declined to put it on until it should be necessary, as it would interfere with my movements.

"Very well," said Mrs. Lecks, "if you think you are safe in gettin' down without it. But Mrs. Aleshine and me will put ours on before we begin sailor-scramblin'. We know how to do it, for we tried 'em on soon after we started from San Francisco. And now, Barb'ry Aleshine, are you sure you've got everythin' you want? for it'll be no use thinkin' about anythin' you've forgot after the ship has sunk out of sight."

"There's nothin' else I can think of," said Mrs. Aleshine; "at least, nothin' I can carry; and so I suppose we may as well begin, for your talk of the ship sinkin' under our feet gives me a sort o' feelin' like an oyster creepin' up and down my back."

Mrs. Lecks looked over the side at the boat, into which I had already descended. "I'll go first, Barb'ry Aleshine," said she, "and show you how."

The sea was quiet, and the steamer had already sunk so much that Mrs. Lecks's voice sounded frightfully near me, although she spoke in a low tone.

"Watch me," said she to her companion. "I'm goin' to do just as he did, and you must follow in the same way."

So saying, she stepped on a bench by the rail; then, with one foot on the rail itself, she seized the ropes which hung from one of the davits to the bow of the boat. She looked down for a moment, and then she drew back.

"It's no use," she said. "We must wait until she sinks more, and I can get in easier."

This remark made me feel nervous. I did not know at what moment there might be a rush for this boat, nor when, indeed, the steamer might go down. The boat amidships on our side had rowed away some minutes before, and through the darkness I could distinguish another boat, near the bows, pushing off. It would be too late now for us to try to get into any other boat, and I did not feel that there was time enough for me to take this one to a place where the two women could more easily descend to her. Standing upright, I urged them not to delay.

"You see," said I, "I can reach you as soon as you swing yourself off the ropes, and I'll help you down."

"If you're sure you can keep us from comin' down too sudden, we'll try it," said Mrs. Lecks; "but I'd as soon be drowned as to get to an island with a broken leg. And as to Mrs. Aleshine, if she was to slip she'd go slam through that boat to the bottom of the sea. Now, then, be ready! I'm comin' down."

So saying, she swung herself off, and she was then so near me that I was able to seize her and make the rest of her descent comparatively easy. Mrs. Aleshine proved to be a more difficult subject. Even after I had a firm grasp of her capacious waist she refused to let go the ropes, for fear that she might drop into the ocean instead of the boat. But the reproaches of Mrs. Lecks and the downward weight of myself made her loosen her nervous grip; and, although we came very near going overboard together, I safely placed her on one of the thwarts.

I now unhooked the tackle from the stern; but before casting off at the bow I hesitated, for I did not wish to desert any of those who might be expecting to embark in this boat. But I could hear no approaching footsteps, and from my position, close to the side of the steamer, I could see nothing. Therefore I cast off, and, taking the oars, I pushed away and rowed to a little distance, where I could get whatever view was possible of the deck of the steamer. Seeing no forms moving about, I called out, and, receiving no answer, I shouted again at the top of my voice. I waited for nearly a minute, and, hearing nothing and seeing nothing, I became convinced that no one was left on the vessel.

"They are all gone," said I, "and we will pull after them as fast as we can."

And I began to row toward the bow of the steamer, in the direction which the other boats had taken.

"It's a good thing you can row," said Mrs. Lecks, settling herself comfortably in the stern-sheets, "for what Mrs. Aleshine and me would ha' done with them oars I am sure I don't know."

"I'd never have got into this boat," said Mrs. Aleshine, "if Mr. Craig hadn't been here."

"No, indeed," replied her friend. "You'd ha' gone to the bottom, hangin' for dear life to them ropes."

When I had rounded the bow of the steamer, which appeared to me to be rapidly settling in the water, I perceived at no great distance several lights, which of course belonged to the other boats, and I rowed as hard as I could, hoping to catch up with them, or at least to keep sufficiently near. It might be my duty to take off some of the people who had crowded into the other boats, probably supposing that this one had been loaded and gone. How such a mistake could have taken place I could not divine, and it was not my business to do so. Quite certain that no one was left on the sinking steamer, all I had to do was to row after

"'WE WILL PULL AFTER THEM.'"

the other boats, and to overtake them as soon as possible. I thought it would not take me very long to do this, but after rowing for half an hour, Mrs. Aleshine remarked that the lights seemed as far off, if not farther, than when we first started after them. Turning, I saw that this was the case, and was greatly surprised. With only two passengers I ought soon to have come up with those heavily laden boats. But after I had thought over it a little, I considered that as each of them was probably pulled by half a dozen stout sailors, it was not so very strange that they should make as good or better headway than I did.

It was not very long after this that Mrs. Lecks said that she thought that the lights on the other boats must be going out, and that this, most probably, was due to the fact that the sailors had forgotten to fill their lanterns before they started. "That sort of thing often happens," she said, "when people leave a place in a hurry."

But when I turned around, and peered over the dark waters, it was quite plain to me that it was not want of oil, but increased distance, which made those lights so dim. I could now perceive but three of them, and as the surface was agitated only by a gentle swell, I could not suppose that any of them were hidden from our view by waves. We were being left behind, that was certain, and all I could do was to row on as long and as well as I could in the direction which the other boats had taken. I had been used to rowing, and thought I pulled a good oar, and I certainly did not expect to be left behind in this way.

"I don't believe this boat has been emptied out since the last rain," said Mrs. Aleshine, "for my feet are wet, though I didn't notice it before."

At this I shipped my oars, and began to examine the boat. The bottom was covered with a movable floor of slats, and as I put my hand down I could feel the water welling up between the slats. The flooring was in sections, and lifting the one beneath me, I felt under it, and put my hand into six or eight inches of water.

The exact state of the case was now as plain to me as if it had been posted up on a bulletin-board. This boat had been found to be unseaworthy, and its use had been forbidden, all the people having been crowded into the others. This had caused confusion at the last moment, and, of course, we were supposed to be on some one of the other boats.

And now here was I, in the middle of the Pacific Ocean, in a leaky boat, with two middle-aged women!

"Anythin' the matter with the floor?" asked Mrs. Lecks.

I let the section fall back into its place, and looked aft. By the starlight I could see that my two companions had each fixed upon me a steadfast gaze. They evidently felt that something was the matter, and wanted to know what it was. I did not hesitate for a moment to inform them. They appeared to me to be women whom it would be neither advisable nor possible to deceive in a case like this.

"This boat has a leak in it," I said. "There is a lot of water in her already, and that is the reason we have got along so slowly."

"And that is why," said Mrs. Aleshine, "it was left empty. We ought to have known better than to expect to have a whole boat just for three of us. It would have been much more sensible, I think, if we had tried to squeeze into one of the others."

"Now, Barb'ry Aleshine," said Mrs. Lecks, "don't you begin findin' fault with good fortune, when it comes to you. Here we're got a comfortable boat, with room enough to set easy and stretch out if we want to. If the water is comin' in, what we've got to do is to get it out again just as fast as we can. What's the best way to do that, Mr. Craig?"

"We must bail her out, and lose no time about it," said I. "If I can find the leak I may be able to stop it."

I now looked about for something to bail with, and the two women aided actively in the search. I found one leather scoop in the bow; but as it was well that we should all go to work, I took two tin cans that had been put in by some one who had begun to provision the boat, and proceeded to cut the tops from them with my jack-knife.

"Don't lose what's in 'em," said Mrs. Lecks; "that is, if it's anythin' we'd be likely to want to eat. If it's tomatoes, pour it into the sea, for nobody ought to eat tomatoes put up in tins."

I hastily passed the cans to Mrs. Lecks, and I saw her empty the contents of one into the sea, and those of the other on a newspaper which she took from her pocket and placed in the stern.

I pulled up the movable floor and threw it overboard, and then began to bail.

"I thought," said Mrs. Aleshine, "that they always had pumps for leaks."

"Now, Barb'ry Aleshine," said Mrs. Lecks, "just gether yourself up on one of them seats, and go to work. The less talkin' we do, and the more scoopin', the better it'll be for us."

I soon perceived that it would have been difficult to find two more valuable assistants in the bailing of a boat than Mrs. Lecks and Mrs. Aleshine. They were evidently used to work, and were able to accommodate themselves to the unusual circumstances in which they were placed. We threw out the water very rapidly, and every little while I stopped bailing and felt about to see if I could discover where it came in. As these attempts met with no success, I gave them up after a time, and set about bailing with new vigor, believing that if we could get the boat nearly dry I should surely be able to find the leak.

But, after working half an hour more, I found that the job would be a long one; and if we all worked at once we would all be tired out at once, and that might be disastrous. Therefore I proposed that we should take turns in resting, and Mrs. Aleshine was ordered to stop work for a time. After this Mrs. Lecks took a rest, and when she went to work I stopped bailing and began again to search for the leak.

For about two hours we worked in this way, and then I concluded it was useless to continue any longer this vain exertion. With three of us bailing we were able to keep the water at the level we first found it; but with only two at work, it slightly gained upon us, so that now there was more water in the boat than when we first discovered it. The boat was an iron one, and the leak in it I could neither find nor remedy. It had probably been caused by the warping of the metal under a hot sun, an accident which, I am told, frequently occurs to iron boats. The little craft, which would have been a life-boat had its air-boxes remained intact, was now probably leaking from stem to stern; and in searching for the leak without the protection of the flooring, my weight had doubtless assisted in opening the seams, for it was quite plain that the water was now coming in more rapidly than it did at first. We were very tired, and even Mrs. Lecks, who had all along counseled us to keep at work, and not to waste one breath in talking, now admitted that it was of no use to try to get the water out of that boat.

It had been some hours since I had used the oars, but whether we had drifted, or remained where we were when I stopped rowing, of course I could not know; but this mattered very little; our boat was slowly sinking beneath us, and it could make no difference whether we went down in one spot or another. I sat and racked my brain to think what could be done in this fearful emergency. To bail any longer was useless labor, and what else was there that we could do?

"When will it be time," asked Mrs. Lecks, "for us to put on the life-preservers? When the water gets nearly to the seats?"

I answered that we should not wait any longer than that, but in my own mind I could not see any advantage in putting them on at all. Why should we wish to lengthen our lives by a few hours of helpless floating upon the ocean?

"Very good," said Mrs. Lecks; "I'll keep a watch on the water. One of them cans was filled with lobster, which would be more than likely to disagree with us, and I've throwed it out; but the other had baked beans in it, and the best thing we can do is to eat some of these right away. They are mighty nourishin', and will keep up strength as well as anythin', and then, as you said there's a keg of water in the boat, we can all take a drink of that, and it'll make us feel like new cre'tur's. You'll have to take the beans in your hands, for we've got no spoons nor forks."

Mrs. Lecks and Mrs. Aleshine were each curled up out of reach of the water, the first in the stern, and the other on the aft thwart. The day now beginning to break, and we could see about us very distinctly. Before reaching out her hands to receive her beans, Mrs. Aleshine washed them in the water in the boat, remarking at the same time that she might as well make use of it since it was there. Having then wiped her hands on some part of her apparel, they were filled with beans from the newspaper held by Mrs. Lecks, and these were passed over to me. I was very hungry, and when I had finished my beans I agreed with my companions that although they would have been a great deal better if heated up with butter, pepper, and salt, they were very comforting as they were. One of the empty cans was now passed to me, and after having been asked by Mrs. Lecks to rinse it out very carefully, we all satisfied our taste from the water in the keg.

"Cold baked beans and lukewarm water ain't exactly company vittles," said Mrs. Aleshine, "but there's many a poor wretch would be glad to get 'em."

I could not imagine any poor wretch who would be glad of the food together with the attending circumstances; but I did not say so.

"The water is just one finger from the bottom of the seat," said Mrs. Lecks, who had been stooping over to measure, "and it's time to put on the life-preservers."

"Very good," said Mrs. Aleshine; "hand me mine."

Each of us now buckled on a life-preserver, and as I did so I stood up upon a thwart and looked about me. It was quite light now, and I could see for a long distance over the surface of the ocean, which was gently rolling in wide, smooth swells. As we rose upon the summit of one of these I saw a dark spot upon the water, just on the edge of our near horizon. "Is that the steamer?" I thought; "and has she not yet sunk?"

At this there came to me a glimmering of courageous hope. If the steamer had remained afloat so long, it was probable that on account of water-tight compartments, or for some other reason, her sinking had reached its limit, and that if we could get back to her we might be saved. But, alas, how were we to get back to her? This boat would sink long, long before I could row that distance.

However, I soon proclaimed the news to my companions, whereupon Mrs. Aleshine prepared to stand upon a thwart and see for herself. But Mrs. Lecks restrained her.

"Don't make things worse, Barb'ry Aleshine," said she, "by tumblin' overboard. If we've got to go into the water, let us do it decently and in order. If that's the ship, Mr. Craig, don't you suppose we can float ourselves to it in some way?"

I replied that by the help of a life-preserver a person who could swim might reach the ship.

"But neither of us can swim," said Mrs. Lecks, "for we've lived where the water was never more'n a foot deep, except in time of freshets, when there's no swimmin' for man or beast. But if we see you swim, perhaps we can follow, after a fashion. At any rate, we must do the best we can, and that's all there is to be done."

"The water now," remarked Mrs. Aleshine, "is so near to the bottom of my seat that I've got to stand up, tumble overboard or no."

"All right," remarked Mrs. Lecks; "we'd better all stand up, and let the boat sink under us. That will save our jumpin' overboard, or rollin' out any which way, which might be awkward."

"Goodness gracious me!" exclaimed Mrs. Aleshine. "You set the oysters creepin' over me again! First you talk of the ship sinkin' under us, and now it's the boat goin' to the bottom under our feet. Before any sinkin' 's to be done I'd ruther get out."

"Now, Barb'ry Aleshine," said Mrs. Lecks, "stand up straight, and don't talk so much. It'll be a great deal better to be let down gradual than to flop into the water all of a bunch."

"Very well," said Mrs. Aleshine; "it may be best to get used to it by degrees; but I must say I wish I was home."

As for me, I would have much preferred to jump overboard at once, instead of waiting in this cold-blooded manner; but as my companions had so far preserved their presence of mind, I did not wish to do anything which might throw them into a panic. I believed there would be no danger from the suction caused by the sinking of a small boat like this, and if we took care not to entangle ourselves with it in any way, we might as well follow Mrs. Lecks's advice as not. So we all stood up, Mrs. Lecks in the stern, I in the bow, and Mrs. Aleshine on a thwart between us. The last did not appear to have quite room enough for a steady footing, but, as she remarked, it did not matter very much, as the footing, broad or narrow, would not be there very long.

I am used to swimming, and have never hesitated to take a plunge into river or ocean, but I must admit that it was very trying to my nerves to stand up this way and wait for a boat to sink beneath me. How the two women were affected I do not know. They said nothing, but their faces indicated that something disagreeable was about to happen, and that the less that was said about it the better.

The boat had now sunk so much that the water was around Mrs. Aleshine's feet, her standing-place being rather lower than ours. I made myself certain that there were no ropes nor any other means of entanglement near my companions or myself, and then I waited. There seemed to be a good deal of buoyancy in the bow and stern of the boat, and it was a frightfully long time in sinking. The suspense became so utterly unendurable that I was tempted to put one foot on the edge of the boat, and, by tipping it, put an end to this nerve-rack; but I refrained, for I probably would throw the women off their balance, when they might fall against some part of the boat, and do themselves a hurt. I had just relinquished this intention, when two little waves seemed to rise one on each side of Mrs. Aleshine, and gently flowing over the side of the boat, they flooded her feet with water.

"Hold your breaths!" I shouted. And now I experienced a sensation which must have been very like that which comes to a condemned criminal at the first indication of the pulling of the drop. Then there

"'STAND UP STRAIGHT, AND DON'T TALK SO MUCH.'"

was a horrible sinking, a gurgle, and a swash, and the ocean over which
I had been gazing appeared to rise up and envelop me.

In a moment, however, my head was out of the water, and, looking
hastily about me, I saw, close by, the heads and shoulders of Mrs. Lecks
and Mrs. Aleshine. The latter was vig-
orously winking her eyes and blowing
from her mouth some sea-water that had
got into it; but as soon as her eyes fell
upon me she exclaimed: "That was ever
so much more suddint than I thought it
was going' to be!"

"Are you both all right?"

"I suppose I am," said Mrs. Aleshine,
"but I never thought that a person with a
life-preserver on would go clean under the
water."

"VIGOROUSLY WINKING
AND BLOWING."

"But since you've come up again, you
ought to be satisfied," said Mrs. Lecks.
"And now," she added, turning her face toward me, "which way
ought we to try to swim? and have we got everythin' we want to take
with us?"

"What we haven't got we can't get," remarked Mrs. Aleshine; "and
as for swimmin', I expect I'm goin' to make a poor hand at it."

I had a hope, which was not quite strong enough to be a belief, that,
supported by their life-preservers, the two women might paddle themselves along; and that, by giving them in turn a helping hand, I might
eventually get them to the steamer. There was a strong probability that
I would not succeed, but I did not care to think of that.

I now swam in front of my companions, and endeavored to instruct
them in the best method of propelling themselves with their arms and
their hands. If they succeeded in this, I thought I would give them
some further lessons in striking out with their feet. After watching me
attentively, Mrs. Lecks did manage to move herself slowly through the
smooth water, but poor Mrs. Aleshine could do nothing but splash.

"If there was anythin' to take hold of," she said to me, "I might get
along; but I can't get any grip on the water, though you seem to do it
well enough. Look there!" she added in a higher voice. "Isn't that an
oar floatin' over there? If you can get that for me, I believe I can row
myself much better than I can swim."

This seemed an odd idea, but I swam over to the floating oar, and
brought it her. I was about to show her how she could best use it, but
she declined my advice.

"If I do it at all," she said, "I must do it in my own way." And taking the oar in her strong hands, she began to ply it on the water very much in the way in which she would handle a broom. At first she dipped the blade too deeply, but, correcting this error, she soon began to paddle herself along at a slow but steady rate.

"Capital!" I cried. "You do that admirably!"

"Anybody who's swept as many rooms as I have," she said, "ought to be able to handle anythin' that can be used like a broom."

"Isn't there another oar?" cried Mrs. Lecks, who had now been left a little distance behind us. "If there is, I want one."

Looking about me, I soon discovered another floating oar, and brought it to Mrs. Lecks, who, after holding it in various positions, so as to get "the hang of it," as she said, soon began to use it with as much skill as that shown by her friend. If either of them had been obliged to use an oar in the ordinary way, I fear they would have had a bad time of it; but, considering the implement in the light of a broom, its use immediately became familiar to them, and they got on remarkably well.

I now took a position a little in advance of my companions, and as I swam slowly they were easily able to keep up with me. Mrs. Aleshine, being so stout, floated much higher out of the water than either Mrs. Lecks or I, and this permitted her to use her oar with a great deal of freedom. Sometimes she would give such a vigorous brush to the water that she would turn herself almost entirely around, but after a little practice she learned to avoid undue efforts of this kind.

I was not positively sure that we were going in the right direction, for my position did not allow me to see very far over the water; but I remembered that when I was standing up in the boat, and made my discovery, the sun was just about to rise in front of me, while the dark spot on the ocean lay to my left. Judging, therefore, from the present position of the sun, which was not very high, I concluded that we were moving toward the north, and therefore in the right direction. How far off the steamer might be I had no idea, for I was not accustomed to judging distances at sea; but I believed that if we were careful of our strength, and if the ocean continued as smooth as it now was, we might eventually reach the vessel, provided she were yet afloat.

"After you are fairly in the water," said Mrs. Aleshine, as she swept along, although without the velocity which that phrase usually implies, "it isn't half so bad as I thought it would be. For one thing, it don't feel a bit salt, although I must say it tasted horribly that way when I first went into it."

"You didn't expect to find pickle-brine, did you?" said Mrs. Lecks. "Though, if it was, I suppose we could float on it settin'."

"And as to bein' cold," said Mrs. Aleshine, "the part of me that's in is actually more comfortable than that which is out."

"THEY GOT ON REMARKABLY WELL."

"There's one thing I would have been afraid of," said Mrs. Lecks, "if we hadn't made preparations for it, and that's sharks."

"Preparations!" I exclaimed. "How in the world did you prepare for sharks?"

"Easy enough," said Mrs. Lecks. "When we went down into our room to get ready to go away in the boats we both put on black stockin's. I've read that sharks never bite colored people, although if they see a white man in the water they'll snap him up as quick as lightnin'; and black stockin's was the nearest we could come to it. You see, I thought as like as not we'd have some sort of an upset before we got through."

"It's a great comfort," remarked Mrs. Aleshine, "and I'm very glad you thought of it, Mrs. Lecks. After this I shall make it a rule: Black stockin's for sharks."

"I suppose in your case," said Mrs. Lecks, addressing me, "dark trousers will do as well."

To which I answered that I sincerely hoped they would.

"Another thing I'm thankful for," said Mrs. Aleshine, "is that I thought to put on a flannel skeert."

"And what's the good of it," said Mrs. Lecks, "when it's soppin' wet?"

"Flannel's flannel," replied her friend, "whether it's wet or dry; and if you'd had the rheumatism as much as I have, you'd know it."

To this Mrs. Lecks replied with a sniff, and asked me how soon I thought we would get sight of the ship; for if we were going the wrong way, and had to turn round and go back, it would certainly be very provoking.

I should have been happy indeed to be able to give a satisfactory answer to this question. Every time that we rose upon a swell I threw a rapid glance around the whole circle of the horizon; and at last, not a quarter of an hour after Mrs. Lecks's question, I was rejoiced to see, almost in the direction in which I supposed it ought to be, the dark spot which I had before discovered. I shouted the glad news, and as we rose again my companions strained their eyes in the direction to which I pointed. They both saw it, and were greatly satisfied.

"Now, then," said Mrs. Aleshine, "it seems as if there was somethin' to work for"; and she began to sweep her oar with great vigor.

"If you want to tire yourself out before you get there, Barb'ry Aleshine," said Mrs. Lecks, "you'd better go on in that way. Now what I advise is that we stop rowin altogether, and have somethin' to eat; for I'm sure we need it to keep up our strength."

"Eat!" I cried. "What are you going to eat? Do you expect to catch fish?"

"And eat 'em raw?" said Mrs. Lecks. "I should think not. But do you suppose, Mr. Craig, that Mrs. Aleshine and me would go off and leave that ship without takin' somethin' to eat by the way? Let's all gether here in a bunch, and see what sort of a meal we can make. And now, Barb'ry Aleshine, if you lay your oar down there on the water, I recommend you to tie it to one of your bonnet-strings, or it'll be floatin' away, and you won't get it again."

As she said this, Mrs. Lecks put her right hand down into the water, and fumbled about, apparently in search of a pocket. I could not but smile as I thought of the condition of food when, for an hour or more, it had been a couple of feet under the surface of the ocean; but my ideas on the subject were entirely changed when I saw Mrs. Lecks hold up in the air two German sausages, and shake the briny drops from their smooth and glittering surfaces.

"There's nothin'," she said, "like sausages for shipwreck and that kind o' thing. They're very sustainin', and bein' covered with a tight

"'THERE'S NOTHIN' LIKE SAUSAGES FOR SHIPWRECK.'"

skin, water can't get at 'em, no matter how you carry 'em. I wouldn't bring these out in the boat, because, havin' the beans, we might as well eat them. Have you a knife about you, Mr. Craig?"

I produced a dripping jack-knife, and after the open blade had been waved in the air to dry it a little, Mrs. Lecks proceeded to divide one of the sausages, handing the other to me to hold meanwhile.

"Now don't go eatin' sausages without bread, if you don't want 'em to give you dyspepsy," said Mrs. Aleshine, who was tugging at a submarine pocket.

"I'm very much afraid your bread is all soaked," said Mrs. Lecks.

To which her friend replied that that remained to be seen, and forthwith produced, with a splash, a glass preserve-jar with a metal top.

"I saw this nearly empty, as I looked into the ship's pantry, and I stuffed into it all the soft biscuits it would hold. There was some sort of jam left at the bottom, so that the one who gets the last biscuit will have somethin' of a little spread on it. And now, Mrs. Lecks," she continued triumphantly, as she unscrewed the top, "that rubber ring has kept 'em as dry as chips. I'm mighty glad of it, for I had trouble enough gettin' this jar into my pocket, and gettin' it out, too, for that matter."

Floating thus, with our hands and shoulders above the water, we made a very good meal from the sausages and soft biscuit.

"Barb'ry Aleshine," said Mrs. Lecks, as her friend proceeded to cut the second sausage, "don't you lay that knife down, when you've done with it, as if 't was an oar; for if you do it'll sink, as like as not, about six miles. I've read that the ocean is as deep as that in some places."

"Goodness gracious me!" exclaimed Mrs. Aleshine, "I hope we are not over one of them deep spots."

"There's no knowin'," said Mrs. Lecks, "but if it's more comfortin' to think it's shallerer, we'll make up our minds that way. Now, then," she continued, "we'll finish off this meal with a little somethin' to drink. I'm not given to takin' spirits, but I never travel without a little whisky, ready mixed with water, to take if it should be needed."

So saying, she produced from one of her pockets a whisky-flask tightly corked, and of its contents we each took a sip, Mrs. Aleshine remarking that, leaving out being chilled or colicky, we were never likely to need it more than now.

Thus refreshed and strengthened, Mrs. Lecks and Mrs. Aleshine took up their oars, while I swam slightly in advance, as before. When, with occasional intermissions of rest, and a good deal of desultory conversation, we had swept and swam for about an hour, Mrs. Lecks suddenly exclaimed: "I can see that thing ever so much plainer now, and I don't believe it's a ship at all. To me it looks like bushes."

"You're mighty long-sighted without your specs," said Mrs. Aleshine, "and I'm not sure but what you're right."

For ten minutes or more I had been puzzling over the shape of the dark spot, which was now nearly all the time in sight. Its peculiar form had filled me with a dreadful fear that it was the steamer, bottom upward, although I knew enough about nautical matters to have no good reason to suppose that this could be the case. I am not far-sighted, but when Mrs. Lecks suggested bushes, I gazed at the distant object with totally different ideas, and soon began to believe that it was not a ship, either right side up or wrong side up, but that it might be an island. This belief I proclaimed to my companions, and for some time we all worked with increased energy in the desire to get near enough to make ourselves certain in regard to this point.

"As true as I'm standin' here," said Mrs. Lecks, who, although she could not read without spectacles, had remarkably good sight at long range, "them is trees and bushes that I see before me, though they do seem to be growin' right out of the water."

"There's an island under them; you may be sure of that!" I cried. "Isn't this ever so much better than a sinking ship?"

"I'm not so sure about that," said Mrs. Aleshine. "I'm used to the ship, and as long as it didn't sink I'd prefer it. There's plenty to eat on board of it, and good beds to sleep on, which is more than can be expected on a little bushy place like that ahead of us. But then, the ship might sink all of a suddint, beds, vittles, and all."

"Do you suppose that is the island the other boats went to?" asked Mrs. Lecks.

This question I had already asked of myself. I had been told that the island to which the captain intended to take his boats lay about thirty miles south of the point where we left the steamer. Now I knew very well that we had not come thirty miles, and had reason to believe, moreover, that the greater part of the progress we had made had been toward the north. It was not at all probable that the position of this island was unknown to our captain; and it must, therefore, have been considered by him as an unsuitable place for the landing of his passengers. There might be many reasons for this unsuitableness: the island might be totally barren and desolate; it might be the abode of unpleasant natives; and, more important than anything else, it was, in all probability, a spot where steamers never touched.

But, whatever its disadvantages, I was most wildly desirous to reach it; more so, I believe, than either of my companions. I do not mean that they were not sensible of their danger, and desirous to be freed from it; but they were women who had probably had a rough time of it during a great part of their lives, and on emerging from their little circle of rural experiences, accepted with equanimity, and almost as a matter of course, the rough times which come to people in the great outside world.

"I do not believe," I said, in answer to Mrs. Lecks, "that that is the island to which the captain would have taken us; but, whatever it is, it is dry land, and we must get there as soon as we can."

"That's true," said Mrs. Aleshine, "for I'd like to have ground nearer to my feet than six miles; and if we don't find anything to eat and any place to sleep when we get there, it's no more than can be said of the place where we are now."

"You're too particular, Barb'ry Aleshine," said Mrs. Lecks, "about your comforts. If you find the ground too hard to sleep on, when you get there, you can put on your life-preserver, and go to bed in the water."

"Very good," said Mrs. Aleshine; "and if these islands are made of coral, as I've heard they are, and if they're as full of small p'ints as some coral I've got at home, you'll be glad to take a berth by me, Mrs. Lecks."

I counseled my companions to follow me as rapidly as possible, and we all pushed vigorously forward. When we had approached near enough to the island to see what sort of place it really was, we perceived that it was a low-lying spot, apparently covered with verdure, and surrounded, as far as we could see as we rose on the swells, by a rocky reef, against which a tolerably high surf was running.

I knew enough of the formation of these coral islands to suppose that within this reef was a lagoon of smooth water, into which there were openings through the rocky barrier. It was necessary to try to find one of these, for it would be difficult and perhaps dangerous to attempt to land through the surf.

Before us we could see a continuous line of white-capped breakers, and so I led my little party to the right, hoping that we would soon see signs of an opening in the reef.

We swam and paddled, however, for a long time, and still the surf rolled menacingly on the rocks before us. We were now as close to the island as we could approach with safety, and I determined to circum-navigate it, if necessary, before I would attempt, with these two women, to land upon that jagged reef. At last we perceived, at no great distance before us, a spot where there seemed to be no breakers; and when we reached it we found, to our unutterable delight, that here was smooth water flowing through a wide opening in the reef. The rocks were piled up quite high, and the reef, at this point at least, was a wide one, but as we neared the opening we found that it narrowed very soon, and made a turn to the left, so that from the outside we could not see into the lagoon.

I swam into this smooth water, followed closely by Mrs. Lecks and Mrs. Aleshine, who, however, soon became unable to use their oars, owing to the proximity of the rocks. Dropping these useful implements, they managed to paddle after me with their hands, and they were as much astonished as I was when, just after making the slight turn, we found stretched across the narrow passage a great iron bar about eight or ten inches above the water. A little farther on, and two or three feet above the water, another iron bar extended from one rocky wall to the other. Without uttering a word I examined the lower bar, and found one end of it fastened by means of a huge padlock to a great staple driven into the rock. The lock was securely wrapped in what appeared to be tarred canvas. A staple through an eyehole in the bar secured the other end of it to the rocks.

"These bars were put here," I exclaimed, "to keep out boats, whether at high or low water. You see they can only be thrown out of the way by taking off the padlocks."

"They won't keep us out," said Mrs. Lecks, "for we can duck under. I suppose whoever put 'em here didn't expect anybody to arrive on life-preservers."

"It's my belief they're not at home," said Mrs. Lecks, after we had waited some time longer, "but perhaps we'll find some of the servants in," and she led the way to the back part of the house.

As we passed the side of the mansion I noticed that all the window-shutters were closed, and my growing belief that the place was deserted became a conviction after we had knocked several times at a door at the back of the building without receiving any answer.

"Well, they're all gone out, that's certain!" said Mrs. Lecks.

"Yes, and they barred up the entrance to the island when they left," I added.

"I wonder if there's another house in the neighborhood?" asked Mrs. Aleshine.

"I don't believe," said I, "that the neighborhood is very thickly settled; but if you will wait here a few minutes, I will run around this wall and see what there is beyond. I may find the huts of some natives or work-people."

I followed a path by the side of the garden wall, but when I reached the end of the inclosure I could see nothing before me but jungle and forest, with paths running in several directions. I followed one of these, and very soon came out upon an open beach, with the reef lying beyond it. From the form of the beach and the reef, and from the appearance of things generally, I began to think that this was probably a very small island, and that the house we had seen was the only one on it. I returned and reported this belief to my companions.

Now that Mrs. Aleshine had no fear of appearing in an untidy condition before "genteel folks," her manner changed very much. "If the family has gone into the country," said she, "or whatever else they've done, I want to get into this house as soon as I can. I expect we can find something to eat, At any rate, we can get ourselves dry, and lay down somewhere to rest, for not a wink has one of us slept since night before last."

"I should think," said Mrs. Lecks, addressing me, "that if you could manage to climb up to them second-story windows, you might find one of them that you could get in, and then come down and open the door for us. Everybody is likely to forget to fasten some of the windows on the upper floors. I know it isn't right to force our way into other people's houses, but there's nothin' else to be done, and there's no need of our talkin' about it."

I agreed with her perfectly, and taking off my coat and shoes, I climbed up one of the columns of the veranda, and got upon its roof. This extended nearly the whole length of two sides of the house. I walked along it and tried all the shutters, and I soon came to one in which some of the movable slats had been broken. Thrusting my hand and arm through the aperture thus formed, I unhooked the shutters and opened them. The sash was fastened down by one of the ordinary contrivances used for such purposes, but with the blade of my jack-knife I easily pushed the bolt aside, raised the sash, and entered. I found myself in a small hall at the head of a flight of stairs. Down these I hurried, and, groping my way through the semi-darkness of the lower story, I reached a side door. This was fastened by two bolts and a bar, and I quickly had it open.

Stepping outside, I called Mrs. Lecks and Mrs. Aleshine.

"Well," said the latter, "I'm sure I'll be glad to get in, and as we've squeezed most of the water out of our clothes, we won't make so much of a mess, after all."

We now entered, and I opened one of the shutters.

"I CLIMBED UP ONE OF THE COLUMNS."

"Let's go right into the kitchen," said Mrs. Lecks, "and make a fire. That's the first thing to do."

But Mrs. Lecks soon discovered that this mansion was very different from a country dwelling in one of our Middle States. Externally, and as far as I had been able to observe its internal arrangements, it resembled the houses built by English residents which I had seen in the West Indies. It was a dwelling in which modern ideas in regard to construction and furnishing adapted themselves to the requirements of a tropical climate. Apparently there was no kitchen. There were no stairs leading to a lower floor, and the darkened rooms into which my companions peered were certainly not used for culinary purposes.

In the meantime I had gone out of the door by which we had entered, and soon discovered, on the other side of the house, a small building with a chimney to it, which I felt sure must be the kitchen. The door and shutters were fastened, but before making any attempt to open them I returned to announce my discovery.

"Door locked, is it?" said Mrs. Aleshine. "Just wait a minute."

She then disappeared, but in a very short time came out, carrying a bunch of large keys.

"It's always the way," said she, as the two followed me round the back of the house, "when people shut up a house and leave it, to put all the door-keys in the back corner of some drawer in the hall, and to take only the front-door key with them. So, you see, I knew just where to go for these."

"It's a poor hen," said Mrs. Lecks, "that begins to cackle when she's goin' to her nest; the wise ones wait till they're comin' away. Now we'll see if one of them keys fit."

Greatly to the triumph of Mrs. Aleshine, the second or third key I tried unlocked the door. Entering, we found ourselves in a good-sized kitchen, with a great fireplace at one end of it. A door opened from the room into a shed where there was a pile of dry twigs and fire-wood.

"Let's have a fire as quick as we can," said Mrs. Lecks, "for since I went into that shet-up house I've been chilled to the bones."

"That's so," said Mrs. Aleshine; "and now I know how a fish keeps comfortable in the water, and how dreadfully wet and flabby it must feel when it's taken out."

I brought in a quantity of wood and kindling, and finding matches in a tin box on the wall, I went to work to make a fire, and was soon rewarded by a crackling blaze. Turning round, I was amazed at the actions of Mrs. Lecks and Mrs. Aleshine. I had expected to see them standing shivering behind me, waiting for the fire to be made; but instead of that, they were moving rapidly here and there, saying not a word, but going as straight to cupboard, closet, and pantry as the hound follows the track of the hare. From a wild chaos of uncongenial surroundings, these two women had dropped into a sphere in which they were perfectly at home. The kitchen was not altogether like those to which they had been accustomed, but it was a well-appointed one, and their instincts and practice made them quickly understand where they would find what they wanted. I gazed on them with delight while one filled a kettle from a little pump in the corner which brought water from a cistern, and the other appeared from the pantry, carrying a tea-caddy and a tin biscuit-box.

"Now, then," said Mrs. Lecks, hanging the kettle on a crane over the fire, and drawing up a chair, "by the time we've got a little dried off the kettle will bile, and we'll have some hot tea, and then the best thing to do is to go to bed."

"We'll take time to have a bite first," said Mrs. Aleshine, "for I was never so near famished in my life. I brought out a box nearly full of biscuits, and there's sardines in this, Mr. Craig, which you can easy open with your knife."

I piled on more wood, and we gathered close around the genial heat.

The sunshine was hot outside, but that did not prevent the fire from being most comforting and refreshing to us.

As soon as the kettle began to simmer, up jumped Mrs. Aleshine. A sugar-bowl and some cups were placed upon a table, and in a short time we were cheered and invigorated by hot tea, biscuits, and sardines.

"This isn't much of a meal," said Mrs. Aleshine, apologetically, "but there's no time to cook nothin', and the sooner we get off our wet things and find some beds, the better."

"If I can once get into bed," said Mrs. Lecks, "all I ask is that the family will not come back till I have had a good long nap. After that, they can do what they please."

We now went back to the house, and ascended the main stairway, which led up to a large central hall.

"We won't go into the front rooms," said Mrs. Lecks, "for we don't want to make no more disturbance than we can help; but if we can find the smallest kind of rooms in the back, with beds in 'em, it is all we can ask."

The first chamber we entered was a good-sized one, neatly furnished, containing a bedstead with uncovered mattress and pillows. Opening a closet door, Mrs. Lecks exclaimed: "This is a man's room, Mr. Craig, and you'd better take it. Look at the trousers and coats! There's no bedclothes in here, but I'll see if I can't find some."

In a few minutes she returned, bearing blankets, sheets, and a pillow-case. With Mrs. Aleshine on one side of the bedstead and Mrs. Lecks on the other, the sheets and blankets were laid with surprising deftness and rapidity, and in a few moments I saw before me a most inviting bed.

While Mrs. Aleshine held a pillow in her teeth as she pulled on the pillow-case with both hands, Mrs. Lecks looked around the room with the air of an attentive hostess. "I guess you'll be comfortable, Mr. Craig," she said, "and I advise you to sleep just as long as you can. We'll take the room on the other side of the hall; but I'm first goin' down to see if the kitchen fire is safe, and to fasten the doors."

I offered to relieve her of this trouble, but she promptly declined my services. "When it's rowin' or swimmin', you can do it, Mr. Craig, but when it's lockin' up and lookin' to fires, I'll attend to that myself."

My watch had stopped, but I suppose it was the middle of the afternoon when I went to bed, and I slept steadily until some hours after sunrise the next morning, when I was awakened by a loud knock at the door.

"It's time to get up," said the voice of Mrs. Lecks, "and if your clothes are not entirely dry, you'd better see if there isn't somethin' in that closet you can put on. After a while, I'll make a big fire in the kitchen, and dry all our things."

I found my clothes were still very damp, and after investigating the contents of the closet and bureau, I was able to supply myself with linen and a light summer suit which fitted me fairly well. I even found socks and a pair of slippers.

When I entered the kitchen, I first opened wide my eyes with delight, and then I burst out laughing. Before me was a table covered with a white cloth, with plates, cups, and everything necessary upon it; at one end was a steaming tea-pot, and at the other a dish of some kind of hot meat, and Mrs. Aleshine was just taking a pan of newly baked biscuits from a small iron oven.

"I don't wonder you laugh," said Mrs. Lecks, "but our clothes was still wet, and we had to take just what we could find. I'm not in the

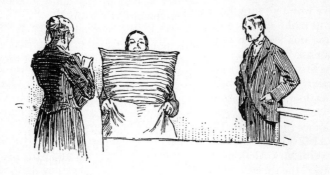

"'I GUESS YOU'LL BE COMFORTABLE, MR. CRAIG.'"

habit of goin' about in a white muslin wrapper with blue-ribbon trimmin's, and as for Mrs. Aleshine, I did think we'd never find anything that she could get into; but there must be one stout woman in the family, for that yeller frock with black buttons fits her well enough, though I must say it's a good deal short."

"I never thought," said Mrs. Aleshine, as she sat down at the tea-pot, "that the heathens had so many conveniences, specially bakin'-powders and Dutch ovens. For my part, I always supposed that they used their altars for bakin', when they wasn't offerin' up victims on 'em."

"Have you got it into your head, Barb'ry Aleshine," said Mrs. Lecks, looking up from the dish of potted beef she was serving, "that this house belongs to common heathen? I expect that most of the savages who live on these desert islands has been converted by the missionaries, but they'd have to take 'em from Genesis to Revelations a good many times before they'd get 'em to the p'int of havin' force-pumps in their kitchens and spring-mattresses on their beds. As far as

I've seen this house, it looks as if the family had always been Christians, and probably either Catholics or Episcopalians."

"On account of the cross on the mantelpiece in our room, I suppose," said Mrs. Aleshine. "But whether they're given to idols or prayer-books, I know they've got a mighty nice house; and considerin' the distance from stores, there's a good deal more in that pantry than you'd expect to find in any house I know of, when the family is away."

"It is my opinion," said I, "that this house belongs to some rich man, probably an American or European merchant, who lives on one of the large islands not far away, and who uses this as a sort of summer residence."

"I thought it was always summer in this part of the world," said Mrs. Lecks.

"So it is in effect," I replied, "but there are some seasons when it is very unpleasant to remain in one of those towns which are found on the larger islands,

"THAT YELLER FROCK." and so the owner of this house may come up here sometimes for fresh sea air."

"Or it's just as like," said Mrs. Aleshine, "that he lives somewhere up in the iceberg regions, and comes here to spend his winters. It would do just as well. But, whichever way it is, I can't help thinkin' it's careless not to leave somebody in the house to take care of it. Why, for all the family would know about it, tramps might break in and stay as long as they like."

"That's just what's happenin' now," said Mrs. Lecks, "and for my part I ain't goin' to find no fault. I don't suppose the people would have been so hard-hearted as to turn us away from their doors, but I've seen enough of folks in this world not to be too sure about that."

"How do you suppose," said Mrs. Aleshine, addressing me, "that the family gets here and goes back? Do they keep a private steamboat?"

"Of course they have a private vessel of some kind," I answered, "probably a yacht. It is quite certain that ordinary steamers never touch here."

"If that's the case," said Mrs. Lecks, "all we can do is to wait here till they come, and get them to send us away in their ship. But whether they've just gone or are just a-comin' back depends, I suppose, on whether they live in a freezin' or a burnin' country; and if they don't like our bein' here when they come back, there's one thing they can make up their minds to, and that is that I'm never goin' to leave this place on a life-preserver."

"Nor me nuther," said Mrs. Aleshine, finishing, with much complacency, her third cup of tea.

When breakfast was over, Mrs. Lecks pushed back her chair, but did not immediately rise. With an expression of severe thought upon her face, she gazed steadfastly before her for a minute, and then she addressed Mrs. Aleshine, who had begun to gather together the cups and the plates. "Now, Barb'ry Aleshine," said she, "don't you begin to clear off the table, nor touch a single thing to wash it up, till we've been over this house. I want to do it now, before Mr. Craig goes out to prospect around and see what else is on the island, which, I suppose, he'll be wantin' to do."

I replied that I had that intention, but I was quite willing to go over the house first.

"It's come to me," said Mrs. Lecks, speaking very gravely, "that it's no use for us to talk of the family bein' here, or bein' there, till we've gone over this house. If we find that they have, as far as we know, gone away in good health and spirits, that's all well enough; but if anything's happened in this house, I don't want to be here with what's happened —at least, without knowin' it, and when we do go over the house, I want a man to go with us."

"If you'd talked that way last night, Mrs. Lecks," exclaimed Mrs. Aleshine, "I'd never slept till after sun-up, and then got up and gone huntin' round among them frocks and petticoats to find somethin' that would fit me, with the quiet pulse I did have, Mrs. Lecks!"

To this remark Mrs. Lecks made no reply, but, rising, she led the way out of the kitchen and into the house.

The rooms on the first floor were very well furnished. There was a large parlor, and back of it a study or library, while on the other side of the hall was a dining-room and an apartment probably used as a family room. We found nothing in these which would indicate that anything untoward had happened in them. Then we went up-stairs, I leading the way, Mrs. Lecks following, and Mrs. Aleshine in the rear.

We first entered one of the front chambers, which was quite dark, but Mrs. Lecks unfastened and threw open a shutter. Then, with a rigid countenance and determined mien, she examined every part of the room, looking into every closet and even under the bed. It was quite plain that it was in one of the chambers that she expected to find what had happened, if anything had happened.

The room on the other side of the hall was very like the one we first examined, except that it had two beds in it. We next visited the chamber recently occupied by my two companions, which was now undergoing the process of "airing".

"We needn't stop here," remarked Mrs. Aleshine.

But Mrs. Lecks instantly replied: "Indeed, we will stop; I'm going to look under the bed."

"Merciful me!" exclaimed Mrs. Aleshine, putting her hand on her friend's shoulder. "Supposin' you should find somethin', and we sleepin' here last night! It curdles me to think of it!"

"It's my duty," said Mrs. Lecks, severely, "and I shall do it."

And do it she did, rising from the task with a sigh of relief.

My room was subjected to the same scrutiny as the others, and then we visited some smaller rooms at the extreme back of the house, which we had not before noticed. A garret, or loft, was reached by a steep stairway in one of these rooms, and into its dusky gloom I ventured by myself.

"Now, don't come down, Mr. Craig," said Mrs. Lecks, "till you're sure there's nothin' there. Of all places in the house, that cockloft, after all, is the most likely."

I had none of the fears which seemed to actuate the two women, but I had a very unpleasant time of it groping about in the darkness and heat, and, as the place was only partly floored, running the continual risk of crashing down through the lath and plaster. I made myself quite sure, however, that nothing had happened in that loft, unless someone had suffocated there, and had dried up and become the dust which I raised at every step.

"Now, then," said Mrs. Lecks, when I descended, "as there is no cellar, we'll go wash up the breakfast things; and if you want to take a walk, to see if there's any genuwine heathens or anybody else a-livin' in this island, we're not afraid to be left alone."

For the whole of the rest of the morning I wandered about the island. I investigated the paths that I had before noticed, and found that each of them led, after a moderate walk, to some wide and pleasant part of the beach. At one of these points I found a rustic bench; and, stuffed in between two of the slats which formed the seat, I found a book. It had been sadly wet and discolored by rain, and dried and curled up by the wind and sun. I pulled it out, and found it to be a novel in French. On one of the fly-leaves was written "Emily". Reasoning from the dilapidated appearance of this book, I began to believe that the family must have left this place some time ago, and that, therefore, their return might be expected at a pro-portionately early period. On second thoughts, however, I considered that the state of this book was of little value as testimony. A few hours of storm, wind, and sun might have inflicted all the damage it had sustained. The two women would be better able to judge by the state of the house and the condition of the provisions how long the family had been away.

I then started out on a walk along the beach, and in little more than an hour I had gone entirely around the island. Nowhere did I see any sign of habitation or occupation except at the house which had given us shelter, nor any opening through the surrounding reef except the barred passageway through which we had come.

When I returned to the house, I found that Mrs. Lecks and Mrs. Aleshine had been hard at work all the morning. They had, so to speak, gone regularly and systematically to housekeeping, and had already divided the labors of the estab-lishment between them. Mrs. Aleshine, who prided herself on her skill in culinary

"MRS. ALESHINE HAD BEEN HARD AT WORK ALL THE MORNING."

matters, was to take charge of the cooking, while Mrs. Lecks assumed the care of the various rooms and the general management of the house-hold. This arrangement was explained to me at length, and when I remarked that all this seemed to indicate that they expected to remain here for a long time, Mrs. Lecks replied:

"In my part of the country I could tell pretty close, by the dust on the tables and on the top of the pianner, how long a family had been out of a house; but dust in Pennsylvany and dust on a sea island, where there's no wagons nor carriages, is quite different. This house has been left in very good order, and though the windows wants washin', and the floors and stairs brushin',—which will be easy considerin' that none of 'em has carpets,—and everything in the house a reg'lar cleanin' up and airin', it may be that the family hasn't been gone away very long, and so it may be a good while before they come back again. Mrs. Aleshine and me has talked it over, and we've made up our minds that the right thing to do is just to go along and attend to things as if we was a-goin' to stay here for a month or two; and it may be even longer than that before the people come back. And I don't think they'll have anything to complain of when they find their house in apple-pie order, their windows washed, their floors clean, and not a speck of dust anywhere."

"For my part," said Mrs. Aleshine, "I don't see what they've got to find fault with, anyway. I look on this as part of the passage To be sure, we ain't movin' a bit on our way to Japan, but that's not my fault, nor yet yours, Mrs. Lecks, nor yours, Mr. Craig. We paid our passage to go to Japan, and if the ship was steered wrong and got sunk, we hadn't anything to do with it. We didn't want to come here, but here we are, and I'd like to know who's got any right to find fault with us."

"And bein' here," said Mrs. Lecks, "we'll take care of the things."

"As far as I'm concerned," added Mrs. Aleshine, "if this island was movin' on to Japan, I'd a great deal rather be on it than on that ship, where, to my way of thinkin', they didn't know much more about housekeepin' than they did about steerin'."

"I think your plans and arrangements are very good," I said. "But how about the provisions? Are there enough to hold out for any time?"

"There's pretty nigh a barrel of flour," said Mrs. Aleshine, "a good deal of tea and coffee and sugar, and lots of things in tins and jars. There's a kind of cellar outside where they keep things cool, and there's more than half a keg of butter down there. It's too strong to use, but I can take that butter and wash it out, and work it over, and salt it, and make it just as good butter as any we got on board the ship."

"But," said I, "you have given me nothing to do. I shall not be content to stand about idle and see you do all the work."

"There's nothin' in the house," said Mrs. Lecks, "which you need put your hand to; but, if you choose to go out into that garden, and see if there's anything can be done in it, or got out of it,—that is, if you know anything about garden work,—I'm sure we'd be very glad of any fresh vegetables we could get."

I replied that I had been accustomed to garden work in an amateur way, and would be glad to do anything that was possible in that direction.

"I never seed into that garden," said Mrs. Aleshine, "but of all the foolish things that ever came under my eye, the buildin' a wall around a garden, when a picket fence would do just as well, is the foolishest."

I explained that in these countries it was the fashion to use walls instead of fences.

"If it's the fashion," said Mrs. Aleshine, "I suppose there's no use sayin' anything ag'in' it; but if the fashion should happen to change, they'd find it a good deal easier to take down a barbed-wire fence than a stone wall."

This conversation took place in the large lower hall, which Mrs. Lecks had been "putting to rights," and where Mrs. Aleshine had just entered from the kitchen. Mrs. Lecks now sat down upon a chair, and, dusting cloth in hand, she thus addressed me:

"There's another thing, Mr. Craig, that me and Mrs. Aleshine has been talkin' about. We haven't made up our minds about it, because we didn't think it was fair and right to do that before speakin' to you and hearin' what you had to say on one side or another of it. Mrs. Aleshine and me has had to bow our heads to afflictions, and to walk sometimes in roads we didn't want to; but we've remembered the ways in which we was brought up, and have kept in them as far as we've been able. When our husbands died, leavin' Mrs. Aleshine with a son, and me without any, which, perhaps, is just as well, for there's no knowin' how he might have turned out—"

"That's so," interrupted Mrs. Aleshine, "for he might have gone as a clerk to Roosher, and then you and me would 'a' had to travel different ways."

"And when our husbands died," continued Mrs. Lecks, "they left us enough, and plenty, to live on, and we wasn't the women to forget them and their ways of thinkin', any more than we'd forget the ways of our fathers and mothers before us."

"That's so!" said Mrs. Aleshine, fervently.

"And now, Mr. Craig," continued Mrs. Lecks, "we don't know how you've been brought up, nor anything about you, in fact, except that you've been as kind to us as if you was some sort of kin, and that we never would have thought of comin' here without you, and so me and Mrs. Aleshine has agreed to leave this whole matter to you, and to do just as you say. When us two started out on this long journey, we didn't expect to find it what you call the path of roses, and, dear only knows, we haven't found it so."

"That's true!" ejaculated Mrs. Aleshine.

"And what we've had to put up with," continued Mrs. Lecks, "we have put up with. So, Mr. Craig, whether you say dinner in the middle of the day at twelve, as we've always been used to, or at six o'clock in the afternoon, as they had it on board that ship,—and how people ever come to turn their meals hind part foremost in that way, I can't say,—we are goin' to do it; if you've been brought up to six o'clock, you won't hear no complainin' from us, think what we may."

I was on the point of laughing aloud at the conclusion of this speech, but a glance at the serious faces of the two women, who, with so much earnest solicitude, awaited my reply, stopped me, and I hastened to assure them that dinner in the middle of the day would be entirely in accordance with my every wish.

"Good!" exclaimed Mrs. Aleshine, her eyes sparkling amid the plumpness of her face, while an expression of calm relief passed over the features of Mrs. Lecks.

"And now I'll be off and get us somethin' to eat in less than no time," said Mrs. Aleshine. "We didn't know whether to make it lunch or dinner till we had seen you, so you can't expect much to-day, but to-morrow we'll begin, and have everything straight and comfortable. I'm goin' to get up early in the mornin' and bake a batch of bread, and you needn't be afraid, Mr. Craig, but what I'll have you a bit of hot meat every night for your supper."

In the afternoon we all visited the garden, which, although a good deal overgrown with luxuriant weeds, showed marks of fair cultivation. Some of the beds had been cleared out and left to the weeds, and we found some "garden truck," as my companions called it, with which we were not familiar. But there were tomato-vines loaded with fruit, plenty of beans of various kinds, and a large patch of potatoes, many of which had been dug.

From the lower end of the garden, Mrs. Aleshine gave a shout of delight. We went to her, and found her standing before a long asparagus bed.

"Well!" she exclaimed. "If there's anything that settles it firm in my mind that these people is Christians, it's this bed of grass. I don't believe there ever was heathens that growed grass."

"I thought that was all settled when we found the bakin'-powders," said Mrs. Lecks.

"But this clinches it," answered her companion. "I can't tell from a sparrowgrass bed what church they belong to, but they're no idolators."

The next morning I delivered to the genial Mrs. Aleshine a large basket full of fresh vegetables, and we had a most excellent dinner.

Somewhat to my surprise, the table was not set in the kitchen, but in the dining-room.

"Me and Mrs. Aleshine have made up our minds," said Mrs. Lecks, in explanation, "that it's not the proper thing for you to be eatin' in the kitchen, nor for us neither. Here's table-cloths, and good glass and china, and spoons and forks, which, although they're not solid silver, are plated good enough for anybody. Neither you nor us is servants and a kitchen is no place for us."

"That's so!" said Mrs. Aleshine. "We paid our money for first-class passages, and it was understood that we'd have everything as good as anybody."

"Which I don't see as that has anything to do with it, Barb'ry Aleshine," said Mrs. Lecks, "for the steamship people don't generally throw in desert islands as part of the accommodation."

"We didn't ask for the island," retorted Mrs. Aleshine, "and if they'd steered the ship right we shouldn't have wanted it."

When we had finished our dinner, Mrs. Lecks pushed back her chair, and sat for a few moments in thought, as was her wont before saying anything of importance.

"There's another thing," said she, "that I've been thinkin' about, though

"'THERE'S ANOTHER THING,' SAID SHE, 'THAT I'VE BEEN THINKIN' ABOUT.'"

I haven't spoke of it yet, even to Mrs. Aleshine. We haven't no right to come here and eat up the victuals and use the things of the people that own this house, without payin' for 'em. Of course, we're not goin' to sleep on the bare ground and starve to death while there's beds and food close to our hands. But if we use 'em and take it, we ought to pay the people that the place belongs to—that is, if we've got the money to do it with—and Mrs. Aleshine and me has got the money. When we went down into our cabin to get ready to leave the ship, the first thing we did was to put our purses in our pockets, and we've both got drafts wrapped up in oil silk, and sewed inside our frock-bodies; and if you didn't think to bring your money along with you, Mr. Craig, we can lend you all you need."

I thanked her for her offer, but stated that I had brought with me all my money.

"Now," continued Mrs. Lecks, "it's my opinion that we ought to pay our board regular each week. I don't know what is commonly charged in a place like this, but I know you can get very good board where I come from for six dollars a week."

"That is for two in a room," said Mrs. Aleshine; "but havin' a room to himself would make it more for Mr. Craig."

"It ain't his fault," said Mrs. Lecks, somewhat severely, "that he ain't got a brother or some friend to take part of the room and pay part of the expense. But, anyway, the room isn't a large one, and I don't think he ought to pay much more for having a room to himself. Seven dollars is quite enough."

"But then you've got to consider," said Mrs. Aleshine, "that we do the cookin' and housework, and that ought to be counted."

"I was comin' to that," said Mrs. Lecks. "Now, if me and Mrs. Aleshine was to go out to service, which you may be sure we wouldn't do unless circumstances was very different from what they are now—"

"That's true!" earnestly ejaculated Mrs. Aleshine.

"But if we was to do it," continued Mrs. Lecks, "we wouldn't go into anybody's family for less than two dollars a week. Now, I've always heard that wages is low in this part of the world, and the work isn't heavy for two of us; so, considering the family isn't here to make their own bargain, I think we'd better put our wages at that, so that'll make four dollars a week for each of us two to pay."

"But how about Mr. Craig?" said Mrs. Aleshine. "He oughtn't to work in that garden for nothin'."

"Fifty cents a day," said Mrs. Lecks, "is as little as any man would work for, and then it oughtn't to take all his time. That will make three dollars to take out of Mr. Craig's board, and leave it four dollars a week, the same as ours."

I declared myself perfectly satisfied with these arrangements, but Mrs. Aleshine did not seem to be altogether convinced that they were just.

"When a woman goes out to service," said she, "she gets her board and is paid wages besides, and it's the same for gardeners."

"Then I suppose, Barb'ry Aleshine," said Mrs. Lecks, "that we ought to charge these people with our wages, and make 'em pay it when they come back!"

This remark apparently disposed of Mrs. Aleshine's objections, and her friend continued: "There's a jar on the mantelpiece there, of the kind the East Indy ginger comes in. It's got nothin' in it now but some brown paper in which fish-hooks is wrapped. We came here on a Wednesday, and so every Tuesday night we'll each put four dollars in that jar, under the fish-hook paper; then if, by night or by day, the family comes back and makes a fuss about our bein' here, all we have to say is, 'The board money's in the ginger-jar,' and our consciences is free."

Mrs. Lecks's plan was adopted as a very just and proper one, and at the expiration of the week we each deposited four dollars in the ginger-jar.

While occupying this house I do not think that any of us endeavored to pry into the private concerns of the family who owned it, although we each had a very natural curiosity to know something about said family. Opportunities of acquiring such knowledge, however, were exceedingly scarce. Even if we had been willing to look into such receptacles, the several desks and secretaries that the house contained were all locked, and nowhere could Mrs. Lecks or Mrs. Aleshine find an old letter or piece of wrapping-paper with an address on it. I explained to my companions that letters and packages were not likely to come to a place like this, but they kept a sharp lookout for anything of the kind, asserting that there could be no possible harm in reading the names of the people whose house they were in.

In some of the books in the library, which were English and French in about equal proportions, with a few volumes in German, I found written on the blank pages the names "Emily" and "Lucille," and across the title-pages of some French histories was inscribed, in a man's hand, "A. Dusante." We discussed these names, but could not make up our minds whether the family were French or English. For instance, there was no reason why an Englishwoman might not be called Lucille, and even such a surname as Dusante was not uncommon either among English or Americans. The labels on the boxes and tins of provisions showed that most of them came from San Francisco, but this was likely to be the case, no matter what the nationality of the family.

The question of the relationship of the three persons, of whose existence we had discovered traces, was a very interesting one to Mrs. Lecks and Mrs. Aleshine.

"I can't make up my mind," said the latter, "whether Emily is the mother of Lucille or her daughter, or whether they are both children of Mr. Dusante, or whether he's married to Lucille and Emily is his sister-in-law, or whether she's his sister and not hers, or whether he's the uncle and they're his nieces, or whether Emily is an old lady and Mr. Dusante and Lucille are both her children, or whether they are two maiden ladies and Mr. Dusante is their brother, or whether Mr. Dusante is only a friend of the family, and boards here because no two women ought to live in such a lonely place without a man in the house."

"Well," said Mrs. Lecks, "whether Mr. Dusante comes back with two nieces, or a wife and daughter, or Mrs. Dusante and a mother-in-law, or a pair of sisters, all we've got to say is, 'The board money's in the ginger-jar,' and let 'em do their worst."

"MRS. LECKS AND MRS. ALESHINE STANDING ON THE END OF THE LITTLE WHARF."

In my capacity as gardener I do not think I earned the wages which my companions had allotted to me, for I merely gathered and brought in such fruits and vegetables as I found in proper condition for use. In other ways, however, I made my services valuable to our little family. In a closet in my chamber I found guns and ammunition, and frequently I was able to bring in a few birds. Some of these were pronounced by Mrs. Aleshine unsuitable for the table, but others she cooked with much skill, and they were found to be very good eating.

Not far from the little wharf which has been mentioned there stood, concealed by a mass of low-growing palms, a boat-house in which was a little skiff hung up near the roof. This I let down and launched, and found great pleasure in rowing it about the lagoon. There was fishing-tackle in the boat-house, which I used with success, the lagoon abounding in fish. Offerings of this kind were much more acceptable to Mrs. Aleshine than birds.

"There's some kinds of fishes that's better than others," said she, "but, as a gen'ral rule, a fish is a fish, and if you catch 'em you can eat 'em; but it's a very different thing with birds. When you've never seen 'em before, how are you goin' to tell but what they're some kin to an owl, a pigeon-hawk, or a crow? And if I once get it into my head that there's any of that kind of family blood in 'em, they disagree with me just the same as if there really was."

One afternoon, as I was returning in the boat from the point on the other side of the island where I had found the rustic seat and Emily's book, I was surprised to see Mrs. Lecks and Mrs. Aleshine standing on the end of the little wharf. This was an unusual thing for them to do, as they were very industrious women and seldom had an idle moment, and it seemed to be one of their greatest pleasures to discuss the work they were going to do when they had finished that on which they were then engaged. I was curious, therefore, to know why they should be standing thus idly on the wharf, and pulled toward them as rapidly as possible.

When I had rowed near enough to hear them, Mrs. Aleshine remarked with cheerful placidity:

"The Dusantes are comin'."

The tide was quite low, and I could not see over the reef; but in a few moments I had grounded the skiff and had sprung upon the wharf. Out on the ocean, about a mile away, I saw a boat, apparently a large one, approaching the island.

"Now, then, Barb'ry Aleshine," said Mrs. Lecks, "you'll soon see whether it's his two nieces, or his daughters, wife and sister-in-law, or whatever of them other relationships which you've got so pat."

"Yes," said Mrs. Aleshine; "but, what's more, we'll find out if he's goin' to be satisfied with the board money we've put in the ginger-jar."

PART III

MRS. *LECKS* AND MRS. *ALESHINE* *WIN* A FIGHT AND *MAKE* A MATCH

WHEN THE BOAT which we saw approaching the island had come near enough for us to distinguish its occupants, we found that it contained five persons. Three sat in the stern, and two were rowing. Of those in the stern, we soon made out one to be a woman, and after putting our eyesight to its very best efforts, we were obliged to admit that there was only one female on board.

"Now, that's disapp'intin'," said Mrs. Aleshine, "for I've wondered and wondered which I should like best, Emily or Lucille, and now that only one of 'em has come, of course I can't tell."

The boat came on, almost directly toward the passageway in the reef, and it was not long before the two women had been able to decide that Mr. Dusante was an elderly man, and that the lady was moderately young, and in all probability his daughter.

"It may be," said Mrs. Aleshine, "that the mother, whether she was Emily, or whether she was Lucille, has died, and for that reason they are comin' back sooner than they expected."

"Well, I hope you're wrong there, Barb'ry Aleshine," said Mrs. Lecks, "for they'll see lots of things here that will freshen up their affliction, and that won't make 'em any too lively people to be with."

"On the other hand," said Mrs. Aleshine, "it may be that Emily, or else Lucille, has got married, and has gone away with her husband to travel, and by the time she's got a little baby she'll come here to live on account of the sea air for the child, and that'll make the house pleasant, Mrs. Lecks."

"I'd like to know how long you expect to live here," said Mrs. Lecks, regarding her friend with some severity.

"That's not for me to say," replied Mrs. Aleshine, "knowin' nothin' about it. But this I will say, that I hope they have brought along with them some indigo blue, for I nearly used up all there was the last time I washed."

During this dialogue I had been thinking that it was a very strange thing for the owners of this place to visit their island in such a fashion. Why should they be in an open boat? And where did they come from? Wherever they might live, it was not at all probable that they would choose to be rowed from that point to this. From the general character and appointments of the house in which we had found a refuge, it was quite plain that its owners were people in good circumstances, who were in the habit of attending to their domestic affairs in a very orderly and proper way. It was to be presumed that it was their custom to come here in a suitable vessel, and to bring with them the stores needed during their intended stay. Now, there could be little or nothing in that boat, and, on the whole, I did not believe it contained the owners of this island.

It would not do, however, to assume anything of the kind. There might have been a disaster; in fact, I knew nothing about it, but it was my immediate duty to go and meet these people at the passage, for, if they were unable to unlock the bars, their boat could not enter, and I must ferry them across the lagoon. Without communicating my doubts to my companions, I hurried into the skiff, and pulled as far as possible into the passage through the reef. The bars, of which there were more than I at first supposed, were so arranged that it was impossible for a boat to go in or out at any stage of the tide.

I had been there but a few minutes when the boat from without came slowly in between the rocks; and almost as soon as I saw it, its progress was suddenly stopped by a sunken bar.

"Hello!" cried several men at once.

"Hello!" cried I, in return. "Have you the key to these bars?"

A stout man with a red beard stood up in the stern. "Key?" said he, "what key?"

"Then you do not belong here?" said I. "Who are you?"

At this, the gentleman who was sitting by the lady arose to his feet. He was a man past middle age, rather tall and slim, and when he stood up the slight rolling of the boat made him stagger, and he came near falling.

"You'd better sit down, sir," said the man with the red beard, who I saw was a sailor. "You can talk better that way."

The gentleman now seated himself, and thus addressed me:

"I am, sir, the Reverend Mr. Enderton, lately missionary to Nan-fouchong, China, and this is my daughter, Miss Enderton. We are returning to the United States by way of the Sandwich Islands, and took passage in a sailing-vessel for Honolulu. About two weeks ago this vessel, in some way which I do not understand, became disabled—"

"Rotten forem'st," interrupted the man with the red beard, "which give way in a gale; strained and leaky, besides."

"I did not know the mast was rotten," said the gentleman, "but, since the occasion of our first really serviceable wind, she has been making very unsatisfactory progress. And, more than that, the whole force of seamen was employed night and day in endeavoring to keep the water out of the tea, thereby causing such a thumping and pounding that sleep was out of the question. Add to this the fact that our meals became very irregular, and were sometimes entirely overlooked—"

"Prog was gettin' mighty short," interpolated the red-bearded man.

"You can easily discern, sir," continued the gentleman, "that it was impossible for myself and my daughter to remain longer on that vessel, on which we were the only passengers. I therefore requested the captain to put us ashore at the nearest land, and, after more than a week of delay and demur, he consented to do so."

"Couldn't do it," said the man, "till there was land nigh enough."

"The captain informed me," continued the gentleman, "that this island was inhabited, and that I could here find shelter and repose until a vessel could be sent from Honolulu to take me off. He furnished me with this boat and three seamen, one of whom," pointing to the red-bearded man, "is a coxswain. We have been rowing ever since early this morning, with but a very moderate quantity of food and much discomfort. Now, sir, you have heard my story; and I ask you, as one man to another, if you still intend to bar your water-gates against us?"

"I did not bar the gates," I said, "and I would gladly unlock them if I could. I belong to a shipwrecked party who took refuge here some two weeks ago."

"And how did you get in?" hastily inquired the red-bearded coxswain.

"Our boat sunk when we were within sight of the island, and we came here on life-preservers, and so got under the bars."

The two men who had been rowing now turned suddenly and looked at me. They both had black beards, and they both exclaimed at the same moment, "By George!"

"I won't stop here to tell any more of our story," said I. "The great point now is to get you all ashore, and have you cared for."

"That's so!" said the coxswain. And the two sailors murmured, "Aye, aye, sir."

The bar which stopped the progress of the larger boat was just under the surface of the water, while another a foot above the water kept my skiff about six feet distant from the other boat. There was some loose flooring in the bottom of the coxswain's boat, and he ordered two of the boards taken out, and with them a bridge was made, one end resting on the bow of the larger boat, and the other on the iron bar by my skiff.

"Now," said the coxswain, "let the lady go first."

The elderly gentleman arose, as if he would prefer to take the lead, but his daughter, who had not yet spoken a word, was passed forward by the coxswain, steadied over the bridge by one of the sailors, and assisted by me into the skiff. Then her father came aboard, and I rowed with them to the wharf.

Mrs. Lecks and Mrs. Aleshine came forward most cordially to meet them.

"Mr. Dusante, I suppose?" said Mrs. Lecks, while Mrs. Aleshine hurriedly whispered in my ear, "Is it Lucille or Emily?"

As quickly as possible I explained the situation. For a few moments Mrs. Lecks and Mrs. Aleshine stood speechless. Nothing which had happened to them, the wreck of the steamer, the sinking of the boat, or our experience with life-preservers, affected them so much as this disappointment in regard to the problem of the Dusante family. Travel by sea was all novel and strange to them, and they had expected all sorts of things to which they were not accustomed, but they had never imagined that Fate would be so hard upon them as to snatch away the solution of this mystery just as they were about to put their hands upon it. But, in spite of this sudden blow, the two good women quickly recovered themselves, and with hearty and kindly words hurried the missionary and his daughter to the house, while I went to bring over the men.

I found the three sailors busy in securing their boat so that it would not be injured by the rocks during the rising and falling of the tide. When they had finished this job, they had to do a good deal of scrambling before they reached my skiff.

"We thought at first, sir," said the coxswain, as I rowed them across the lagoon, "that it was all gammon about your not livin' here, and havin' no keys to them bars; but we've come to the 'pinion that if you'd been able to unlock 'em you'd have done it sooner than take all this trouble."

I now related my story more fully, and the men were greatly

astonished when they heard that my companions in this adventure were two women. Upon my asking the coxswain why he had come to this island, he replied that his captain had heard that people lived on it, although he knew nothing about them; and that, as it would be almost impossible to get his brig here with the wind that was then prevailing, and as he did not wish to go out of his course anyway, he made up his mind that he would rather lose the services of three men than keep that missionary on board a day longer.

"You see, sir," said the coxswain, as we went ashore, "the parson wouldn't never take it into account that we were short of prog, and leakin' like Sam Hill; and because things were uncomfortable he growled up and he growled down, till he was wuss for the spirits of the men than the salt water comin' in or the hard-tack givin' out, and there was danger, if he wasn't got rid of, that he'd be pitched overboard and left to take his chances for a whale. And then, by sendin' us along, that give the crew three half-rations a day extry, and that'll count for a good deal in the fix they're in."

When I reached the house I took the men into the kitchen, where Mrs. Aleshine already had the table spread. There were bread and cold meat, while the tea-kettle steamed by the fire. In a very short time three happy mariners sat round that table, while Mrs. Aleshine, with beaming face, attended to their wants, and plied them with innumerable questions. They had not finished eating when Mrs. Lecks entered the kitchen.

"I put that minister and his daughter in the two front bedrooms," said she to me, after hospitably greeting the three men, "which me and Mrs. Aleshine had run and got ready for the Dusantes, as soon as you went in your boat to meet 'em. The young lady was mighty nigh worn out, and glad enough of the tea and things, and to get into bed. But the gentleman he wanted a soft-boiled egg, and when I told him I hadn't come across no hen-house yet on this island, he looked at me as if he didn't half believe me, and thought I was keepin' the eggs to sell."

"Which it would be ridiculous to do," said Mrs. Aleshine, "in the middle of an ocean like this."

"If he lets you off with soft-b'iled eggs, ma'am," said the coxswain, very respectfully, "I think you may bless your stars."

"Aye, aye, sir," said the two sailors with black beards.

Miss Ruth Enderton and her father did not make their appearance until the next morning at breakfast-time. I found the young lady a very pleasant person. She was rather slight in figure, inclined to be pretty, and was what might be called a warm-colored blonde. Her disposition was quite sociable, and she almost immediately stepped into the favor of Mrs. Lecks and Mrs. Aleshine.

Mr. Enderton, however, was a person of another sort. He was a prim and somewhat formal man, and appeared to be entirely self-engrossed, with very vague notions in regard to his surroundings. He was not by any means an ill-tempered man, being rather inclined to be placid than otherwise; but he gave so little attention to circumstances and events that he did not appear to understand why he should be incommoded by the happenings of life. I have no doubt that he made existence on board the disabled brig a hundred times more unsatisfactory than it would otherwise have been. With his present condition he seemed very well satisfied, and it was quite plain that he looked upon Mrs. Lecks, Mrs. Aleshine, and myself as the proprietors of the establishment, having forgotten, or paid no attention to, my statement in regard to our coming here.

" MR. ENDERTON WAS A PERSON OF ANOTHER SORT. "

As soon as she thought it fit and proper—and this moment arrived in the course of the first forenoon—Mrs. Lecks spoke to Mr. Enderton on the subject of the board which should be paid to the Dusantes. She stated the arrangements we had made in the matter, and then told him that as he and his daughter had the best accommodations in the house, each occupying a large, handsome room, she thought that he should pay fifteen dollars a week for the two.

"Now, if your daughter," she continued, "can do anything about the house which will be of real help, though for the life of me I don't see what she can find to do, with me and Mrs. Aleshine here, somethin' might be took off on account of her services; but of course you, sir, can't do nothin', unless you was to preach on Sundays, and not knowin' what denomination the Dusantes belong to, it wouldn't be fair to take their money to pay for the preachin' of doctrines which, perhaps, they don't believe in."

This financial proposal aroused Mr. Enderton's opposition. "When I came here, madam," he said, "I did not expect to pay any board whatever, and I think, moreover, that your rates are exorbitant. In Nanfouchong, if I remember rightly, the best of board did not cost more than two or three dollars a week."

"I don't want to say anything, sir," said Mrs. Lecks, "which might look disrespectful, but as long as I've got a conscience inside of me I'm not goin' to stay here and see the Dusantes lose money by Chinese cheapness."

"I don't know anything about the Dusantes," said Mr. Enderton, "but I am not going to pay fifteen dollars a week for board for myself and daughter."

The discussion lasted for some time, with considerable warmth on each side, and was at last ended by Mr. Enderton agreeing to pay board at the same rate as the two women and myself, and each week to deposit in the ginger-jar eight dollars for himself and daughter.

"You may not care to remember, sir," said Mrs. Lecks, with cold severity, "that Mr. Craig and me and Mrs. Aleshine puts in services besides, although, to be sure, they don't go into the jar."

"I only remember," said Mr. Enderton, "that I am paying an un-justifiable price as it is."

Mrs. Lecks and Mrs. Aleshine, however, were not at all of this opinion, and they agreed that, if it should be in their power, they would see to it that the Dusantes lost nothing by this close-fisted missionary.

After dinner—and I may remark that the newcomers were not con-sulted in regard to the hours for meals—Mrs. Lecks had an interview with the coxswain on the subject of board for himself and his two com-panions. This affair, however, was very quickly settled, for the three mariners had among them only one dollar and forty-three cents, and this, the coxswain explained, they would like to keep for tobacco. It was therefore settled that, as the three sailors could pay no money, as much work as possible should be got out of them, and to this plan they agreed heartily and cheerfully.

"There's only one thing we'll ask, ma'am," said the coxswain to Mrs. Lecks, "and that is that we be put in a different mess from the parson. We've now eat two meals with the passengers, and me and my mates is agreed that that's about as much as we can go."

After this, therefore, the three men had their meals in the kitchen, where they were generally joined by Mrs. Aleshine, who much de-lighted in their company. But she made it a point sometimes to sit down with us in the dining-room, merely to show that she had as much right there as anybody.

"As to the work for them sailormen," said Mrs. Aleshine, "I don't see what they're goin' to do. Of course they don't know nothin' about gardenin', and it seems to me that the best thing to be done is to put 'em to fishin'."

Mrs. Lecks considered this a good suggestion, and accordingly the coxswain and his companions were told that thereafter they would be expected to fish for eight hours a day, Sundays excepted. This plan, however, did not work very well. During the first two days the sailors caught so many fish that, although the fishermen themselves had excellent appetites for such food, it was found utterly impossible to consume what they brought in. Consequently, it was ordered that thereafter they should catch only as many fish as should be needed, and then make themselves useful by assisting Mrs. Aleshine and Mrs. Lecks in any manner they might direct.

I found it quite easy to become acquainted with Miss Ruth Enderton, as she was very much inclined to conversation. "It's ever so long," she said, "since I've had anybody to talk to."

She had left the United States when she was quite a little girl, and had since seen nothing of her native land. She was, consequently, full of questions about America, although quite willing to talk of her life in China. Society, at least such kind as she had ever cared for, had been extremely scarce in the little missionary station at which she had lived so long, and now, coming from a wearisome sojourn on a disabled sailing-vessel, with no company but the crew and a preoccupied father, she naturally was delighted to get among people she could talk to. With Mrs. Lecks, Mrs. Aleshine, and myself she soon became very friendly and showed herself to be a most lively and interesting young person.

I did all that I could to make Miss Ruth's time pass agreeably. I rowed with her on the lagoon, taught her to fish, and showed her all the pleasant points on the island which could be easily reached by walking. Mr. Enderton gave us very little of his company, for, having discovered that there was a library in the house, he passed most of his time in that room.

"You have made a very fair selection of books, sir," he remarked to me, "but it may readily be conceived, from the character of the works, that your tastes are neither ecclesiastic nor scientific."

Several times I explained to him the ownership of the library and the house, but he immediately forgot what I had said, or paid no attention to it. When he paid his board, at the end of the week, he handed the money to Mrs. Lecks; and although before his eyes she put it into the ginger-jar, beneath the paper of fish-hooks, I know very well that he considered he was paying it to her for her own use and behoof. He was comfortably lodged, he had all that he needed—and very nearly all that he wanted—to eat, and I do not know that I ever saw a man more contented with his lot.

As for the coxswain and the two sailors, they had a very pleasant time of it, but Mrs. Lecks and Mrs. Aleshine would not think of such a thing as allowing them to eat in idleness the bread of the Dusantes.

"I DID ALL THAT I COULD TO MAKE MISS RUTH'S TIME PASS
AGREEABLY."

After they had been with us a few days, Mrs. Lecks told me that she
thought she could show the coxswain and his mates how to dig and
gather the garden-stuff which was daily needed.

"To be sure," said she, "that work goes ag'in' part of your board,
but fishin' and bringin' in fire-wood don't take up quarter of the time
of them sailors, and so that the garden work is done, I don't suppose it
matters to the Dusantes who does it. And that'll give you more time to
make things pleasant for Miss Ruth, for, as far as I can see, there isn't
a thing for her to do, even if she knows how to do it."

The three mariners were more than willing to do anything desired by
Mrs. Lecks or Mrs. Aleshine, to whom they looked up with great admiration and respect. The latter was their favorite, not only because
she was with them a great deal during their meals and at other times,
but because of her genial nature and easy sociability. The men were
always trying to lighten her labors, and to do something that would
please her.

One of them climbed to the top of what she called a "palm-leaf-fan tree," and brought therefrom some broad leaves, which he cut and trimmed and sewed, in true nautical fashion, until he made some fans which were heavy and clumsy, but, as he said, they would stand half a gale of wind if she chose to raise it. The coxswain caught or trapped two sea-birds, and, having clipped their wings, he spent days in endeavoring to tame them, hoping to induce them, as far as the power in them lay, to take the place of the barn-yard fowls whose absence Mrs. Aleshine continually deplored. Every evening the two black-bearded sailors would dance hornpipes for her, much to her diversion and delight.

"THEY WERE EVIDENTLY WAITING FOR ME."

"I've often heard," she remarked, "that in these hot cocoanut countries the tricks of the monkeys was enough to keep everybody on a steady laugh, but I'm sure sailormen is a great deal better. When you get tired of their pranks and their tomfooleries you can tell 'em to stop, which with monkeys you can't."

It was about ten days after the arrival of the missionary's party that, as I was going to get ready the boat in which Miss Ruth and myself generally rowed in the cool of the evening, I saw Mrs. Lecks and Mrs. Aleshine sitting on the beach in the shade of some low-growing trees. They were evidently waiting for me, and as soon as I appeared Mrs. Lecks beckoned to me; whereupon I joined them.

"Sit down," said Mrs. Lecks; "there's somethin' I want to talk to you about. Mrs. Aleshine and me have made up our minds that you ought to be hurried up a little about poppin' the question to Miss Ruth."

This remark astounded me. "Popping the question!" I exclaimed.

"Yes," continued Mrs. Lecks, "and me and Mrs. Aleshine know very well that you haven't done it yet, for both of us havin' been through that sort of thing ourselves, we know the signs of it after it has happened."

"And we wouldn't say nothin' to hurry you," added Mrs. Aleshine, "if it wasn't that the groceries, especially the flour, is a-gettin' low. We've been talkin' to them sailormen, and they're pretty well agreed that there's no use now in expectin' their captain to send for 'em; for if he was a-goin' to do it at all, he'd 'a' done it before this. And perhaps he never got nowhere himself, in which case he couldn't. And they say the best thing we can all do when the victuals has nearly give out, provided the Dusantes don't come back in time, is to take what's left, and all get into their big boat, and row away to that island, which I don't know just how far it is, that the captain of our ship was goin' to. There we can stay pretty comfortable till a ship comes along and takes us off."

"But what has all that to do," I asked, "with Miss Ruth and me?"

"Do?" cried Mrs. Lecks. "It has everythin' to do. When it's all settled and fixed between you and Miss Ruth, there'll be nothin' to hinder us from gettin' ready to start when we please."

"But, my dear friends," I said with much earnestness, "I have not the slightest idea of proposing to Miss Enderton."

"That's just what I said to Mrs. Aleshine," said Mrs. Lecks, "and that's the reason we let our irons cool, and come out here to talk to you. It's just like a young man to keep puttin' off that sort of thing, but this can't be put off."

"That's so!" cried Mrs. Aleshine; "and I'll just let you see how the matter stands. There is housekeepers who allows a pint of flour a day to each person, but this is for farm-hands and people who works hard and eats hearty, and I've found that three quarters of a pint will do very well, if the dough is kneaded conscientious and made up light, so that it'll rise well when it's put into the oven. Now I've measured all the flour that's left, and me and Mrs. Lecks we've calculated that, allowin' three-quarters of a pint of flour a day to each one of us, there's just eight days more that we can stay here—that is, if the Dusantes don't come back before that time, which, of course, can't be counted on. So you can see for yourself, Mr. Craig, there's no time to be lost, even considerin' that she hasn't to make up anything to be married in."

"No," said Mrs. Lecks; "just for us and three sailors, that wouldn't be needed."

I looked from one to the other in dumb astonishment. Mrs. Lecks gave me no time to say anything.

"In common cases," said she, "this might all be put off till we got somewhere; but it won't do now. Here you are, with everythin' in your hands, but just get away from here, and there's an end of that. She's as pretty a girl as you'll see in a month of Sundays, and if she leaves here without your gettin' her, there's no knowing who'll snap her up. When we've got to that island, you may see her once a week, but maybe you won't. She may go away in one ship, and you in another, and there may be somebody right there—a missionary, for all I know—who'll have her before you have a chance to put in a word."

"And that's not the worst of it," said Mrs. Aleshine. "Supposin' them Dusantes come back before we go. There's no knowin' what that Mr. Dusante is. He may be a brother of Emily and Lucille. And what sort of a chance would you have then, I'd like to know, with Miss Ruth right here in his own house, and he ownin' the rowboat, and every-thin'? Or it may be he's a widower, and that'll be a mighty sight worse, I can tell you."

"No matter whether they're widowers or never been married," said Mrs. Lecks, "there'll be plenty that'll want her as soon as they see her; and if it isn't for the girl's own pretty face, it'll be for her father's money."

"Her father's money!" I exclaimed. "What are you talking of?"

"There's no good tellin' me anything about that," said Mrs. Lecks, very decidedly. "There never was a man as close-fisted as Mr. Enderton who hadn't money."

"And you know as well as we do," said Mrs. Aleshine, "that in them countries where he's been the heathens worship idols of silver and idols of gold, and when them heathens is converted, don't you suppose the missionaries get any of that? I expect that Mr. Enderton has converted thousands of heathens."

At this suggestion I laughed outright. But Mrs. Lecks reproved me.

"Now, Mr. Craig," said she, "this is no laughin' matter. What me and Mrs. Aleshine is sayin' is for your good, and for the good of Miss Ruth along with you. I haven't much opinion of her father, but his money is as good as anybody else's, and though they had to leave their trunks on board their ship, what little they brought with them shows that they've been used to havin' the best there is. Mrs. Aleshine and me has set up till late into the night talkin' over this thing, and we are both of one mind that you two need never expect to have the same chance again that you've got now. The very fact that the old gentleman is a preacher, and can marry you on the spot, ought to make you tremble when you think of the risks you are runnin' by puttin' it off."

"I've got to go into the house now to see about supper," said Mrs.

Aleshine, rising, "and I hope you'll remember, Mr. Craig, when your
bread is on your plate, and Miss Ruth is sittin' opposite to you, that
three quarters of a pint of flour a day is about as little as anybody can
live on, and that time is flyin'."

Mrs. Lecks now also rose. But I detained the two for a moment.

"I hope you have not said anything to Miss Enderton on this subject," I said.

"No," replied Mrs. Aleshine, "we haven't. We are both agreed that
as you're the one that's to do what's to be done, you are the one that's
to be spoke to. And havin' been through it ourselves, we understand
well enough that the more a woman don't know nothin' about it, the
more likely she is to be ketched if she wants to be."

The two women left me in an amused but also somewhat annoyed
state of mind. I had no intention whatever of proposing to Miss Ruth
Enderton. She was a charming girl, very bright and lively, and withal,
I had reason to believe, very sensible. But it was not yet a fortnight
since I first saw her, and no thought of marrying her had entered into
my head. Had Mrs. Lecks and Mrs. Aleshine, or, more important than
all, had Miss Enderton, any reason to believe that I was acting the part
of a lover?

The latter portion of this question was almost immediately answered
to my satisfaction by the appearance of Miss Ruth, who came skipping
down to me and calling out to me in that free and hearty manner with
which a woman addresses a friend or near acquaintance, but never a
suspected lover. She betrayed no more notion of the Lecks and Aleshine
scheme than on the day I first met her.

But, as I was rowing her over the lagoon, I felt a certain constraint
which I had not known before. There was no ground whatever for the
wild imaginings of the two women, but the fact that they had imagined
interfered very much with the careless freedom with which I had previously talked to Miss Ruth. I do not think, however, that she noticed
any change in me, for she chatted and laughed, and showed, as she had
done from the first, the rare delight which she took in this novel island
life.

When we returned to the house, we were met by Mrs. Aleshine.
"I am goin' to give you two your supper," she said, "on that table
there under the tree. We all had ours a little earlier than common, as
the sailormen seemed hungry; and I took your father's to him in the
libr'ry, where I expect he's a-sittin' yet, holdin' a book in one hand and
stirrin' his tea with the other, till he's stirred out nearly every drop on
the floor; which, however, won't matter at all, for in the mornin' I'll
rub up that floor till it's as bright as new."

This plan delighted Miss Ruth, but I saw in it the beginning of the workings of a deep-laid scheme. I was just about to sit down when Mrs. Aleshine said to me in a low voice, as she left us:

"Remember that the first three quarters of a pint apiece begins now!"

"Don't you think that Mrs. Lecks and Mrs. Aleshine are perfectly charming?" said Miss Ruth, as she poured out the tea. "They always seem to be trying to think of some kind thing to do for other people."

I agreed entirely with Miss Enderton's remark, but I could not help thinking of the surprise she would feel if she knew of the kind thing that these two women were trying to do for her.

"Have you taken any steps yet?" asked Mrs. Lecks of me, the next day. On my replying that I had taken no steps of the kind to which I supposed she alluded, she walked away with a very grave and serious face.

A few hours later Mrs. Aleshine came to me. "There's another reason for hurryin' up," said she, "Them sailormen seems able to do without 'most anything in this world except tobacco, and Mrs. Lecks has been sellin' it to 'em out of a big box she found in a closet up-stairs, at five cents a teacupful,—which I think is awful cheap, but she says prices in islands is always low,—and wrapping the money up in a paper, with 'Cash paid by sailormen for tobacco' written on it, and puttin' it into the ginger-jar with the board money. But their dollar and forty-three cents is nearly gone, and Mrs. Lecks she says that not a whiff of Mr. Dusante's tobacco shall they have if they can't pay for it. And when they have nothin' to smoke they'll be wantin' to leave this island just as quick as they can, without waitin' for the flour to give out."

Here was another pressure brought to bear upon me. Not only the waning flour, but the rapidly disappearing tobacco money was used as a weapon to urge me forward to the love-making which Mrs. Lecks and Mrs. Aleshine had set their hearts upon.

I was in no hurry to leave the island, and hoped very much that when we did go we should depart in some craft more comfortable than a ship's boat. In order, therefore, to prevent any undue desire to leave on the part of the sailors, I gave them money enough to buy a good many teacups full of tobacco. By this act I think I wounded the feelings of Mrs. Lecks and Mrs. Aleshine, although I had no idea that such would be the effect of my little gift. They said nothing to me on the subject, but their looks and manners indicated that they thought I had not been acting honorably. For two days they had very little to say to me, and then Mrs. Aleshine came to me to make what, I suppose, was their supreme effort.

"Mrs. Lecks and me is a-goin' to try," she said,—and as she spoke she looked at me with a very sad expression and a watery appearance about the eyes,—"to stretch out the time for you a little longer. We are goin' to make them sailor men eat more fish; and as for me and her, we'll go pretty much without bread, and make it up, as well as we can on other things. You and Miss Ruth and the parson can each have your three quarters of a pint of flour a day, just the same as ever, and what we save ought to give you three or four days longer."

This speech moved me deeply. I could not allow these two kind-hearted women to half starve themselves in order that I might have more time to woo, and I spoke very earnestly on the subject to Mrs. Aleshine, urging her to give up the fanciful plans which she and Mrs. Lecks had concocted.

"Let us drop this idea of love-making," I said, "which is the wildest kind of vagary, and all live happily together, as we did before. If the provisions give out before the Dusantes come back, I suppose we shall have to leave in the boat; but, until that time comes let us enjoy life here as much as we can, and be the good friends that we used to be."

I might as well have talked to one of the palm-trees which waved over us.

"As I said before," remarked Mrs. Aleshine, "what is saved from Mrs. Lecks's and mine and the three sailormen's three quarters of a pint apiece ought to give you four days more." And she went into the house.

"SMOKING THEIR PIPES IN PEACE."

All this time the Reverend Mr. Enderton had sat and read in the library, or meditatively had walked the beach with a book in his hand; while the three mariners had caught fish, performed their other work, and lain in the shade, smoking their pipes in peace. Miss Ruth and I had taken our daily rows and walks, and had enjoyed our usual hours of pleasant converse, and all the members of the little colony seemed happy and contented except Mrs. Lecks and Mrs. Aleshine. These two went gravely and sadly about their work, and the latter asked no more for the hornpipes and the sea-songs of her sailormen.

But, for some unaccountable reason, Mr. Enderton's condition of tranquil abstraction did not continue. He began to be fretful and discontented. He found fault with his food and his accommodations, and instead of spending the greater part of the day in the library, as had been his wont, he took to wandering about the island, generally with two or three books under his arm, sometimes sitting down in one place, and sometimes in another, and then rising suddenly to go grumbling into the house.

One afternoon, as Miss Ruth and I were in the skiff in the lagoon, we saw Mr. Enderton approaching us, walking on the beach. As soon as he was near enough for us to hear him, he shouted to his daughter:

"Ruth, come out of that boat! If you want to take the air, I should think you might as well with me as to go rowing round with—with anybody."

This rude and heartless speech made my blood boil, while my companion turned pale with mortification. The man had never made the slightest objection to our friendly intercourse, and this unexpected attack was entirely indefensible.

"Please put me ashore," said Miss Ruth, and without a word, for I could not trust myself to speak, I landed her; and, petulantly complaining that she never gave him one moment of her society, her father led her away.

An hour later, my soul still in a state of turmoil, but with the violence of its tossings somewhat abated, I entered one of the paths which led through the woods. After a few turns, I reached a point where I could see for quite a long distance to the other end of the path, which opened out upon the beach. There I perceived Mr. Enderton sitting upon the little bench on which I had found Emily's book. His back was toward me, and he seemed to be busily reading. About midway between him and myself I saw Miss Ruth slowly walking toward me. Her eyes were fixed upon the ground, and she had not seen me.

Stepping to one side, I awaited her approach. When she came near I accosted her.

"Miss Ruth," said I, "has your father been talking to you of me?"

She looked up quickly, evidently surprised at my being there. "Yes," she said, "he has told me that it is not—suitable that I should be with you as much as I have been since we came here."

There was something in this remark that roused again the turmoil which had begun to subside within me. There was so much that was unjust and tyrannical, and—what perhaps touched me still deeper— there was such a want of consideration and respect in this behavior of Mr. Enderton's, that it brought to the front some very incongruous emotions. I had been superciliously pushed aside, and I found I was angry. Something was about to be torn from me, and I found I loved it.

"Ruth," said I, stepping up close to her, "do you like to be with me as you have been?"

If Miss Ruth had not spent such a large portion of her life in the out-of-the-world village of Nanfouchong, if she had not lived among those simple-hearted missionaries, where it was never necessary to conceal her emotions or her sentiments, if it had not been that she never had had emotions or sentiments that it was necessary to conceal, I do not believe that when she answered me she would have raised her eyes to me with a look in them of a deep-blue sky seen through a sort of Indian-summer mist, and that, gazing thus, she would have said:

"Of course I like it."

"Then let us make it suitable," I said, taking both her hands in mine.

There was another look, in which the skies shone clear and bright, and then, in a moment, it was all done.

About five minutes after this I said to her, "Ruth, shall we go to your father?"

"Certainly," she answered. And together we walked along the thickly shaded path.

The missionary still sat with his back "IT WAS PERFECTLY SAFE." toward us, and, being so intent upon his book, I found that by keeping my eyes upon him it was perfectly safe to walk with my arm around Ruth until we had nearly reached him. Then I took her hand in mine, and we stepped in front of him.

"Father," said Ruth, "Mr. Craig and I are going to be married."

There was something very plump about this remark, and Mr. Enderton immediately raised his eyes from his book and fixed them first upon his daughter and then upon me; then he let them drop, and through the narrow space between us he gazed out over the sea.

"Well, father," said Ruth, a little impatiently, "what do you think of it?"

Mr. Enderton leaned forward and picked up a leaf from the ground. This he placed between the open pages of his book, and closed it.

"It seems to me," he said, "that on many accounts the arrangement you propose may be an excellent one. Yes," he added more decidedly; "I think it will do very well indeed. I shall not be at all surprised if we are obliged to remain on this island for a considerable time, and, for my part, I have no desire to leave it at present. And when you shall place yourself, Ruth, in a position in which you will direct the domestic economies of the establishment, I hope that you will see to it that things generally are made more compatible with comfort and gentility, and, as regards the table, I may add with palatability."

Ruth and I looked at each other, and then together we promised that as far as in us lay we would try to make the life of Mr. Enderton a happy one, not only while we were on the island, but ever afterward.

We were promising a great deal, but at that moment we felt very grateful.

Then he stood up, shook us both by the hands, and we left him to his book.

When Ruth and I came walking out of the woods and approached the house, Mrs. Aleshine was standing outside, not far from the kitchen. When she saw us she gazed steadily at us for a few moments, a strange expression coming over her face. Then she threw up both her hands, and without a word she turned and rushed indoors.

We had not reached the house before Mrs. Lecks and Mrs. Aleshine came hurrying out together. Running up to us with a haste and an excitement I had never seen in either of them, first one and then the other took Ruth into her arms and kissed her with much earnestness. Then they turned upon me and shook my hands with hearty vigor, expressing, more by their looks and actions than their words, a triumphant approbation of what I had done.

"The minute I laid eyes on you," said Mrs. Aleshine, "I knowed it was all right. There wasn't no need of askin' questions."

I now became fearful lest, in the exuberance of their satisfaction, these good women might reveal to Ruth the plans they had laid for our matrimonial future, and the reluctance I had shown in entering into them. My countenance must have expressed my apprehensions, for Mrs. Aleshine, her ruddy face glowing with warmth, both mental and physical, gave me a little wink, and drew me to one side.

"You needn't suppose that we've ever said anything to Miss Ruth, or that we're goin' to. It's a great deal better to let her think you did it all yourself."

I felt like resenting this imputation upon the independence of my

"'I KNOWED IT WAS ALL RIGHT.'"

love-making, but at this happy moment I did not want to enter into a discussion, and therefore merely smiled.

"I'm so glad, I don't know how to tell it," continued Mrs. Aleshine, as Mrs. Lecks and Ruth walked toward the house.

I was about to follow, but my companions detained me.

"Have you spoke to the parson?" she asked.

"Oh, yes," said I, "and he seemed perfectly satisfied. I am rather surprised at this, because of late he has been in such a remarkably bad humor."

"That's so," said Mrs. Aleshine; "there's no gettin' round the fact that he's been a good deal crosser than two sticks. You see, Mr. Craig, that Mrs. Lecks and me we made up our minds that it wasn't fair to the Dusantes to let that rich missionary go on payin' nothin' but four dollars a week apiece for him and his daughter, and if we couldn't get no more out of him one way, we'd do it another. It was fair enough that if he didn't pay more he ought to get less; and so we gave him more fish and not so much bread, the same as we did the sailormen; and we weakened his tea, and sent him just so much sugar, and no more; and as for openin' boxes of sardines for him, which there was no reason why they shouldn't be left here, for the Dusantes, I just wouldn't do it, though he said he'd got all the fresh fish he wanted when he was in China. And then we agreed that it was high time that that libr'ry should be cleaned up, and we went to work at it, not mindin' what he said; for it's no use tellin' me that four dollars a week will pay for a front room and good board, and the use of a libr'ry all day. And as there wasn't no need of both of us cleanin' one room, Mrs. Lecks she went into the parlor, where he'd took his books, and begun there. And then, again, we shut down on Mr. Dusante's dressing-gown. There was no sense includin' the use of that in his four dollars a week, so we brushed it up, and camphored it, and put it away. We just wanted to let him know that if he undertook to be skinflinty, he'd better try it on somebody else besides us. We could see that he was a good deal upset, for if ever a man liked to have things quiet and comfortable around him, and everything his own way, that man is that missionary. But we didn't care if we did prod him up a little. Mrs. Lecks and me we both agreed that it would do him good. Why, he'd got into such a way of shettin' himself up in himself that he didn't even see that his daughter was goin' about with a young man, and fixin' her affections on him more and more every day, when he never had no idea, as could be proved by witnesses, of marryin' her."

"Mrs. Aleshine," said I, looking at her very steadfastly, "I believe, after all, that you and Mrs. Lecks had your own way in regard to hurrying up this matter."

"Yes," said she, with happy complacency; "I shouldn't wonder if we had. Stirrin' up the parson was our last chance, and it wasn't much trouble to do it."

Mrs. Lecks, whose manner toward me for the last few days had been characterized by cold severity, now resumed her former friendly demeanor, although she was not willing to let the affair pass over without some words of reproach.

"I must say, Mr. Craig," she remarked the next morning, "that I was gettin' pretty well outdone with you. I was beginnin' to think that a young man that couldn't see and wouldn't see what was good for him didn't deserve to have it; and if Miss Ruth's father had just come down with a heavy foot and put an end to the whole business, I'm not sure I'd been sorry for you. But it's all right at last, and bygones is bygones. And now, what we've got to do is to get ready for the weddin'."

"The wedding!" I exclaimed.

Mrs. Lecks regarded me with an expression in which there was something of virtuous indignation and something of pity. "Mr. Craig," said she, "if there ever was anybody that wanted a guardeen, it's you. Now, just let me tell you this. That Mr. Enderton ain't to be trusted no further than you can see him, and not so fur, neither, if it can be helped. He's willin' for you to have Miss Ruth now, because he's pretty much made up his mind that we're goin' to stay here, and as he considers you the master of this island, of course he thinks it'll be for his good for his daughter to be mistress of it. For one thing, he wouldn't expect to pay no board then. But just let him get away from this island, and just let him set his eyes on some smooth-faced young fellow that'll agree to take him into the concern and keep him for nothin' on books and tea, he'll just throw you over without winkin'. And Miss Ruth is not the girl to marry you against his will, if he opens the Bible and piles texts on her, which he is capable of doin'. If in any way you two should get separated when you leave here, there's no knowin' when you'd ever see each other again, for where he'll take her nobody can tell. He's more willin' to set down and stay where he finds himself comfortable than anybody I've met yet."

"Of course," I said, "I'm ready to be married at any moment; but I don't believe Miss Ruth and her father would consent to anything so speedy."

"Don't you get into the way," said Mrs. Lecks, "of beforehand believin' this or that. It don't pay. Just you go to her father and talk to him about it, and if you and him agree, it'll be easy enough to make her see the sense of it. You attend to them, and I'll see that everythin' is got ready. And you'd better fix the day for to-morrow, for we can't stay here much longer, and there's a lot of house-cleanin' and bakin' and cookin' to be done before we go."

I took this advice, and broached the subject to Mr. Enderton.

"Well, sir," said he, laying down his book, "your proposition is decidedly odd; I may say, very odd, indeed. But it is, perhaps, after all, no odder than many things I have seen. Among the various denominational sects I have noticed occurrences quite as odd, sir. For my part, I have no desire to object to an early celebration of the matrimonial rites. I may say, indeed, that I am of the opinion that a certain amount of celerity in this matter will conduce to the comfort of all concerned. It has been a very unsatisfactory thing to me to see my daughter occupying a subordinate position in our little family, where she has not even the power to turn household affairs into the channels of my comfort. To-morrow, I think, will do very well indeed. Even if it should rain, I see no reason why the ceremony should be postponed."

The proposition of a wedding on the morrow was not received by Ruth with favor. She was unprepared for such precipitancy. But she finally yielded to arguments; not so much to mine, I fear, as to those offered by Mrs. Lecks and Mrs. Aleshine.

For the rest of that day the three mariners were kept very busy, bringing in green things to deck the parlor, and doing every imaginable kind of work necessary to a wedding which Mrs. Aleshine was willing to give into their hands. As for herself and her good friend, they put themselves upon their mettle as providers of festivals. They made cakes, pies, and I never knew half so well as the three sailors how many other kinds of good things. Besides all this, they assisted Ruth to array herself in some degree in a manner becoming a bride. Some light and pretty adornments of dress were borrowed from Emily or Lucille, they knew not which, and, after having been "done up" and fluted and crimped by Mrs. Lecks, were incorporated by Ruth into her custume with so much taste that on the wedding morning she appeared to me to be dressed more charmingly than any bride I had ever seen.

The three sailors had done their own washing and ironing, and appeared in cleanly garb, and with hair and beards well wet and brushed. Mrs. Lecks and Mrs. Aleshine put on their best bibs and tuckers, and Mr. Enderton assumed his most clerical air as he stood behind a table in the parlor and married Ruth and me.

"This," said Mr. Enderton, as we were seated at the wedding-feast, "is a most creditable display of attractive viands, but I may say, my dear Ruth, that I think I perceived the influence of the happy event of to-day even before it took place. I have lately had a better appetite for my food, and have experienced a greater enjoyment of my surroundings."

"I should think so," murmured Mrs. Aleshine in my ear, "for we'd no sooner knowed that you two were to make a match of it than we put an extry spoonful of tea into his pot, and stopped scrubbin' the libr'ry."

For the next two days all was bustle and work on the island. Mrs. Lecks and Mrs. Aleshine would not consent to depart without leaving everything in the best possible order, so that the Dusantes might not be dissatisfied with the condition of their house when they returned. It was in fact, the evident desire of the two women to gratify their pride in their housewifely abilities by leaving everything better than they found it.

Mr. Enderton was much surprised at these preparations for immediate departure. He was very well satisfied with his life on the island, and had prepared his mind for an indefinite continuance of it, with the position of that annoying and obdurate Mrs. Lecks filled by a compliant and affectionate daughter. He had no reasonable cause for complaint, for the whole subject of the exhaustion of our supply of

"THEY ASSISTED RUTH TO ARRAY HERSELF."

provisions, and the necessity of an open-boat trip to an inhabited island, had been fully discussed before him; but he was so entirely engrossed in the consideration of his own well-being that this discussion of our plans had made no impression upon him. He now became convinced that a conspiracy had been entered into against him, and fell into an unpleasant humor. This, however, produced very little effect upon any of us, for we were all too busy to notice his whims. But his sudden change of disposition made me understand how correct were the opinions of Mrs. Lecks and Mrs. Aleshine concerning him. If I had left that island with my marriage with Ruth depending upon Mr. Enderton's cooperation, my prospects of future happiness would have been at the mercy of his caprices.

Very early on a beautiful morning Ruth and I started out on our wedding journey in the long-boat. Mr. Enderton was made as comfortable as possible in the stern, with Ruth near him. Mrs. Lecks and Mrs. Aleshine sat facing each other, each with a brown-paper package by her side, containing the life-preserver on which she had arrived. These were to be ever cherished as memorials of a wonderful experience. The three sailors and I took turns at the oars. The sea was smooth, and there was every reason to believe that we should arrive at our destination before the end of the day. Mrs. Aleshine had supplied us with an abundance of provisions, and, with the exception of Mr. Enderton, who had not been permitted to take away any of the Dusante books, we were a contented party.

"As long as the flour held out," remarked Mrs. Aleshine, "I'd never been willin' to leave that island till the Dusantes came back, and we could have took Emily or Lucille, whichever it was that kept house, and showed her everythin', and told her just what we had done. But when they do come back," she added, "and read that letter which Mr. Craig wrote and left for them, and find out all that happened in their country-place while they was away; and how two of us was made happy for life; and how two more of us, meanin' Mrs. Lecks and me, have give up goin' to Japan, intendin', instid of that, writin' to my son to come home to America and settle down in the country he ought to live in,—why, then, if them Dusantes ain't satisfied, it's no use for anybody to ever try to satisfy 'em."

"I should think not," said Mrs. Lecks, "with the weddin'-cards on the parlor table, not a speck of dust in any corner, and the board money in the ginger-jar."

PART IV

MR. *ENDERTON* MANAGES AFFAIRS

WHEN THE LITTLE party, consisting of Mrs. Lecks and Mrs. Aleshine, Mr. Enderton, my newly made wife, and myself, with the red-bearded coxswain and the two sailormen, bade farewell to that island in the Pacific where so many happy hours had been passed, where such pleasant friendships had been formed, and where I had met my Ruth and made her my wife, we rowed away with a bright sky over our heads, a pleasant wind behind us, and a smooth sea beneath us. The long-boat was comfortable and well appointed, and there was even room enough in it for Mr. Enderton to stretch himself out and take a noon-day nap. We gave him every advantage of this kind, for we had found by experience that our party was happiest when my father-in-law was best contented.

Early in the forenoon the coxswain rigged a small sail in the bow of the boat, and with this aid to our steady and systematic work at the oars we reached, just before nightfall, the large island whither we were bound, and to which, by means of the coxswain's pocket-compass, we had steered a direct course. Our arrival on this island, which was inhabited by some white traders and a moderate population of natives, occasioned great surprise; for when the boats containing the crew and passengers of our unfortunate steamer had reached the island, it was found that Mrs. Lecks, Mrs. Aleshine and myself were missing. There were many suppositions as to our fate. Some persons thought we had been afraid to leave the steamer, and, having secreted ourselves on board, had gone down with her. Others conjectured that in the darkness we had fallen overboard, either from the steamer or from one of the boats; and there was even a surmise that we might have embarked in the leaky small boat—in which we really did leave the steamer—and so had been lost. At any rate, we had disappeared, and our loss was a good deal talked about and, in a manner, mourned. In less than a week after their arrival the people from the steamer had been taken on board a sailing-vessel and carried westward to their destination.

We, however, were not so fortunate, for we remained on this island for more than a month. During this time but one ship touched there, and she was western bound and of no use to us, for we had determined to return to America. Mrs. Lecks and Mrs. Aleshine had given up their journey to Japan, and were anxious to reach once more their country homes, while my dear Ruth and I were filled with a desire to found a home on some pleasant portion of the Atlantic seaboard. What Mr. Enderton intended to do we did not know. He was on his way to the United States when he left the leaking ship on which he and his daughter were passengers, and his intentions regarding his journey did not appear to have been altered by his mishaps.

By the western-bound vessel, however, Mrs. Aleshine sent a letter to her son.

Our life on this island was monotonous and to the majority of the party uninteresting; but as it was the scene of our honeymoon, Mrs. Craig and I will always look back to it with the most pleasurable recollections. We were comfortably lodged in a house belonging to one of the traders, and although Mrs. Lecks and Mrs. Aleshine had no household duties to occupy their time, they managed to supply themselves with knitting-materials from the stores on the island, and filled up their hours of waiting with chatty industry. The pipes of our sailor friends were always well filled, while the sands of the island were warm and pleasant for their backs, and it was only Mr. Enderton who showed any signs of impatient repining at our enforced stay. He growled, he grumbled, and he inveighed against the criminal neglect of steamship companies and the owners of sailing-craft in not making it compulsory in every one of their vessels to stop on every voyage at this island, where, at any time, intelligent and important personages might be stranded.

At last, however, we were taken off by a three-masted schooner bound for San Francisco, at which city we arrived in due time and in good health and condition.

We did not remain long in this city, but soon started on our way across the continent, leaving behind us our three sailor companions, who intended to ship from this port as soon as an advantageous opportunity offered itself. These men heard no news of their vessel, although they felt quite sure that she had reached Honolulu, where she had probably been condemned and the crew scattered. As some baggage belonging to my wife and my father-in-law had been left on board this vessel, I had hopes that Mr. Enderton would remain in San Francisco and order it forwarded to him there; or that he would even take a trip to Honolulu to attend to the matter personally. But in this I was disappointed. He seemed to take very little interest in his missing trunks, and wished only to press on to the East. I wrote to Honolulu, desiring the necessary steps to be taken to forward the baggage in case it had arrived there; and soon afterward our party of five started eastward.

It was now autumn, but, although we desired to reach the end of our journey before winter set in, we felt that we had time enough to visit some of the natural wonders of the California country before taking up our direct course to the East. Therefore, in spite of some petulant remonstrances on the part of Mr. Enderton, we made several trips to points of interest.

From the last of these excursions we set out in a stage-coach, of which we were the only occupants, toward a point on the railroad where we expected to take a train. On the way we stopped to change horses at a small stage-station at the foot of a range of mountains; and when I descended from the coach I found the driver and some of the men at the station discussing the subject of our route. It appeared that there were two roads, one of which gradually ascended the mountain for several miles, and then descended to the level of the railroad, by the side of which it ran until it reached the station where we wished to take the train. The other road pursued its way along a valley or notch in the mountain for a considerable distance, and then, by a short but somewhat steep ascending grade, joined the upper road.

It was growing quite cold, and the sky and the wind indicated that bad weather might be expected; and as the upper road was considered the better one at such a time, our driver concluded to take it. Six horses, instead of four, were now attached to our stage; and as two of these animals were young and unruly, and promised to be unusually difficult to drive in the ordinary way, our driver concluded to ride one of the wheel-horses, postilion fashion, and to put a boy on one of the leaders. Mr. Enderton was very much afraid of horses, and objected strongly to the young animals in our new team. But there were no others to take their places, and his protests were disregarded.

My wife and I occupied a back seat, having been ordered to take this comfortable position by Mrs. Lecks and Mrs. Aleshine, who had constituted themselves a board of instruction and admonition to Mrs. Craig, and incidentally to myself. They fancied that my wife's health was not vigorous, and that she needed coddling, and if she had had two mothers she could not have been more tenderly cared for than by these good women. They sat upon the middle seat with their faces towards the horses, while Mr. Enderton had the front seat all to himself. He was, however, so nervous and fidgety, continually twisting himself about endeavoring to get a view of the horses or of the bad places on the road, that Mrs. Lecks and Mrs. Aleshine found that a position facing him and in close juxtaposition was entirely too uncomfortable; and consequently the back of their seat being adjustable, they turned themselves about and faced us.

"THE ASCENT OF THE MOUNTAIN WAS SLOW AND TEDIOUS."

The ascent of the mountain was slow and tedious, and it was late in the afternoon when we reached the highest point in our route, from which the road descended for some eight miles to the level of the railroad. Now our pace became rapid, and Mr. Enderton grew wildly excited. He threw open the window, and shouted to the driver to go more slowly; but Mrs. Lecks seized him by the coat and jerked him back on his seat before he could get any answer to his appeals.

"If you want your daughter to ketch her death o' cold you'll keep that window open!" As she said this, she leaned back and pulled the window down with her own strong right arm. "I guess the driver knows what he is about," she continued, "this not bein' the first time he's gone over the road."

"Am I to understand, madam," said Mr. Enderton, "that I am not to speak to my driver when I wish him to know my will?"

To this question Mrs. Lecks made no answer, but sat up very straight and stiff, with her back square upon the speaker. For some time she and Mr. Enderton had been "out," and she made no effort to conceal the fact.

Mr. Enderton's condition now became pitiable, for our rapid speed and the bumping over rough places in the road seemed almost to deprive him of his wits, notwithstanding my assurance that stage-coaches were generally driven at a rapid rate down long inclines. In a short time, however, we reached a level spot in the road, and the team was drawn up and stopped. Mr. Enderton popped out in a moment, and I also got down to have a talk with the driver.

"These hosses won't do much at holdin' back," he said, "and it worries 'em less tö let 'em go ahead with the wheels locked. You needn't be afraid. If nothin' breaks, we're all right."

Mr. Enderton seemed endeavoring to satisfy himself that everything about the running-gear of the coach was in a safe condition. He examined the wheels, the axles, and the whiffletrees, much to the amusement of the driver, who remarked to me that the old chap probably knew as much now as he did before. I was rather surprised that my father-in-law subjected the driver to no further condemnation. On the contrary, he said nothing except that for the rest of this downhill drive he should take his place on the driver's unoccupied seat. Nobody offered any objection to this, and up he climbed.

When we started again, Ruth seemed disturbed that her father should be in such an exposed position, but I assured her that he would be perfectly safe, and would be much better satisfied at being able to see for himself what was going on.

We now began to go downhill again at a rate as rapid as before. Our speed, however, was not equal. Sometimes it would slacken a little where the road was heavy or more upon a level, and then we would go jolting and rattling over some long downward stretch. After a particularly unpleasant descent of this kind the coach seemed suddenly to change its direction, and with a twist and an uplifting of one side it bumped heavily against something, and stopped. I heard a great shout outside, and from a window which now commanded a view of the road I saw our team of six horses, with the drivers pulling and tugging at the two they rode, madly running away at the top of their speed.

Ruth, who had been thrown by the shock into the arms of Mrs. Aleshine, was dreadfully frightened, and screamed for her father. I had been pitched forward upon Mrs. Lecks, but I quickly recovered myself, and as soon as I found that none of the occupants of the coach had been hurt, I opened the door and sprang out.

In the middle of the road stood Mr. Enderton, entirely uninjured, with a jubilant expression on his face, and in one hand a large closed umbrella.

"What has happened?" I exclaimed, hurrying around to the front of the coach, where I saw that the pole had been broken off about the middle of its length.

"Nothing has happened, sir," replied Mr. Enderton. "You cannot speak of a wise and discreet act, determinately performed, as a thing which has happened. We have been saved, sir, from being dashed to pieces behind that wild and unmanageable team of horses; and I will add that we have been saved by my forethought and prompt action."

I turned and looked at him in astonishment. "What do you mean?" I said. "What could you have had to do with this accident?"

"Allow me to repeat," said Mr. Enderton, "that it was not an accident. The moment that we began to go downhill I perceived that we were in a position of the greatest danger. The driver was reckless, the boy incompetent, and the horses unmanageable. As my remonstrances and counsels had no effect upon the man, and as you seemed to have no desire to join me in efforts to restrain him to a more prudent rate of speed,

"'WHAT HAS HAPPENED?' I EXCLAIMED."

I determined to take the affair into my own hands. I knew that the first thing to be done was to rid ourselves of those horses. So long as we were connected with them disaster was imminent. I knew exactly what ought to be done. The horses must be detached from the coach. I had read, sir, of inventions especially intended to detach runaway horses from a vehicle. To all intents and purposes our horses were runaways, or would have become so in a very short time. I now, made it my object to free ourselves from those horses."

"What!" I exclaimed. "You freed us?"

"Yes, sir," he answered; "I did. I got out at our first stop, and thoroughly examined the carriage attachments. I found that the movable bar to which the whiffletrees were attached was connected to the vehicle by two straps and a bolt, the latter having a ring at the top and an iron nut at the bottom. While you and that reckless driver were talking together, and paying no attention to me, the only person in the party who thoroughly comprehended our danger, I unbuckled those straps, and with my strong, nervous fingers, without the aid of implements, I unscrewed the nut from the bolt. Then, sir, I took my seat on the outside of the coach, and felt that I held our safety in my own hands. For a time I allowed our vehicles to proceed; but when we approached this long slope which stretches before us, and our horses showed signs of increasing impetuosity, I leaned forward, hooked the handle of my umbrella in the ring of the bolt, and with a mighty effort jerked it out. I admit to you, sir, that I had overlooked the fact that the horses were also attached to the end of the pole, but I have often noticed that when we are discreet in judgment and prompt in action we are also fortunate. Thus was I fortunate. The hindermost horses, suddenly released, rushed upon those in front of them, and, in a manner, jumbled up the whole team, which seemed to throw the animals into such terror that they dashed to one side and snapped off the pole, after which they went madly tearing down the road, entirely beyond the control of the two riders. Our coach turned and ran into the side of the road with but a moderate concussion, and as I looked at those flying steeds, with their riders vainly endeavoring to restrain them, I could not sir, keep down an emotion of pride that I had been instrumental in freeing myself, my daughter, and my traveling companions from their dangerous proximity."

The speaker ceased, a smile of conscious merit upon his face. For the moment I could not say a word to him, I was so angry. But had I been able to say or do anything to indicate the wild indignation that filled my brain, I should have had no opportunity, for Mrs. Lecks stepped up to me and took me by the arm. Her face was very stern, and her expression gave one the idea of the rigidity of Bessemer steel.

"I've heard what has been said," she remarked, "and I wish to talk to this man. Your wife is over there with Mrs. Aleshine. Will you please take a walk with her along the road? You may stay away for a quarter of an hour."

"Madam," said Mr. Enderton, "I do not wish to talk to you."

"I didn't ask you whether you did or not," said Mrs. Lecks. "Mr. Craig, will you please get your wife away as quick and as far as you can?"

I took the hint, and, with Ruth on my arm, walked rapidly down the road. She was very glad to go, for she had been much frightened, and wanted to be alone with me to have me explain to her what had occurred. Mrs. Lecks, imagining from the expression of his countenance that Mr. Enderton had, in some way, been at the bottom of the trouble, and fearing that she should not be able to restrain her indignation when she found how he had done it, had ordered Mrs. Aleshine to keep Ruth away from her father. This action had increased the poor girl's anxiety, and she was glad enough to have me take her away and tell her all about our accident.

I did tell her all that had happened, speaking as mildly as I could of Mr. Enderton's conduct. Poor Ruth burst into tears.

"I do wish," she exclaimed, "that father would travel by himself! He is so nervous, and so easily frightened, that I am sure he would be happier when he could attend to his safety in his own way; and I know, too, that we should be happier without him."

I agreed most heartily with these sentiments, although I did not deem it necessary to say so, and Ruth now asked me what I supposed would become of us.

"If nothing happens to the driver and the boy," I replied, "I suppose they will go on until they get to the station to which we were bound and there they will procure a pole, if such a thing can be found, or, perhaps, get another coach, and come back for us. It would be useless for them to return to our coach in its present condition."

"And how soon do you think they will come back?" she said.

"Not for some hours," I replied. "The driver told me there were no houses between the place where we last stopped and the railroad-station, and I am sure he will not turn back until he reaches a place where he can get either a new pole or another vehicle."

Ruth and I walked to a turn at the bottom of the long hill down which our runaway steeds had sped. At this point we had an extended view of the road as it wound along the mountain-side, but we could see no signs of our horses, nor of any living thing. I did not, in fact, expect to see our team, for it would be foolish in the driver to come back until he was prepared to do something for us, and even if he had succeeded in controlling the runaway beasts, the quicker he got down the mountain the better.

By the time we had returned we had taken quite a long walk, but we were glad of it, for the exercise tranquilized us both. On our way back we noticed that a road which seemed to come up from below us joined the one we were on a short distance from the place where our accident occurred. This, probably, was the lower road which had been spoken of when we changed horses.

We found Mr. Enderton standing by himself. His face was of the hue of wood-ashes, his expression haggard. He reminded me of a man who had fallen from a considerable height, and who had been frightened and stupefied by the shock. I comprehended the situation without difficulty, and felt quite sure that had he had the choice he would have much preferred a thrashing to the plain talk he had heard from Mrs. Lecks.

"What is the matter, father?" exclaimed Ruth. "Were you hurt?"

Mr. Enderton looked in a dazed way at his daughter, and it was some moments before he appeared to have heard what she said. Then he answered abruptly: "Hurt? Oh, no! I am not hurt in the least. I was just thinking of something. I shall walk on to the village or town, which-ever it is, to which that man was taking us. It cannot be more than seven or eight miles away, if that. The road is down hill, and I can easily reach the place before nightfall. I will then personally attend to your rescue, and will see that a vehicle is immediately sent to you. There is no trust-ing these ignorant drivers. No," he continued, deprecatingly raising his hand; "do not attempt to dissuade me. Your safety and that of others is always my first care. Exertion is nothing."

Without further words, and pay-ing no attention to the remon-strances of his daughter, he strode off down the road.

I was very glad to see him go. At any time his presence was undesir-able to me, and under the present circumstances it would be more objectionable than ever. He was a good walker, and there was no doubt he would easily reach the station, where he might possibly be of some use to us.

Mrs. Lecks was sitting on a stone by the roadside. Her face was still stern and rigid, but there was an expression of satisfaction upon it which had not been there when I left her. Ruth went to the coach to get a shawl, and I said to Mrs. Lecks:

"'MRS. LECKS WAS SITTING ON A STONE.'"

"I suppose you had your talk with Mr. Enderton?"

"Talk!" she replied. "I should say so! If ever a man understands what people think of him, and knows what he is, from his crown to his feet, inside and outside, soul, body, bones, and skin, and what he may expect in this world and the next, he knows it. I didn't keep to what he has done for us this day. I went back to the first moment when he began to growl at payin' his honest board on the island, and I didn't let him off for a single sin that he has committed since. And now I feel that I've done my duty as far as he is concerned; and havin' got through with that, it's time we were lookin' about to see what we can do for our-selves."

It was indeed time, for the day was drawing toward its close. For a moment I had thought we would give Mr. Enderton a good start, and then follow him down the mountain to the station. But a little reflection showed me that this plan would not answer. Ruth was not strong enought to walk so far, and although Mrs. Aleshine had plenty of vigor, she was too plump to attempt such a tramp. Besides, the sky was so heavily overcast that it was not safe to leave the shelter of the coach.

As might have been expected, Mrs. Lecks and Mrs. Aleshine took immediate charge of the personal comfort of the party, and the first thing they did was to make preparations for a meal. Fortunately, we had plenty of provisions. Mrs. Aleshine had had charge of what she called our lunch-baskets—which were, indeed, much more like market-baskets than anything else,—and having small faith in the resources of roadside taverns, and great faith in the unlimited capabilities of Mr. Enderton in the mater of consuming food on a journey, she had provided bounteously and even extravagantly.

One side of the road was bordered by a forest, and on the ground was an abundance of dead wood. I gathered a quantity of this, and made a fire, which was very grateful to us, for the air was growing colder and colder. When we had eaten a substantial supper and had thoroughly warmed ourselves at the fire, we got into the coach to sit there and wait until relief should come. We sat for a long time—all night, in fact. We were not uncomfortable, for we each had a corner of the coach, and we were plentifully provided with wraps and rugs.

Contrary to their usual habit, Mrs. Lecks and Mrs. Aleshine did not talk much. When subjected to the annoyances of an ordinary accident, even if it should have been the result of carelessness, their disposition would have prompted them to take events as they came, and to make the best of whatever might happen to them. But this case was entirely different. We were stranded and abandoned on the road, on the side of a lonely, desolate mountain, on a cold, bleak night; and all this was the result of what they considered the deliberate and fiendish act of a man who was afraid of horses, and who cared for no one in the world but himself. Their minds were in such a condition that if they said any-thing they must vituperate, and they were so kindly disposed toward my wife, and had such a tender regard for her feelings, that they would not, in her presence, vituperate her father. So they said very little, and, nestling into their corners, were soon asleep.

After a time Ruth followed their example, and, though I was very anxiously watching out of the window for an approaching light, and listening for the sound of wheels, I, too, fell into a doze. It must have been ten or eleven o'clock when I was awakened by some delicate but cold touches on my face, the nature of which, when I first opened my eyes, I could not comprehend. But I soon understood what these cold touches meant. The window in the door of the coach on my side had been slightly lowered from the top to give us air, and through the narrow aperture the cold particles had come floating in. I looked through the window. The night was not very dark, for, although the sky was overcast, the moon was in its second quarter, and I could plainly see that it was snowing, and that the ground was already white.

This discovery sent a chill into my soul, for I was not unfamiliar with snows in mountain regions, and knew well what this might mean to us. But there was nothing that we could now do, and it would be useless and foolish to awaken my companions and distress them with this new disaster. Besides, I thought our situation might not be so very bad, after all. It was not yet winter, and the snowfall might prove to be but a light one. I gently closed the window, and made my body comfortable in its corner; but my mind continued very uncomfortable for I do not know how long.

When I awoke I found that there had been a heavy fall of snow in the night, and that the flakes were still coming down thick and fast. When Ruth first looked out upon the scene she was startled and dismayed. She was not accustomed to storms of this kind, and the snow frightened her. Upon Mrs. Lecks and Mrs. Aleshine the sight of the storm produced an entirely different effect. Here was a difficulty, a discomfort, a hardship; but it came in a natural way, and not by the hand of a dastardly coward of a man. With natural-happening difficulties they were accustomed to combat without fear or repining. They knew all about snow, and were not frightened by this storm. The difficulties which it presented to their minds actually raised their spirits, and from the grim and quiet beings of the last evening they became the same cheerful, dauntless, ready women that I had known before.

"Upon my word," exclaimed Mrs. Aleshine, as she clapped her face to a window of the coach, "if this isn't a reg'lar old-fashioned snowstorm! I've shoveled my own way through many a one like it to git to the barn to do my milkin' afore the men-folks had begun makin' paths, and I feel jus' like as though I could do it ag'in."

"Now, Barb'ry Aleshine," said Mrs. Lecks, "if you're thinkin' of

"I SOON HAD A CRACKLING FIRE."

shovelin' your way from this place to where your cows is, you'd better step right out and get at it, and I really do think that if you felt they were sufferin' for want of milkin' you'd make a start."

"I don't say," answered Mrs. Aleshine, with an illuminating grin, "that if the case was that way I mightn't have the hankerin', though not the capableness; but I don't know that there's any place to shovel our way to, jus' now."

Mrs. Lecks and I thought differently. Across the road, under the great trees, the ground was comparatively free from snow, and in some places, owing to the heavy evergreen foliage, it was entirely bare. It was very desirable that we should get to one of these spots and build a fire, for, though we had been well wrapped up, we all felt numbed and cold. In the boot at the back of the coach I knew that there was an ax, and I thought I might possibly find there a shovel. I opened the coach door, and saw that the snow was already above the lower step. By standing on the spokes of the back wheel I could easily get at the boot, and I soon pulled out the ax, but found no shovel. But this did not deter me. I made my way to the front wheel, and climbed up to the driver's box, where I knocked off one of the thin planks of the foot-board. and this, with the ax, I shaped into a rude shovel, with a handle rather too wide, but serviceable. With this I went vigorously to work, and soon had made a pathway across the road. Here I chopped off some low dead branches, picked up others, and soon had a crackling fire, around which my three companions gathered with delight.

A strong wind was now blowing, and the snow began to form into heavy drifts. The fire was very cheery and pleasant, but the wind was cutting, and we soon returned to the shelter of the coach, where we had our breakfast. This was not altogether a cold meal, for Mrs. Aleshine had provided a little tea-kettle, and, with some snow-water which I brought in boiling from the fire in the woods, we had all the hot and comforting tea we wanted.

We passed the morning waiting and looking out, and wondering what sort of conveyance would be sent for us. It was generally agreed that nothing on wheels could now be got over the road, and that we must be taken away in a sleigh.

"I like sleigh-ridin'," said Mrs. Aleshine, "if you're well wrapped up, with good hosses, and a hot brick for your feet; but I must say I don't know but what I'm goin' to be a little skeery goin' down these long hills. If we git fairly slidin', hosses, sleigh, and all together, there's no knowin' where we'll fetch up."

"There's one comfort, Barb'ry," remarked Mrs. Lecks, "and that is that when we do fetch up it'll be at the bottom of the hills, and not at the top; and as the bottom is what we want to get to, we oughtn't to complain."

"That depends a good deal whether we come down hind part foremost, or fore part front. But nobody's complainin' so fur, 'specially as the sleigh isn't here."

I joined in the outlooking and the conjectures, but I could not keep up the cheerful courage which animated my companions; for not only were the two elder women bright and cheery, but Ruth seemed to be animated and encouraged by their example, and showed herself as brave and contented as either of them. She was convinced that her father must have reached the railroad-station before it began to snow, and therefore she was troubled by no fears for his safety. But my mind was filled with many fears.

The snow was still coming down thick and fast, and the wind was piling it into great drifts, one of which was forming between the coach and a low embankment on that side of the road near which it stood.

About every half-hour I took my shovel and cleared out the path across the road from the other side of the coach to the woods. Several times after doing this I made my way among the trees, where the snow did not impede my progress, to points from which I had a view some distance down the mountain; and I could plainly see that there were several places where the road was blocked up by huge snow-drifts. It would be a slow, laborious and difficult undertaking for any relief-party to come to us from the station; and who was there at that place

to come? This was the question which most troubled me. The settlement at the station was probably a very small one, and that there should
be found at that place a sleigh or a sled with enough men to form a party
sufficiently strong to open a road up the mountain-side was scarcely to
be expected. Men and vehicles might be obtained at some point farther
along the railroad, but action of this kind would require time, and it
was not unlikely that the railroad itself was blocked up with snow. I
could form no idea satisfactory to myself of any plan by which relief
could come to us that day. Even the advent of a messenger on horseback was not to be expected. Such an adventurer would be lost in the
storm and among the drifts. On the morrow relief might come, but I
did not like to think too much about the morrow; and of any of my
thoughts and fears I said nothing to my companions.

At intervals, after I had freshly cleared out the pathway, the three
women, well bundled up, ran across the road to the fire under the trees.
This was the only way in which they could keep themselves warm, for
the coach, although it protected us from the storm, was a very cold
place to sit in. But the wind and the snow which frequently drove in
under the trees made it impossible to stay very long by the fire, and the
frequent passages to and from the coach were attended with much
exposure and wetting of feet. I therefore determined that some better
way must be devised for keeping ourselves warm; and, shortly after our
noonday meal, I thought of a plan, and immediately set to work to
carry it out.

The drift between the coach and the embankment had now risen
higher than the top of the vehicle, against one side of which it was
tightly packed. I dug a path around the back of the coach, and then
began to tunnel into the huge bank of snow. In about an hour I had
made an excavation nearly high enough for me to stand in, and close to
the stage door on that side; and I cleared away the snow so that this
door could open into the cavern I had formed. At the end opposite the
entrance of my cave, I worked a hole upward until I reached the outer
air. This hole was about a foot in diameter, and for some time the light,
unpacked snow from above kept falling and filling it up; but I managed
by packing and beating the sides with my shovel, to get the whole into a
condition in which it would retain the form of a rude chimney.

Now I hurried to bring wood and twigs, and having made a hearth
of green sticks, which I cut with my ax, I built a fire in this snowy fireplace. Mrs. Lecks, Mrs. Aleshine, and Ruth had been watching my
proceedings with great interest; and when the fire began to burn, and
the smoke to go out of my chimney, the coach door was opened, and
the genial heat gradually pervaded the vehicle.

"Upon my word," exclaimed Mrs. Aleshine, "if that isn't one of the brightest ideas I ever heard of! A fire in the middle of a snowbank, with a man there attendin' to it, an' a chimney! 'T isn't every day that you can see a thing like that!"

"I should hope not," remarked Mrs. Lecks, "for if the snow drifted this way every day, I'd be ready to give up the seein' business out and out! But I think, Mr. Craig, you ought to pass that shovel in to us so that we can dig you out when the fire begins to melt your little house and it all caves in on you."

"You can have the shovel," said I, "but I don't believe this snow-bank will cave in on me. Of course the heat will melt the snow, but I think it will dissolve gradually, so that the caving in, if there is any, won't be of much account, and then we shall have a big open space here in which we can keep up our fire."

"Oh, dear!" exclaimed Ruth, "you talk as if you expected to stay here ever so long, and we certainly can't do that. We should starve to death, for one thing."

"Don't be afraid of that," said Mrs. Aleshine. "There's plenty of victuals to last till the people come for us. When I pack baskets for travelin' or picnickin', I don't do no scrimpin'. An' we've got to keep up a fire, you know, for it wouldn't be pleasant for those men, when they've cut a way up the mountain to git at us, to find us all froze stiff."

Mrs. Lecks smiled. "You're awful tender of the feelin's of other people, Barb'ry," she said, "and a heart as warm as yourn ought to keep from freezin'."

"Which it has done, so far," said Mrs. Aleshine, complacently.

As I had expected, the water soon began to drip from the top and the sides of my cavern, and the chimney rapidly enlarged its dimensions. I made a passage for the melted snow to run off into a hollow, back of the coach; and as I kept up a good strong fire, the drops of water and occasional pieces of snow which fell into it were not able to extinguish it. The cavern enlarged rapidly, and in a little more than an hour the roof became so thin that while I was outside collecting wood it fell in and extinguished the fire. This accident, however, interrupted my operations but for a short time. I cleared away the snow at the bottom of the excavation, and rebuilt my fire on the bare ground. The high snow walls on three sides of it protected it from the wind, so that there was no danger of the flames being blown against the stage-coach, while the large open space above allowed a free vent for the smoke.

About the middle of the afternoon, to the great delight of us all, it stopped snowing, and when I had freshly shoveled out the path across the road my companions gladly embraced the opportunity of walking over to the comparatively protected ground under the trees and giving themselves a little exercise. During their absence I was busily engaged in arranging the fire, when I heard a low crunching sound on one side of me, and, turning my head, I saw in the wall of my excavation opposite to the stage-coach, and at a distance of four or five feet from the ground, an irregular hole in the snow, about a foot in diameter, from which protruded the head of a man. This head was wrapped, with the exception of the face, in a brown woolen comforter. The features were those of a man of about fifty, a little sallow and thin, without beard, whiskers, or mustache; although the cheeks and chin were darkened with a recent growth.

The astounding apparition of this head projecting itself from the snow wall of my cabin utterly paralyzed me, so that I neither moved nor spoke, but remained crouching by the fire, my eyes fixed upon the head. It smiled a little, and then spoke.

"Could you lend me a small iron pot?" it said.

I rose to my feet, almost ready to run away. Was this a dream? Or was it possible that there was a race of beings who inhabited snowbanks?

The face smiled again very pleasantly. "Do not be frightened," it said. "I saw you were startled, and spoke first of a familiar pot in order to reassure you."

"Who, in the name of Heaven, are you?" I gasped.

"I am only a traveler, sir," said the head, "who has met with an accident similar, I imagine, to that which has befallen you. But I cannot further converse with you in this position. Lying thus on my breast in a tunnel of snow will injuriously chill me. Could you conveniently lend me an iron pot?"

I was now convinced that this was an ordinary human being, and my courage and senses returned to me; but my astonishment remained boundless. "Before we talk of pots," I said, "I must know who you are, and how you got into that snowbank."

"I do not believe," said my visitor, "that I can get down, head foremost, to your level. I will therefore retire to my place of refuge, and perhaps we can communicate with each other through this aperture."

"Can I get through to your place of refuge?" I asked.

"Certainly," was the answer. "You are young and active, and the descent will not be so deep on my side. But I will first retire, and will then project toward you this sheepskin rug, which, if kept under you as you move forward, will protect your breast and arms from direct contact with the snow."

It was difficult to scramble up into the hole, but I succeeded in doing

"'COULD YOU LEND ME A SMALL IRON POT?'"

it, and found awaiting me the sheepskin rug, which, by the aid of an umbrella, the man had pushed toward me for my use. I was in a horizontal tunnel barely large enough for the passage of my body, and about six feet in length. When I had worked my way through this, and had put my head out of the other end, I looked into a small wooden shed, into which light entered only through a pane of glass set in a rude door opposite to me. I immediately perceived that the whole place was filled with the odor of spirituous liquors. The man stood awaiting me, and by his assistance I descended to the floor. As I did so I heard something which sounded like a titter, and looking around I saw in a corner a bundle of clothes and traveling-rugs, near the top of which appeared a pair of eyes. Turning again, I could discern in another corner a second bundle, similar to, but somewhat larger than, the other.

"These ladies are traveling with me," said the man, who was now wrapping about him a large cloak, and who appeared to be of a tall though rather slender figure. His manner and voice were those of a gentleman, extremely courteous and considerate. "As I am sure you are curious—and this I regard as quite natural, sir—to know why we are here, I will at once proceed to inform you. We started yesterday in a carriage for the railway-station, which is, I believe, some miles beyond this point. There were two roads from the last place at which we stopped, and we chose the one which ran along a valley, and which we supposed would be the pleasanter of the two. We there engaged a pair of horses which did not prove very serviceable animals, and, at a point about a hundred yards from where we now are, one of them gave out entirely. The driver declared that the only thing to be done was to turn loose the disabled horse, which would be certain, in time, to find his way back to his stable, and for him to proceed on the other animal to the station to which we were going, where he would procure some fresh horses and return as speedily as possible. To this plan we were obliged to consent, as there was no alternative. He told us that if we did not care to remain in the carriage, there was a shed by the side of the road, a little farther on, which was erected for the accommodation of men who are sometimes here in charge of relays of horses. After assuring us that he would not be absent more than three hours, he rode away, and we have not seen him since.

"Soon after he left us I came to this shed, and finding it tight and comparatively comfortable, I concluded it would give us relief from our somewhat cramped position in the carriage, and so conducted the ladies here. As night drew on it became very cold, and I determined to make a fire, a proceeding which, of course, would have been impossible in a vehicle. Fortunately I had with me, at the back of the carriage, a case of California brandy. By the aid of a stone I knocked the top off this case, and brought hither several of the bottles. I found in the shed an old tin pan, which I filled with the straw coverings of the bottles, and on this I poured brandy, which, being ignited, produced a fire without smoke, but which, as we gathered around it, gave out considerable heat."

As the speaker thus referred to his fuel, I understood the reason of the strong odor of spirits which filled the shed, and I experienced a certain relief in my mind.

The gentleman continued: "at first I attributed the delay of the driver's return to those ordinary hindrances which so frequently occur in rural and out-of-the-way places; but after a time I could not imagine any reasonable cause for his delay. As it began to grow dark I brought here our provision-baskets, and we partook of a slight repast. I then made the ladies as comfortable as possible, and awaited with much anxiety the return of the driver.

"After a time it began to snow, and feeling that the storm might interrupt communication with the carriage, I brought hither, making many trips for the purpose, the rest of the brandy, our wraps and rugs, and the cushions of the carriage. I did not believe that we should be left here all night, but thought it prudent to take all precautions, and to prepare for remaining in a place where we could have a fire. The morning showed me that I had acted wisely. As you know, sir, I found the road in each direction completely blocked up by snow, and I have since been unable to visit the carriage."

"Have you not all suffered from cold?" I inquired. "Have you food enough?"

"I will not say," replied the gentleman, "that in addition to our anxiety we have not suffered somewhat from cold, but for the greater part of this day I have adopted a plan which has resulted in considerable comfort to my companions. I have wrapped them up very closely and warmly, and they hold in each hand a hard-boiled egg. I thought it better to keep these for purposes of warmth than to eat them. About every half-hour I reboil the eggs in a little travelling tea-pot which we have. They retain their warmth for a considerable period, and this warmth in a moderate degree is communicated through the hands to the entire person."

As he said this a low laugh again burst forth from the bundle in one corner of the room, and I could not help smiling at this odd way of keeping warm. I looked toward the jocose bundle, and remarked that the eggs must be pretty hard by this time.

"These ladies," said the gentleman, "are not accustomed to the cold atmosphere of this region, and I have therefore forbidden them to talk, hoping thus to prevent injury from the inhalation of frosty air. So far we have not suffered, and we still have some food left. About noon I noticed smoke floating over this shed, and I forced open the door and made my way for some little distance outside, hoping to discover whence it came. I then heard voices on the other side of the enormous snow-drift behind us; but I could see no possible way of getting over the drift. Feeling that I must, without fail, open communication with any human beings who might be near us, I attempted to shout; but the cold had so affected my voice that I could not do so. I thereupon set my wits to work. At the back of this shed is a small window closed by a wooden shutter. I opened this shutter, and found outside a wall of snow packed closely against it. The snow was not very hard, and I believed that it would not be difficult to tunnel a way through it to the place where the voices seemed to be. I immediately set to work, for I feared that if we were obliged to remain here another night without assistance we should be compelled to-morrow morning to eat those four hard-boiled eggs which the ladies are holding, and which, very shortly, I must boil again."

"How did you manage to cut through the snow?" I asked. "Had you a shovel?"

"Oh, no," replied the other. "I used the tin pan. I found it answered very well as a scoop. Each time that I filled it I threw the contents out of our door."

"It must have been slow and difficult work," I said.

"Indeed it was," he replied. "The labor was arduous, and occupied me several hours. But when I saw a respectable man at a fire, and a stage-coach near by, I felt rewarded for all my trouble. May I ask you, sir, how you came to be thus snow-bound?"

I then briefly related the circumstances of our mishap, and had scarcely finished when a shrill sound came through the tunnel into the shed. It was the voice of Mrs. Aleshine.

"Hello!" she screamed, "are you in there? An' you don't mean to tell me there are other people in that hole?"

Feeling quite certain that my wife and her companions were in a state of mental agitation on the other side of the drift, I called back that I would be with them in a moment, and then explained to the gentleman why I could not remain with him longer. "But before I go," I said, "is there anything I can do for you? Do you really want an iron pot?"

"The food that remains to us," he answered, "is fragmentary and rather distasteful to the ladies, and I thought if I could make a little stew of it, it might prove more acceptable to them. But do not let me detain you another instant from your friends, and I advise you to go through that tunnel feet foremost, for you might, otherwise, experience difficulties in getting out at the other end."

I accepted his suggestion, and by his assistance and the help of the rough window-frame, I got into the hole feet first, and soon ejected myself into the midst of my alarmed companions. When they heard where I had been, and what I had seen, they were naturally astounded.

"Another party deserted at this very point!" exclaimed Ruth, who was both excitable and imaginative. "This looks like a conspiracy! Are we to be robbed and murdered?"

At these words Mrs. Aleshine sprang toward me. "Mr. Craig," she exclaimed, "if it's robbers, don't lose a minute! Never let 'em get ahead of you! Pull out your pistol and fire through the hole!"

"Gracious me! Barb'ry Aleshine," said Mrs. Lecks, "you don't suppose the robbers is them poor unfortunates on the other side of the drift! And I must say,

" WE WERE ABOUT TO

Mrs. Craig, that if there was any such thing as a conspiracy, your father must have been in it, for it was him who landed us just here. But of course none of us supposes nothin' of that kind, and the first thing we've got to think of is what we can do for them poor people."

"They seem to have some food left, but not much," I said, "and I fear they must be suffering from cold."

"Couldn't we poke some wood to them through this hole?" said Mrs. Aleshine, whose combative feelings had changed to the deepest compassion. "I should think they must be nearly froze, with nothin' to warm 'em but hard-b'iled eggs."

I explained that there was no place in their shed where they could build a fire, and proposed that we should give them some hot tea and some of our provisions.

"That's so!" said Mrs. Aleshine. "Just shout in to them that if they'll shove them eggs through the hole, I'll bile 'em fur 'em as often as they want 'em."

"I've just got to say this," ejaculated Mrs. Lecks, as she and Mrs. Aleshine were busily placing a portion of our now very much reduced stock of provisions in the smallest of our baskets: "this is the first time in my life that I ever heard of people warmin' themselves up with hens' eggs and spirits, excep' when mixed up into egg-nog; and that they resisted that temptation and contented themselves with plain honest heat, though very little of it, shows what kind of people they must be. And now, do you suppose we could slide this basket in without up-settin' the little kittle?"

I called to the gentleman that we were about to send him a basket, and then, by the aid of an umbrella, I gently pushed it through the snow tunnel to a point where he could reach it. Hearty thanks came back to us through the hole, and when the basket and kettle were returned, we prepared our own evening meal.

SEND HIM A BASKET."

"For the life of me," said Mrs. Lecks, as she sipped a cup of tea, "I can't imagine, if there was a shed so near us, why we didn't know it."

"That has been puzzling me," I replied; "but the other road, on which the shed is built is probably lower than this one, so that the upper part of the shed could not have projected far above the embankment between the two roads, and if there were weeds and dead grasses on the bank, as there probably were, they would have prevented us from noticing the top of a weather-worn shed."

"Especially," said Mrs. Lecks, "as we wasn't lookin' for sheds, and, as far as I know, we wasn't lookin' for anything on that side of the coach, for all my eyes was busy starin' about on the side we got in and out of, and down the road."

"Which mine was too," added Mrs. Aleshine. "And after it begun to snow we couldn't see nothin' anyhow, partic'larly when everything was all covered up."

"Well," added Mrs. Lecks, in conclusion, "as we didn't see the shed, it's a comfort to think there was reasons for it, and that we are not born fools."

It was now growing dark, and but few further communications took place through the little tunnel.

"Before we get ready to go to sleep," said Mrs. Aleshine, "for, havin' no candles, I guess we won't sit up late, hadn't we better rig up some kind of a little sled to put in that hole, with strings at both ends, so that we kin send in mustard-plasters and peppermint to them poor people if they happen to be sick in the night?"

This little project was not considered necessary, and after receiving

assurances from the gentleman on the other side that he would be able
to keep his party warm until morning, we bade each other good night;
and, after having replenished the fire, I got into the stage, where my
companions had already established themselves in their corners. I slept
very little, while I frequently went out to attend to the fire, and my
mind was racked by the most serious apprehensions. Our food was
nearly gone, and if relief did not come to us very soon I could see
nothing but a slow death before us, and, so far as I could imagine, there
was no more reason to expect succor on the following day than there
had been on the one just passed. Where were the men to be found who
could cut a road to us through those miles of snow-drifts?

Very little was said during the night by my companions, but I am
sure that they felt the seriousness of our situation, and that their
slumbers were broken and unrefreshing. If there had been anything to
do, Mrs. Lecks and Mrs. Aleshine would have been cheered up by the
prospect of doing it; but we all felt that there was nothing we could do.

PART V

A *JOYFUL MEETING* ENDS
IN A *DISPUTE*

AFTER A SECOND night spent in the stage-coach on that lonely
and desolate mountain road where we were now snow-bound, I arose
early in the morning, and went into the forest to collect some fuel; and
while thus engaged I made the discovery that the snow was covered
with a hard crust which would bear my weight. After the storm had
ceased the day before, the sun had shone brightly and the temperature
had moderated very much, so that the surface of the snow had slightly
thawed. During the night it became cold again, and this surface froze
into a hard coating of ice. When I found I could walk where I pleased,
my spirits rose, and I immediately set out to view the situation. The
aspect of the road gave me no encouragement. The snowfall had been
a heavy one, but had it not been for the high wind which accompanied
it, it would have thrown but moderate difficulties in the way of our
rescue. Reaching a point which commanded a considerable view along
the side of the mountain, I could see that in many places the road was
completely lost to sight on account of the great snow-drifts piled up on
it. I then walked to the point where the two roads met, and crossing
over, I climbed a slight rise in the ground which had cut off my view
in this direction, and found myself in a position from which I could
look directly down the side of the mountain below the road.

Here, the mountain-side, which I had supposed to be very steep and
rugged, descended in a long and gradual slope to the plains below, and

for the greater part of the distance was covered by a smooth, shining surface of frozen snow, unbroken by rock or tree. This snowy slope apparently extended for a mile or more, and then I could see it gradually blended itself into the greenish-brown turf of the lower country. Down in the valley there still were leaves upon the trees, and there were patches of verdure over the land. The storm which had piled its snows up here had given them rain down there and had freshened everything. It was like looking down into another climate and on another land. I saw a little smoke coming up behind a patch of trees. It must be that there was a house there! Could it be possible that we were within a mile or two of a human habitation? Yet, what comfort was there in that thought? The people in that house could not get to us, nor we to them, nor could they have heard of our situation, for the point where our road reached the lower country was miles farther on.

As I stood thus and gazed, it seemed to me that I could make a run and slide down the mountain-side into green fields, into safety, into life. I remembered those savage warriors who, looking from the summits of the Alps upon the fertile plains of Italy, seated themselves upon their shields and slid down to conquest and rich spoils.

An idea came into my mind, and I gave it glad welcome. There was not time to be lost. The sun was not yet high, but it was mounting in a clear sky, and should its rays become warm enough to melt the crust on which I stood, our last chance of escape would be gone. To plow our way to any place through deep, soft snow would be impossible. I hurried back to our coach, and found three very grave women standing around the fire. They were looking at a small quantity of food at the bottom of a large basket.

"That's every crumb there is left," said Mrs. Aleshine to me, "and when we pass in some to them unfortunates on the other side of the drift,—which, of course, we're bound to do,—we'll have what I call a skimpy meal. And that's not the worst of it. Until somebody gets up to us, it will be our last meal."

I took my poor Ruth by the hand, for she was looking very pale and troubled, and I said: "My dear friends, nobody can get up to this place for a long, long time; and before help could possibly reach us we should all be dead. But do not be frightened. It is not necessary to wait for any one to come to us. The snow is now covered with a crust which will bear our weight. I have thought of a way in which we can slide down the mountain-side, which, from a spot where I have been standing this morning, is no steeper than some coastal-hills, though very much longer. In a few minutes we can pass from this region of snow, where death from cold and starvation must soon overtake us, to a

grassy valley where there is no snow, and where we shall be within
walking distance of a house in which people are living."

Ruth grasped my arm. "Will it be safe?" she exclaimed.

"I think so," I answered. "I see no reason why we should meet with
any accident. At any rate, it is much safer than remaining here for
another hour; for if the crust melts, our last chance is gone."

"Mr. Craig," said Mrs. Lecks, "me and Mrs. Aleshine is no hands at
coastin' downhill, havin' given up that sort of thing since we was little
girls with short frocks and it didn't make no matter anyway. But you
know more about these things than we do; and if you say we can get
out of this dreadful place by slidin' downhill, we're ready to follow, if
you'll just go ahead. We followed you through the ocean, with nothin'
between our feet and the bottom but miles o' water and nobody knows
what sorts of dreadful fish; and when you say it's the right way to save
our lives, we're ready to follow you again. And as for you, Mrs. Ruth,
don't you be frightened. I don't know what we're goin' to slide on, but,
whatever it is, even if it's our own selves, me and Mrs. Aleshine will
take you between us, and if anything is run against, we'll get the bumps,
and not you."

I was delighted to see how rapidly my proposition was accepted, and
we made a hasty breakfast, first sending in some of our food to the other
party. The gentleman reported through the hole of communication
that they were all fairly well, but a good deal stiffened by cold and want
of exercise. He inquired, in a very anxious voice, if I had discovered any
signs of approaching relief. To this I replied that I had devised a plan
by which we could get ourselves out of our present dangerous situation,
and that in a very short time I would come round to the door of his
shed—for I could now walk on the crusted snow—and tell him about it.
He answered that these words cheered his heart, and that he would do
everything possible to cooperate with me.

I now went to work vigorously. I took the cushions from the coach,
four of them all together, and carried them to the brink of the slope
down which I purposed to make our descent. I also conveyed thither a
long coil of rawhide rope which I had previously discovered in the boot
of the coach. I then hurried along the other road, which, as has been
said before, lay at a somewhat lower level than the one we were on, and
when I reached the shed I found the door had been opened, and the
gentleman, with his tin pan, had scooped away a good deal of the snow
about it, so as to admit of a moderately easy passage in and out. He met
me outside, and grasped my hand.

"Sir, if you have a plan to propose," he said, "state it quickly. We
are in a position of great danger. Those two ladies inside the shed

cannot much longer endure this exposure, and I presume that the ladies in your party—although their voices, which I occasionally hear, do not seem to indicate it—must be in a like condition."

I replied that, so far, my companions had borne up very well, and without further waste of words proceeded to unfold my plan of escape.

When he had heard it the gentleman put on a very serious expression. "It seems hazardous," he said. "but it may be the only way out of our danger. Will you show me the point from which you took your observations?"

"Yes," said I; "but we must be in haste. The sun is getting up in the sky, and this crust may soon begin to melt. It is not yet really winter, you know."

We stepped quickly to the spot where I had carried the cushions. The gentleman stood and silently gazed first at the blocked-up roadway, then at the long, smooth slope of the mountain-side directly beneath us, and then at the verdure of the plain below, which had grown greener under the increasing brightness of the day. "Sir," said he, turning to me, "there is nothing to be done but to adopt your plan, or to remain here and die. We will accompany you in the descent, and I place myself under your orders."

"The first thing," said I, "is to bring here your carriage cushions, and help me to arrange them."

When he had brought the three cushions from the shed, the gentleman and I proceeded to place them with the others on the snow, so that the whole formed a sort of wide and nearly square mattress. Then with the rawhide rope, we bound them together in a rough but secure network of cordage. In this part of the work I found my companion very apt and skilful.

When this rude mattress was completed, I requested the gentleman to bring his ladies to the place, while I went for mine.

"What are we to pack up to take with us?" said Mrs. Aleshine, when I reached our coach.

"We take nothing at all," said I, "but the money in our pockets, and our rugs and wraps. Everything else must be left in the coach, to be brought down to us when the roads shall be cleared out."

With our rugs and shawls on our arms, we left the coach, and as we were crossing the other road we saw the gentleman and his companions approaching. These ladies were very much wrapped up, but one of them seemed to step along lightly and without difficulty, while the other moved slowly and was at times assisted by the gentleman.

A breeze had sprung up which filled the air with fine frozen particles blown from the uncrusted beds of snow along the edge of the forest, and I counseled Ruth to cover up her mouth and breathe as little of this snow powder as possible.

"If I'm to go coastin' at all," said Mrs. Aleshine, "I'd as lief do it with strangers as friends; and a little liefer, for that matter, if there's any bones to be broken. But I must say that I'd like to make the acquaintance of them ladies afore I git on to the sled, which"—at that moment catching sight of the mattress—"you don't mean to say that that's it?"

"Barb'ry Aleshine," said Mrs. Lecks, from underneath her great woolen comforter, "if you want to get your lungs friz, you'd better go on talkin'. Manners is manners, but they can wait till we get to the bottom of the hill."

Notwithstanding this admonition, I noticed that as soon as the two parties met, both Mrs. Lecks and Mrs. Aleshine advanced and shook hands with the ladies who had been their neighbors under such peculiar circumstances, and that Mrs. Lecks herself expressed a muffled hope that they might all get down safely.

I now pushed the mattress which was to serve as our sled as close as was prudent to the edge of the descent, and requested the party to seat themselves upon it. Without hesitation Mrs. Lecks and Mrs. Aleshine sat down, taking Ruth between them, as they had promised to do. My young wife was very nervous, but the cool demeanor of her companions, and my evident belief in the practicability of the plan, gave her courage and she quietly took her seat. The younger of the two strange ladies stepped lightly on the cushions, and before seating herself stood up for a good look at the far-extending bed of snow over which we were to take our way. The prospect did not appear to deter her, and she sat down promptly and with an air that seemed to say that she anticipated a certain enjoyment from the adventure. The elder lady, however, exhibited very different emotions. She shrank back from the cushions toward which the gentleman was conducting her, and turned her face away from the declivity. Her companion assured her that it was absolutely necessary that we should descend from the mountain in this way, for there was no other; and asserting his belief that our slide would be a perfectly safe one, he gently drew her to the mattress and induced her to sit down.

I now noticed, for the first time, that the gentleman carried under one arm, and covered by his long cloak, a large package of some sort, and I immediately said to him: "It will be very imprudent for us to attempt to carry any of our property except what we can put in our pockets or wrap around us. Everything else should be left here, either in your carriage or our coach, and I have no fear that anything will be lost. But even if our luggage were in danger of being molested, we cannot afford to consider it under circumstances such as these."

"My dear sir," said the gentleman, speaking very gravely, "I appreciate the hazards of our position as keenly as yourself. Our valises, and all the light luggage which we had with us in our carriage, I have left there, and shall not give them another thought. But with the parcel I hold under this arm I cannot part, and if I go down the mountain-side on these cushions, it must go with me. If you refuse in such a case to allow me to be one of your party, I must remain behind, and endeavor to find a board or something else on which I can make the descent of the mountain."

He spoke courteously, but with an air of decision which showed me that it would be of no use to argue with him. Besides, there was no time for parleying, and if this gentleman chose to take his chances with but one arm at liberty, it was no longer my affair. I therefore desired him to sit down, and I arranged the company so that they sat back to back, their feet drawn up to the edge of the mattress. I then took the place which had been reserved for me as steersman, and having tied several shawls together, end to end, I passed them around the whole of us under our arms, thus binding us all firmly together. I felt that one of our greatest dangers would be that one or more of the party might slip from the mattress during the descent.

When all was ready I asked the gentleman, who, with the elder lady, sat near me at the back of the mattress, to assist in giving us a start by pushing outward with his heels while I thrust the handle of my wooden shovel into the crust and thus pushed the mattress forward. The starting was a little difficult, but in a minute or two we had pushed the mattress partly over the brink, and then, after a few more efforts, we began to slide downward.

The motion, at first slow, suddenly became quite rapid, and I heard behind me a cry or exclamation, from whom I knew not, but I felt quite sure it did not come from any of my party. I hoped to be able to make some use of my shovel in the guidance of our unwieldy raft or mattress-sled, but I soon found this impossible, and down we went over the smooth, hard-frozen slope, with nothing to direct our course but the varying undulations of the mountain-side. Every moment we seemed to go faster and faster, and soon we began to revolve, so that sometimes I was in front and sometimes behind. Once, when passing over a very smooth sheet of snow, we fairly spun around, so that in every direction feet were flying out from a common center and heels grating on the frozen crust. But there were no more cries or exclamations. Each one of us grasped the cordage which held the cushions together, and the rapidity of the motion forced us almost to hold our breath.

Down the smooth, white slope we sped, as a bird skims through the air. It seemed to me as if we passed over miles and miles of snow. Sometimes my face was turned down the mountain, where the snow-surface seemed to stretch out illimitably, and then it was turned upward toward the apparently illimitable slopes over which we had passed.

Presently, my position now being in front of the little group that glanced along its glittering way, I saw at some distance below me a long

"WE BEGAN TO SLIDE DOWNWARD."

rise or terrace, which ran along the mountain-side for a considerable distance, and which cut off our view of everything below us. As we approached this hillock the descent became much more gradual and our progress slower, and at last I began to fear that our acquired velocity would not be sufficient to carry us up the side of this elevation and so enable us to continue our descent. I therefore called to everybody in the rear to kick out vigorously, and with my shovel I endeavored to assist our progress. As we approached the summit of the elevation we moved slower and slower. I became very anxious, for, should we slide backward, we might find it difficult or impossible to get ourselves and the mattress up this little hill. But the gentleman and myself worked valiantly, and as for Mrs. Lecks and Mrs. Aleshine, they kicked their heels through the frozen crust with such energy that we moved sidewise almost as much as upward. But in a moment the anxious suspense was over, and we rested on the ridge of the long hillock, with the mountain-side stretching down to the plain, which lay not very far below us.

I should have been glad to remain here a few minutes to regain breath, and give some consideration to the rest of our descent, but as some of those behind continued to push, the mattress slid over the edge of the terrace, and down again we went. Our progress was not so rapid, but it was very much more unpleasant. The snow was thinner; there was little or no crust upon it, and we very soon reached a wide extent of exposed turf, over which we slid, but not without a good deal of bumping against stones and protuberances. Then there was another sheet of snow, which quickened our downward impetus; and, after that, the snow was seen only in occasional patches, and our progress continued over a long slope of short, partly dried grass, which was very slippery, and over which we passed with considerable quickness.

I wished now to bring our uncouth sled to a stop, and to endeavour to make the rest of the descent on foot. But although I stuck out my heels, and tried to thrust the handle of my shovel into the ground, it was of no use. On we went, and the inequalities of the surface gave an irregularity of motion which was uncomfortable and alarming. We turned to this side and that; we bounced and bumped; and the rawhide ropes, which must have been greatly frayed and cut by the snow-crust, now gave way in several places, and I knew that the mattress would soon separate into its original cushions, if indeed they still could be called cushions. Fearing increased danger should we now continue bound together in a bunch, I jerked apart the shawl-knot under my arms, and the next moment, it seemed to me, there was a general dissolution of our connection with each other. Fortunately, we were now near the bottom of the slope, for while some of us stuck fast to the cushions, others rolled over, or slid, independent of any projection, while I, being thrown forward on my feet, actually ran downhill! I had just succeeded in stopping myself when down upon me came the rest of the company, all prostrate in some position or other.

Now from an unwieldy mass of shawls came a cry:

"Oh, Albert Dusante! Where are you? Lucille! Lucille!"

Instantly sprang to one foot good Mrs. Aleshine, her other foot being entangled in a mass of shawls which dragged behind her. Her bonnet was split open and mashed down over her eyes. In her left hand she waved a piece of yellow flannel, which in her last mad descent she had torn from some part of the person of Mrs. Lecks, and in the other a bunch of stout dead weeds, which she had seized and pulled up by the roots as she had passed them. Her dress was ripped open down her rotund back, and the earth from the weed roots had bespattered her face. From the midst of this dilapidation her round eyes sparkled with excitement. Hopping on one foot, the shawls and a part of a cushion dragging behind her, she shouted:

"The Dusantes! They are the Dusantes!"

Then, pitching forward on her knees before the two strange ladies, who had now tumbled into each other's arms, she cried:

"Oh, which is Emily, and which is Lucille?"

"'OH, WHICH IS EMILY, AND WHICH IS LUCILLE?'"

I had rushed toward Ruth, who had clung to a cushion and was now sitting upon it, when Mrs. Lecks, who was close beside her, arose to her feet and stood upright. One foot was thrust through her own bonnet, and her clothes gave evidence of the frenzy and power of Mrs. Aleshine's grasp, but her mien was dignified and her aspect stately.

"Barb'ry Aleshine!" she exclaimed, "if them Dusantes has dropped down from heaven at your very feet, can't you give 'em a minute to feel their ribs and see if their legs and arms is broken?"

The younger lady now turned her head toward Mrs. Aleshine. "I am Lucille," she said.

In a moment the good woman's arms were around her neck. "I always liked you the best of the two," she whispered into the ear of the astonished young lady.

Having found that Ruth was unhurt, I ran to the assistance of the others. The gentleman had just arisen from a cushion, upon which, lying flat on his back, he had slid over the grass, still holding under one arm the package from which he had refused to part. I helped him to raise the elder lady to her feet. She had been a good deal shaken, and much frightened, but although a little bruised, she had received no important injury.

I went to fill a leather pocket-cup from a brook near by, and when I returned I found the gentleman standing, confronted by Mrs. Lecks, Mrs. Aleshine, and Ruth, while his own companions were regarding the group with eager interest.

"Yes," he was saying, "my name is Dusante. But why do you ask at this moment? Why do you show such excited concern on the subject?"

"Why?" exclaimed Mrs. Lecks. "I will tell you why, sir. My name is Mrs. Lecks, and this is Mrs. Aleshine, and if you are the Mr. Dusante with the house on the desert island, this is the Mrs. Craig who was married in that very house, and the gentleman here with the water is Mr. Craig, who wrote you the letter, which I hope you got. And if that isn't reason enough for our wanting to know if you are Mr. Dusante, I'd like to be told what more there could be!"

"It's them! Of course it's them!" cried Mrs. Aleshine. "I had a feelin' while we were scootin' downhill that they was near and dear to us, though exactly why and how, I didn't know. And she's told me she's Lucille, and of course the other must be Emily, though what relations—"

"Am I to understand," interrupted the gentleman, looking with earnest animation from one to the other of us, "that these are the good people who inhabited my house on the island?"

"The very ones!" cried Mrs. Aleshine. "And what relation are you to Emily? and Lucille to her?"

The gentleman stepped backward and laid down the package which he had held under his arm, and advancing toward me with outstretched hands, and with tears starting to his eyes, he exclaimed:

"And this man, then, to whom I owe so much, is Mr. Craig!"

"Owe me!" I said. "It is to you that we owe our very lives, and our escape from death in mid-ocean."

"Do not speak of it," he said, shaking his head, with a sorrowful expression on his face. "You owe me nothing. I would to Heaven it were not so! But we will not talk of that now. And this is Mrs. Craig," he continued, taking Ruth by the hand, "the fair lady whose nuptials were celebrated in my house. And Mrs. Lecks, and Mrs. Aleshine." As he spoke he shook hands with each. "How I have longed to meet you! I have thought of you every day since I returned to my island and discovered that you had been—I wish I could say—my guests. And where is the reverend gentleman? and the three mariners? I hope that nothing has befallen them!"

"Alas!—for three of them at least," ejaculated Mrs. Aleshine; "they have left us, but they are all right. And now, sir, if you could tell us what relation you are to Emily, and what Lucille—"

"Barb'ry!" cried Mrs. Lecks, making a dash toward her friend, "can't you give the man a minute to breathe? Don't you see he's so dumflustered that he hardly knows who he is himself? If them two women was to sink down dead with hunger and hard slidin' right afore your very eyes while you was askin' what relation they was to each other and to him, it would no more'n serve you right! We'd better be seein' if anythin' 's the matter with 'em, and what we can do for 'em."

At this moment the younger of Mr. Dusante's ladies quickly stepped forward. "Oh, Mrs. Craig, Mrs. Lecks, and Mrs. Aleshine!" she exclaimed, "I'm just dying to know all about you!"

"And which, contrariwise," cried Mrs. Aleshine, "is the same with us, exactly."

"And of all places in the world," continued the young lady, "that we should meet here!"

No one could have been more desirous than I was to know all about these Dusantes, and to discuss the strange manner of our meeting; but I saw that Ruth was looking very pale and faint, and that the elder Dusante lady had sat down again upon the ground as though obliged to do so by sheer exhaustion, and I therefore hailed with a double delight the interruption of further explanations by the appearance of two men on horseback who came galloping toward us.

They belonged to the house which I had noticed from the road above, and one of them had seen our swift descent down the mountain-side.

At first he had thought the black object he saw sliding over the snow-slopes was a rock or a mass of underbrush, but his keen eye soon told him that it was a group of human beings, and summoning a companion, he had set out for the foot of the mountain as soon as horses could be caught and saddled.

The men were much surprised when they heard the details of our adventure, but as it was quite plain that some members of our party needed immediate nourishment and attention, the questions and explanations were made very short. The men dismounted from their horses, and the elder Dusante lady was placed upon one of them, one man leading the animal and the other supporting the lady. Ruth mounted the other horse, and I walked by her to assist her in keeping her seat; but she held fast to the high pommel of the saddle, and got on very well. Mr. Dusante took his younger companion on one arm, and his package under the other, while Mrs. Lecks, having relieved her foot from the encircling bonnet, and Mrs. Aleshine, now free from the entangling shawls, followed in the rear. The men offered to come back with the horses for them, if they would wait; but the two women declared that they were quite able to walk, and intended to do no waiting, and they trudged vigorously after us. The sun was now high, and the air down here was quite different from that of the mountain-side, being pleasant and almost warm. The men said that the snows above would probably soon melt, as it was much too early in the season for snow to lie long on these lower sides of the mountains.

Our way lay over an almost level plain for about a mile. A portion of it was somewhat rough, so that when we reached the low house to which we were bound, we were all very glad indeed to get there. The house belonged to the two men, who owned a small ranch here. One of them was married, and his wife immediately set herself to work to attend to our needs. Her home was small, its rooms few, and her larder very plain in quality; but everything she had was placed at our disposal. Her own bed was given to the elder Dusante lady, who took immediate possession of it; and after a quickly prepared but plentiful meal of fried pork, corn-bread, and coffee, the rest of us stretched ourselves out to rest wherever we could find a place. Before lying down, however, I had, at Ruth's earnest solicitation, engaged one of the men to ride to the railroad-station to inquire about Mr. Enderton, and to inform him of our safety. By taking a route which ran parallel with the mountain-chain, but at some distance from it, the station, the man said, could be reached without encountering snow.

None of us had had proper rest during the past two nights, and we slept soundly until dark, when we were aroused to partake of supper.

All of us, except the elder Dusante lady, who preferred to remain in bed, gathered around the table. After supper a large fire, principally of brushwood, was built upon the hearth; and with the bright blaze, two candles, and a lamp, the low room appeared light and cheery. We drew

"WE DREW UP ABOUT THE FIRE."

up about the fire—for the night was cool—on whatever chairs, stools, or boxes we could find, and no sooner had we all seated ourselves than Mrs. Aleshine exclaimed:

"Now, Mr. Dusante, it ain't in the power of mortal man, nor woman neither,—an' if put the other way it might be stronger,—to wait any longer before knowin' what relation Lucille is to Emily, an' you to them, an' all about that house of yours on the island. If I'd blown up into bits this day through holdin' in my wantin' to know, I shouldn't have wondered! An' if it hadn't been for hard sleep, I don't believe I could have held in, nohow!"

"That's my mind exactly," said Mrs. Lecks; "and though I know there's a time for all things, and don't believe in crowdin' questions on played-out people, I do think, Mr. Dusante, that if I could have caught up with you when we was comin' over here, I'd have asked you to speak out on these p'ints. But you're a long-legged walker, which Mrs. Aleshine is not, and it wouldn't have done to leave her behind."

"Which she wouldn't 'a' been," said Mrs. Aleshine, "long legs or short."

Ruth and I added our entreaties that Mr. Dusante should tell his story, and the good ranchman and his wife said that if there was anything to be done in the story-telling line they were in for it, strong; and quitting their work of clearing away supper things, they brought an old hair trunk from another room, and sat down just behind Mrs. Lecks.

The younger Dusante lady, who, having been divested of her wraps, her veil, and the woolen shawl that had been tied over her head, had proved to be a very pretty girl with black eyes, here declared that it had been her intention at the first opportunity to get us to tell our story, but as we had asked first, she supposed we ought to be satisfied first.

"I do not wish, my good friends," said Mr. Dusante, "to delay for a moment longer than necessary your very pardonable curiosity concerning me and my family; and I must say at the same time that, although your letter, sir, gave me a very clear account of your visit to my island, there are many things which naturally could not be contained within the limits of a letter, and about which I am most anxious to make inquiries. But these I will reserve until my own narration is finished.

"My name is Albert Dusante. It may interest you to know that my father was a Frenchman and my mother an American lady from New England. I was born in France, but have lived very little in that country, and for a great part of my life have been a merchant in Honolulu. For the past few years, however, I have been enabled to free myself in a great degree from the trammels of business, and to devote myself to the pursuits of a man of leisure. I have never married, and this young lady is my sister."

"Then what relation," began Mrs. Aleshine, "is she to—?"

At this moment the hand of Mrs. Lecks, falling heavily into the lap of the speaker, stopped this question, and Mr. Dusante proceeded:

"Our parents died when Lucille was an infant, and we have no near blood relations."

At this the faces of both Mrs. Aleshine and Mrs. Lecks assumed expressions as if they had each just received a letter superscribed in an unknown hand, and were wondering who it could possibly be from.

"The lady who is now resting in the adjoining room," continued Mr. Dusante, "is a dear friend who has been adopted by me as a mother."

"Upon my word! " burst from Mrs. Lecks and Mrs. Aleshine, in as much unison of time and tone as if the words had been a response in a church service, while Miss Lucille leaned back against the wall near which she sat, and laughed gleefully. Mr. Dusante, however, continued his statements with the same quiet gravity with which he had begun.

"This lady was a dear friend of my mother, although younger than she. I adopted her as a mother to my little orphan sister, and, consequently, placed her in the same maternal relation to myself, doing this with much earnest satisfaction, for I hoped to be able to return, as a son, something of the tender care and affection which she would bestow on Lucille as a daughter."

"And she is Emily?" cried Mrs. Aleshine.

"She adopted our name," answered the speaker, "and she is Mrs. Emily Dusante."

"And she is your adopted *mother*?" said Mrs. Aleshine.

"Adopted mother!" ejaculated Mrs. Lecks.

"Yes," answered Mr. Dusante.

"And that is the only relation she is to you two?" said Mrs. Lecks.

"And you to her?" added Mrs. Aleshine.

"Most assuredly," answered Mr. Dusante.

Here Mrs. Lecks leaned back in her chair, folded her hands in her lap, and ejaculated, "Well, well!" and then allowed her face to assume a rigid intention of having nothing more to say at the present moment.

"One thing is certain," remarked Mrs. Aleshine, in a tone which indicated that she did not care who heard her; "I always liked Lucille the best!"

At this Ruth and I exchanged smiles with Miss Lucille, and Mr. Dusante proceeded:

"I do not wish to occupy too much of your time with our personal affairs, and will therefore state that the island on which you found refuge, and where I wish most heartily I had been present to act as host, was bought by me as a retreat from the annoyances of business and the exactions of society. I built there a good house—"

"Which it truly was," said Mrs. Aleshine, "with fixtures in it for water, and letting it off, which I never saw in a house so far out of town."

"I furnished it suitably," said Mr. Dusante. "We had books and music, and for several years we passed vacations there which were both enjoyable and profitable. But of late my sister has found the place lonely, and we have traveled a good deal, making intermittent and often short visits to the island.

"As I never cared to leave anyone on that lonely spot during our absences from it, I arranged a gateway of bars across the only opening in the reef, with the intention of preventing marauding visits from fishing-boats or other small craft which might be passing that way. As the island was out of the ordinary track of vessels, I did not imagine that my bars would ever prove an obstacle to unfortunate castaways who might seek a refuge there."

"Which they didn't," remarked Mrs. Aleshine, "for under we bobbed."

"I never exactly understood," said Mr. Dusante, "and I hope to have it explained to me in due time, how you passed my bars without removing them; and I have had a sore weight upon my conscience since I discovered that shipwrecked persons, fleeing to my house from the perils of the sea, should have found those inhospitable bars in their way—"

"Which is a weight you might as well cast off, and be done with it," said Mrs. Lecks, her deep-set notions on the rights of property obliging her to speak; "for if a man hasn't a right to lock up his house when he goes away and leaves it, I don't know what rights anybody has about anything. Me, or Mrs. Aleshine, or anybody else here who has a house, might just as well go off travelin', or to town visitin', and leave our front door unlocked, and the yard gate swinging' on its hinges, because we was afraid that some tramp or other body with no house or home might come along and not be able to get in and make himself comfortable. Your business, sir, when you left that house and all your belongin's on that island, was to leave everything tight and safe; and the business of people sailin' in ships was to go on their proper way, and not be runnin' into each other. And if these last mentioned didn't see fit to do that, and so got into trouble, they should have gone to some island where there were people to attend to 'em, just as the tramps should go to the poorhouse. And this is what we would have done—not meanin' the poorhouse—if we hadn't been so over long-headed as to get into a leaky boat, which, I wish it understood, is sayin' nothin' against Mr. Craig."

"That's true," said Mrs. Aleshine, "for nobody has got a right to complain that a fellow-bein' locks his own door after him. But it does seem to me, sir, that in such scattered neighborhoods as your island is in, it might be a good thing to leave something to eat an' drink— perhaps in a bottle or in a tin pail—at the outside of your bars for them as might come along shipwrecked, an' not be able to get inside on account of bein' obliged to come in a boat, an' not as we did; an' so, when they found they'd have to go on, they might have somethin' to keep up their strength till they got to another house."

"Now, Barb'ry Aleshine," said Mrs. Lecks, "when you start off on a journey to Japan or any other place an' leave mince-pies and buttered toast a-stickin' on the p'ints of your pickets for tramps that might come along and need 'em, you can do that kind of talkin'. But as that time hasn't come, let's hear the rest of Mr. Dusante's story."

"When I first visited my island this year," continued the narrator, "we made but a short stay, as we were all desirous of taking a somewhat extended sea-voyage in my steam-yacht. We visited several places of interest, and when we returned, just six weeks ago to-day—"

"Just one week, lackin' a day," exclaimed Mrs. Lecks, "after we left that spot!"

"If I'd 'a' knowed," said Mrs. Aleshine, rising to her feet, "that you'd be back so soon, I'd 'a' made them sailormen live on fish, I'd 'a' eat garden-truck myself, and I'd be bound I'd 'a' made the flour hold out for six days more for the rest of 'em, if I'd 'a' had to work my fingers to the skin and bone to do it!" Then she sat down solemnly.

"When we returned," continued Mr. Dusante, "I was pleased to find my bars intact; and when these were unlocked, and the boat from our yacht went through with ourselves and our servants, it was very agreeable to notice the good order which seemed to prevail everywhere. As we passed from the wharf to the house, not even fallen boughs or weeds were seen to indicate that we had been away from the place for more than two months. When we entered the house, my mother and sister immediately ascended to their chambers, and when the windows had been opened I heard them from above calling to each other and remarking upon the freshness and cleanliness of the rooms. I went to my library, and when I had thrown open the window I was struck with the somewhat peculiar air of order which seemed to obtain in the room. The books stood upon their shelves with a remarkable regularity, and the chairs and other furniture were arranged with a precision which impressed me as unusual. In a moment, sir, I saw your letter upon the table addressed to me. Greatly astonished, I opened and read it.

"When I had finished it my amazement was great indeed; but obeying an instant impulse, I stepped into the dining-room, which a servant had opened, and took the ginger-jar from the mantelpiece. When I lifted from it the little brown-paper parcel, and beneath it saw the money which had been mentioned in the letter, you may imagine the condition of my mind. I did not take out the money, nor count it; but covering it again with the paper parcel, which I believed contained fish-hooks, and with the jar in my hands, I returned to the library, where I sat down to ponder upon these most astounding revelations. While so doing my mother and sister hastily entered the room. Lucille declared in an excited manner that she believed that the brownies or some other fairies had been there while we were away and had kept the house in order. The whole place was actually cleaner, she said, than when we left it. She had taken down a thin dress from her closet, and it looked as if it had just come from the hand of a laundress, with the ruffles ironed smoother and more evenly than they had ever been since it was first stitched together. 'Albert,' said my mother, her face pale, 'there has been somebody in this house!' Then she went on to say that the windows, which were left unwashed because we went away in somewhat of a hurry, were as bright and clean as if the maids had just been rubbing them; the floors and furniture were cleaner and freer from dust than they had ever been before; and the whole house looked as if we had just left it yesterday. 'In fact,' she said, 'it is unnaturally clean!'"

During this part of Mr. Dusante's story Mrs. Lecks and Mrs. Aleshine sat very quiet, with an air of sedate humility upon their faces; but I could see by the proud light in their eyes that they felt their superiority to ordinary women, although they were properly resolved not to show such feeling.

"At that moment," continued Mr. Dusante, "a servant came hurrying into the room, and informed us that the flour was all gone, and that there was scarcely anything in the pantries to eat. At this my mother and my sister, who knew that an abundance of provisions had been left in the house, looked at each other aghast. But before they could express their consternation in words, I addressed them. 'My dear mother,' said I, 'and Lucille, there truly has been some one in this house. By this letter I am informed that for several weeks eight persons have lived here under this roof; a marriage has been solemnized, and the happy couple have gone forth from our doors. These persons have eaten our food, they have made use of our property, and this has been their temporary home. But they are good people, honest and true-hearted, for they have left the house in better order than they found it, and more than the price of all they have consumed is in that ginger-jar.' And thereupon I read them your letter, sir.

"I cannot undertake to describe the wonder and absorbing interest with which this letter filled our minds. All needful stores were brought ashore from the yacht, which lay outside the reef, and we began our usual life on the island; but none of the occupations or recreations in which we formerly employed our time now possessed any attractions for us. Our minds were filled with thoughts of the persons who had been so strangely living in our house; and our conversation was mainly made up of surmises as to what sort of people they were, whether or not we should ever see them, and similar suppositions."

"Yes, indeed!" exclaimed Miss Lucille. "I thought of you by day and by night, and pictured you all in various ways, but never as you really are. Sometimes I used to think that the boat in which you went away had been sunk in a storm in which you were all drowned, and that perhaps your ghosts would come back and live in our house, and sleep in our beds, and clean our windows, and wash and iron our clothes, and do all sorts of things in the night."

"Goodnessful, gracious me!" cried Mrs. Aleshine, "don't talk that way! The idea of bein' a cold ghost, goin' about in the dark, is worse than slidin' down a snow-mountain, even if you had to do it on the bare of your back."

"Barb'ry!" said Mrs. Lecks, severely.

"The idea is jus' as chillin'," replied her undaunted friend.

"Two things connected with this matter," continued Mr. Dusante, "weighed heavily on my mind. One of these I have already mentioned —the cruel inhospitality of the barred entrance."

I had refrained from adding to the interruptions to Mr. Dusante's narrative, but I now felt impelled to assure the gentleman, on behalf of myself and wife, that we shared the opinions of Mrs. Lecks and Mrs. Aleshine, and felt that he could in no way be blamed for thus protecting his private property.

"You are very good," said Mr. Dusante, "but I will say here that there are now no bars to that entrance. I have left some people on the island, who will take care of my property and succor any unfortunate castaways who may arrive there. The other matter to which I alluded was, however, the heavier load which oppressed me. This was the money in the ginger-jar. I could not endure to reflect that I had been paid actual money for the hospitality I would have been so glad to offer to you poor shipwrecked people. Every sentiment of my being rebelled against such a thing. I was grieved. I was ashamed. At last I determined I would bear no longer the ignominy of this brand of inhospitality, and that, with the ginger-jar in my hand, I would search over the world, if necessary, for the persons who in my absence had paid board to me, and return to them the jar with its contents uncounted and untouched. Your letter informed me of the island to which you were bound, and if I did not find you there I could discover to what port you had taken your departure. There I could make further inquiries, and so follow you. When I proposed this plan to my family they agreed to it instantly, for their interest in the matter was almost as great as mine; and in a day or two we started on our quest.

"I easily traced you to San Francisco, and found the hotel at which you had stopped. Here I obtained fresh news of you, and learned that you had started East, and that the destination of the party was believed to be Philadelphia. I had hoped that I should meet with you before you left California; but supposing that by that time you had reached your destination, or were, at least, far on your way, I yielded to the

solicitations of my sister and made some excursions in California, in-
tending then to follow you to Philadelphia, and there to advertise for
Mr. Craig, if he could not otherwise be found. However, by the rarest
and most fortunate of chances, we have met thus early, and for this I
can never be too devoutly thankful."

"Nor we," said I, earnestly; "for our greatly desired acquaintance
with you and your family could not have begun too soon."

"Now," said Mr. Dusante, "I will perform the duty for which my
journey was undertaken, and I assure you it is a great pleasure to me to
be able so soon to carry out this cherished purpose."

" REVEALING THE FAMILIAR
FAT LITTLE GINGER-JAR."

He then took up from the floor by
his side the package which he had so
safely guarded during his swift and
perilous descent of the mountainside,
and which he had since kept close by
him. Placing this upon his knee, he removed the light shawl in which it had
been rolled, and then several pieces of
wrapping-paper, revealing to our eyes
the familiar fat little ginger-jar which
had stood on the mantelpiece of the
dining-room in the house on the island,
and in which we had deposited our
board money.

"It would be simply impossible for
me," said Mr. Dusante, "to consent to
retain in my possession money paid for
the aid which I involuntarily rendered
to shipwrecked people. Had I been
present on the island, that aid would
have been most heartily and freely
given, and the fact of my absence makes no difference whatever in regard to my feelings on the subject of your paying for the food and
shelter you found at my house. Having understood from Mr. Craig's
letter that it was Mrs. Lecks who superintended the collection and
depositing of the money, I now return to you, madam, this jar with its
contents."

"And which," said Mrs. Lecks, sitting up very rigidly, with her
hands clasped behind her, "I don't take. If it had been a day and a
night, or even two nights and over a Sunday, it wouldn't have mattered
but when me and Mrs. Aleshine—and the rest of the party can speak
for themselves—stays for weeks and weeks, without leave or license, in a

man's house, we pay our board—of course deductin' services. Good night."

With that she arose, and walked, very erect, into the adjoining room.

"It was all very well, Mr. Dusante," said Mrs. Aleshine, "for you to try to carry out what you thought was right; but we have our ideas as to what our duty is, an' you have your ideas as to what your duty is, an' consciences is even."

Having said this, she followed her friend.

Mr. Dusante looked surprised and troubled, and he turned toward me. "My dear sir," said I, "those two good women are very sensitive in regard to right and justice, and I think it will be well not to press this subject upon them. As for my wife and me, neither of us would consent to touch money which was placed in that jar by Mrs. Lecks with the expectation that no one but you or one of your family would take it out."

"Very well, sir," said Mr. Dusante, replacing the wrapping-paper around the jar; "I will drop the subject for the present. But you will allow me to say, sir, that I also am very sensitive in regard to right and justice."

Early the next morning the man who had been sent to the railroad-station came back, bringing news that a four-horse wagon would shortly be sent for us, and also bearing a letter from Mr. Enderton to Ruth. In this that gentleman informed his daughter that he was quite well, but that he had suffered anxiety on account of her probable hardships in the abandoned stage-coach. He had hoped, however, that the snow which had precluded his return with assistance had fallen lightly in the elevated position in which she had been left; and he had trusted also that Mr. Craig had bethought himself to build a fire somewhere near the coach, where his daughter might be warmed; and that the provisions, of which he knew an ample quantity had been packed for the trip, had been properly heated for her and given to her at suitable intervals. This anxiety, he said, had added very much to his own mental disquietude occasioned by the violent vituperations and unjust demands of the driver of the stage coach, who had seen fit to attack him with all manner of abuse, and might even have resorted to personal violence had it not been for the interference of bystanders and the locking of his room door. He was now, however, much relieved by the departure of this driver, and by the news that his daughter had reached a place of safety, which, of course, he had supposed she would do, her detention having occurred on an ordinary route of travel.

While waiting for the arrival of the wagon, the adventures of Mrs. Lecks, Mrs. Aleshine, and myself, as well as those of Ruth and her father, from the time the one party left America and the other China, were related at length to the Dusantes, who showed a deep interest in every detail, and asked many questions.

Mrs. Dusante, whose nervous equilibrium had been fully restored by her night's rest, and who, although feeling a little stiff and bruised, now declared herself quite well, proved to be a very pleasant lady of fifty-five or thereabouts. She was of a quiet disposition, but her speech and manner showed that in former years, at least, she had been a woman of society, and I soon found out that she was much interested in the study of character. This interest was principally shown in the direction of Mrs. Lecks and Mrs. Aleshine, whom she evidently looked upon as most remarkable women. If any of her sentiments were those of admiration, however, they were not returned in kind; Mrs. Lecks and Mrs. Aleshine had but a small opinion of her.

"There's mother-in-laws, and stepmothers, and real mothers, and grandmothers, and sometimes great-grandmothers livin'," said Mrs. Lecks to me, apart; "but though Mr. Dusante may be a well-meanin' man,—and I don't doubt he is,—and wishin', I haven't the least reason to disbelieve, to do his whole duty by his fellow-men, still I must say, bein' brought up as I was, he hasn't any right to make a new kind of mother. To be sure, a man can adopt children, but that isn't goin' backward, like this, which is ag'in' nat'ral law and gospel."

"I expect," said Mrs. Aleshine, who was with us, "that them French has got fashions that we don't know about, and thankful we ought to be that we don't! I never had no patience with French heels an' French arsenic-green beans; an' now, if there's to be adoptin' of mothers in this country, the next thing will be gullotynes."

"I don't see," said I, "why you look upon the Dusantes as French people. They are just as much American as French."

"Well," said Mrs. Lecks, "it's not for me and Mrs. Aleshine to set ourselves up to judge other people. In our part of the country we don't adopt mothers; but if they do it in France, or the Sandwich Islands, or down East, I don't know that we ought to have anything to say."

"He might as well have adopted a father at the same time," said Mrs. Aleshine, "although, to be sure, he would 'a' had to been particular to take one that was acquainted with Mrs. Dusante, and not had 'em strangers to each other, though parents to him."

"If I was you, Barb'ry Aleshine," said Mrs. Lecks, "I'd adopt some sort of rag to the top of my head to serve for a bonnet; for here comes the wagon, and I suppose now we'll be off."

We took leave of the kind-hearted ranch people, who looked upon us as a godsend into their lonely life, and disposed ourselves as comfortably as we could in the large wagon. Our journey of seven or eight miles

to the railroad-station was slow, and over ways that were rough. Mrs.
Dusante was a delicate woman and not used to hardship, whereas Mrs.
Lecks and Mrs. Aleshine were exceedingly vigorous and tough. The
consequence of this difference was that the kindly hearts of the latter
prompted them to do everything they could to prevent Mrs. Dusante
feeling the bumps and jolts, and to give her such advantages of wraps
and position as would help her to bear better the fatigues of the journey.

In doing this these good women gradually forgot the adopted mother,
and came to think only of the very pleasant lady who needed their
attentions, and who took such a lively and agreeable interest in their
family histories, their homes, their manner of living, and everything

" RUTH AND MISS LUCILLE STRUCK UP A WARM ACQUAINTANCE. "

that pertained to them; and before we reached the end of our trip these
three were talking together like old friends. Ruth and Miss Lucille had
also struck up a warm acquaintance, while I found Mr. Dusante a very
entertaining man—of sedate and careful speech, ingenious ideas, and
of a very courteous disposition.

When we arrived at the railroad-station we were met by Mr.
Enderton, who showed a moderate degree of pleasure at seeing us, and
an immoderate amount of annoyance, exhibited principally to me, in
being obliged to give up to the women of our party the large room he
had occupied in the only lodging-house in the little settlement.

When I informed him that the strangers with us were the Dusantes,
on whose island we had been staying, he at first listened vaguely. He
had always looked upon the Dusante family as a sort of fable used by
Mrs. Lecks to countenance her exactions of money from the unfortunate sojourners on the island. But when I told him what Mr. Dusante
had done, and related how he had brought the board money with him,
and had offered to pay it back to us, an eager interest was aroused in
him.

"I do not wonder," he exclaimed, "that the conscience-stricken man wishes to give the money back, but that any one should refuse what actually belongs to him or her is beyond my comprehension! One thing is certain—I shall receive my portion. Fifteen dollars a week for my daughter and myself that woman charged me, and I will have it back."

"My dear sir," I said, "your board was reduced to the same sum as that paid by the rest of us—four dollars a week each."

"I call to mind no reduction," said Mr. Enderton. "I remember distinctly the exorbitant sum charged me for board on a desert island. It made a deep impression upon me."

"I do not care to talk any further on this subject," I said. "You must settle it with Mrs. Lecks."

Mr. Enderton gave a great sniff, and walked away with dignity. I could not but laugh as I imagined his condition two minutes after he had stated his opinions on this subject to Mrs. Lecks.

When Mr. Dusante had started from San Francisco on his search for us, he had sent his heavy baggage ahead of him to Ogden City, where he purposed to make his first stop. He supposed that we might possibly here diverge from our homeward-bound route in order to visit the Mormon metropolis; and, if we had done so, he did not wish to pass us. It was therefore now agreed that we should all go to Ogden City, and there await the arrival of our effects left in the snowed-up vehicles on the mountain-side. We made arrangements with the station-master that these should be forwarded to us as soon as the stage-coach and the carriage could be brought down. All the baggage of my party was on the coach, and it consisted only of a few valises bought in San Francisco, and a package containing two life-preservers, which Mrs. Lecks and Mrs. Aleshine said they would take home with them, if they took nothing else.

On the morning after our arrival at Ogden City, Mr. Dusante took me aside. "Sir," he said, "I wish to confide to you my intentions regarding the jar containing the money left by your party in my house, and I trust you will do nothing to thwart them. When your baggage arrives, you, with your party, will doubtless continue your eastern way, and we shall return to San Francisco. But the jar, with its contents, shall be left behind to be delivered to Mrs. Lecks. If you will take charge of the jar, and hand it to her, sir, I shall be obliged greatly."

I promised Mr. Dusante that I would not interfere with his intentions, but asserted that I could, on no account, take charge of the jar. The possession of that piece of pottery, with its contents, was now a matter of dispute between him and Mrs. Lecks, and must be settled by them.

"Very well, then, sir," he said. "I shall arrange to depart before you and your company, and I shall leave the jar, suitably packed, in the care of the clerk of this hotel, with directions to hand it to Mrs. Lecks after I am gone. Thus there will be nothing for her to do but to receive it."

Some one now came into the smoking-room, where we were sitting, and no more was said on this subject. Mr. Dusante's statement of his intention very much amused me, for Mrs. Lecks had previously taken me into her confidence in regard to her intentions in this matter. "Mr. Dusante," she had said, "hasn't dropped a word more about the money in that ginger-jar, but I know just as well as he does what he's goin' to do about it. When the time comes to go, he's goin' to slip off quietly, leavin' that jar behind him, thinkin' then I'll be obliged to take it, there bein' nobody to give it back to. But he'll find me just as sharp as he is. I've got the street and number of his business place in Honolulu from his sister,—askin' about it in an offhand way, as if it didn't mean anything,—an' if that jar is left for me, I'll pack it in a box, money and all, and I'll express it to Mr. Dusante; and when he gets to Honolulu he'll find it there, and then he'll know that two can play at that sort of game."

Knowing Mr. Dusante, and knowing Mrs. Lecks, I pictured to myself a box containing a ginger-jar, and covered with numerous half-obliterated addresses, traveling backward and forward between the Sandwich Islands and Pennsylvania during the lifetime of the contestants, and, probably, if testamentary desires should be regarded, during a great part of the lifetime of their heirs. That the wear and tear of the box might make it necessary to inclose it in a keg, and that, eventually, the keg might have to be placed in a barrel, and that, after a time, in a hogshead, seemed to me as likely as any other contingencies which might befall this peregrinating ginger-jar.

We spent three days in Ogden City, and then, the weather having moderated very much, and the snow on the mountains having melted sufficiently to allow the vehicles to be brought down, our effects were forwarded to us, and my party and that of Mr. Dusante prepared to proceed on our different ways. An eastward-bound train left that evening an hour after we received our baggage, but we did not care to depart upon such short notice, and so determined to remain until the next day.

In the evening Mr. Dusante came to me to say that he was very glad to find that the westward train would leave Ogden City early in the morning, so that he and his family would start on their journey some hours before we should leave. "This suits my plans exactly." he said.

"I have left the ginger-jar, securely wrapped, and addressed to Mrs. Lecks, with the clerk of the hotel, who will deliver it to-morrow immediately after my departure. All our preparations are made, and we purpose this evening to bid farewell to you and our other kind friends, from whom, I assure you, we are most deeply grieved to part."

I had just replied that we also regretted extremely the necessity for this separation, when a boy brought me a letter. I opened it, and found it was from Mr. Enderton. It read as follows:

DEAR SIR: I have determined not to wait here until to-morrow, but to proceed eastward by this evening's train. I desire to spend a day in Chicago, and as you and the others will probably not wish to stop there, I shall, by this means, attain my object without detaining you. My sudden resolution will not give me time to see you all before I start, but I have taken a hurried leave of my daughter, and this letter will explain my departure to the rest.

I will also mention that I have thought it proper, as the natural head of our party both by age and position, to settle the amicable dispute in regard to the reception and disposition of the money paid, under an excusable misapprehension, for our board and lodging upon a desert island. I discovered that the receptacle of this money had been left in the custody of the clerk, addressed to Mrs. Lecks, who has not only already refused to receive it, and would probably do so again, but who is, in my opinion, in no wise entitled to hold, possess, or dispose of it. I therefore, without making any disturbance whatever, have taken charge of the package, and shall convey it with me to Chicago. When you arrive there, I will apportion the contents among us according to our several claims. This I regard as a very sensible and prudent solution of the little difficulty which has confronted us in regard to the disposition of this money. Yours hurriedly,   DAVID J. ENDERTON.

P. S. I shall stop at Brandiger's Hotel, where I shall await you.

PART VI

THE *CONTENTS* OF A *GINGER-JAR* *MAKE* EVERYBODY *HAPPY*

MR. ENDERTON'S LETTER astonished and angered me, but in spite of my indignation, I could not help smiling at the unexpected way in which he had put a stop to the probable perpetual peregrinations of the ginger-jar. I handed the letter to Mr. Dusante, and when he had read it his face flushed, and I could see that he was very angry, although he kept his temper under excellent control.

"Sir," he said presently, "This shall not be allowed. That jar, with its contents, is my property until Mrs. Lecks has consented to receive it. It is of my own option that I return it at all, and I have decided to return it to Mrs. Lecks. Any one interfering with my intentions steps entirely beyond the line of just and warrantable procedure. Sir, I shall not go westward to-morrow morning, but, with my family, will accompany you to Chicago, where I shall require Mr. Enderton to return to me my property, which I shall then dispose of as I see fit. You must excuse me, sir, if anything I have said regarding this gentleman with whom you are connected has wounded your sensibilities."

"Oh, don't think of that," I exclaimed. "Pitch into Enderton as much as you please, and you may be sure that I shall not object. When I took the daughter to wife, I did not marry the father. But, of course, for my wife's sake I hope this matter will not be made the subject of public comment."

"You need have no fear of that," said Mr. Dusante; "and you will allow me to remark that Mr. Enderton's wife must have been a most charming lady."

"Why do you think so?" I asked.

"I judge so," he answered, with a bow, "from my acquaintance with Mrs. Craig."

I now went immediately to Ruth, who, I found, knew nothing of what had occurred, except that her father had gone on to Chicago in advance of our party, and had had time only to bid her a hasty good-by. I made no remarks on this haste, which would not allow Mr. Enderton to take leave of us, but which gave him time to write a letter of some length; and as Ruth knew nothing of this letter, I determined not to mention it to her. Her father's sudden departure surprised her but little, for she told me that he always liked to get to places before the rest of the party with whom he might be journeying.

"Even when we go to church," she said, "he always walks ahead of the rest of us. I don't understand why he likes to do so, but this is one of his habits."

When I informed Mrs. Lecks and Mrs. Aleshine of what had happened, they fairly blazed.

"I don't know what Mr. Dusante calls it," exclaimed Mrs. Lecks, "but I know what I call it."

"Yes, indeed!" cried Mrs. Aleshine, her round eyes sparkling with excitement; "if that isn't ex-honesty, then he ain't no ex-missionary! I pity the heathen he converted!"

"I'll convert him," said Mrs. Lecks, "if ever I lay eyes on him! Walkin' away with a package with my name on it! He might as well take my gold spectacles or my tortoise-shell comb! I suppose there's no such thing as ketchin' up with him, but I'll telegraph after him; an' I'll let him know that if he dares to open a package of mine, I'll put the law on him!"

"That's so," said Mrs. Aleshine. "You kin send telegraphs all along the line to one station an' another for conductors to give to him in the cars, an' directed to Mr. Enderton, a tall man with gray-mixed hair an' a stolen bundle. That's the way they did in our place when Abram Marly's wife fell into the cistern, an' he'd jus' took the cars to the city, an' they telegraphed to him at five different stations to know where he'd left the ladder."

"Which ain't a bad idea," said Mrs. Lecks, "though his name will be enough on it without no description; an' I'll do that this minute, an' find out about the stations from the clerk."

"You must be very careful," I said, "about anything of that kind, for the telegrams will be read at the stations, and Mr. Enderton might be brought into trouble in a way which we all should regret; but a despatch may be worded so that he, and no one else, would understand it."

"Very well," said Mrs. Lecks, "an' let's get at it; but I must say that he don't deserve bein' saved no trouble, for I'm as sure as that I'm a livin' woman that he never saved nobody else no trouble sence the first minute he was born."

The following despatch was concocted and sent on to Bridger, to be delivered to Mr. Enderton on the train:

The package you know of has been stolen. You will recognize the thief. If he leaves it at Chicago hotel, let him go. If he opens it, clap him in jail.

MRS. LECKS.

"I think that will make him keep his fingers off it," said Mrs. Lecks; "an' if Mr. Dusante chooses to send somethin' of the same kind to some other station, it won't do no harm. An' if that Enderton gets so skeered that he keeps out of sight and hearin' of all of us, it'll be the best thing that's happened yet. An' I want you to understan', Mr. Craig, that nothin's goin' to be said or done to make your wife feel bad; an' there's no need of her hearin' about what's been done or what's goin' to be done. But I'll say for her that though, of course, Mr. Enderton is her father, and she looks up to him as such, she's a mighty deal livelier and gayer-hearted when he's away than when he's with her. An' as for the rest of us, there's no use sayin' anything about our resignedness to the loss of his company."

"I should say so," said Mrs. Aleshine; "for if there ever was a man who thought of himself ninety-nine times before he thought of anybody else once, an' then as like as not to forgit that once, he's the man. An' it's not, by no means, that I'm down on missionaries, for it's many a box I've made up for 'em, an' never begrudged neither money nor trouble, an' will do it ag'in many times, I hope. But he oughtn't to be called one, havin' given it up,—unless they gave him up, which there's no knowin' which it was,—for if there's anything which shows the good in a man, it's his bein' willin' to give up the comforts of a Christian land an' go an' convert heathens; though bein' willin' to give up the heathens an' go for the comforts shows him quite different, besides, as like as not, chargin' double, an' only half convertin'.'"

Mr. Dusante was fully determined to go on with us until he had recovered possession of the ginger-jar. His courteous feelings toward Mrs. Craig and myself prevented his saying much about Mr. Enderton, but I had good reason to believe that his opinions in regard to my father-in-law were not very different from those of Mrs. Lecks and Mrs. Aleshine. Ever since Mr. Enderton had shown his petulant selfishness, when obliged to give up his room at the railroad-station for the use of the women of his party, Mr. Dusante had looked upon him coldly, and the two had had but little to say to each other.

We were all very glad that our pleasant party was not to be broken up; and although there was no resignation at the absence of the ginger-jar, we started on our journey the next day in a pleasanter mood for the absence of Mr. Enderton. Before we left, Mr. Dusante sent a telegram to Kearney Junction, to be delivered to Mr. Enderton when he arrived there. What this message was I do not know, but I imagine its tone was decided.

Our journey to Chicago was a pleasant one. We had now all become very well acquainted with each other, and there was no discordant element in the combined party. Some of us were a little apprehensive of trouble, or annoyance at least, awaiting us in Chicago, but we did not speak of it; and while Ruth knew nothing of her father's misbehaviour, it might have been supposed that the rest had forgotten it.

At Chicago we went at once to Brandiger's Hotel, and there we found, instead of Mr. Enderton, a letter from him to Ruth. It read as read as follows:

My dear Daughter: I have determined not to wait here, as originally intended, but to go on by myself. I am sorry not to meet you here, but it will not be long before we are together again, and you know I do not like to travel with a party. Its various members always incommode me in one way or another. I had proposed to go to Philadelphia and wait for you there, but have since concluded to stop at Meadowville, a village in the interior of Pennsylvania, where, as they have informed me, the two women, Mrs. Lecks and Mrs. Aleshine, reside. I wish to see the party all together before I take final leave of them, and I suppose the two women will not consent to go any farther than the country town in which they live. Inclosed is a note to your husband relating to business matters. I hope that he will take the best of care of you during the rest of the journey, and thus very much oblige   Your affectionate Father.

This was my note:

Mr. Craig. Sir: I should have supposed that you would have been able to prevent the insolent messages which have been telegraphed to me from some members of your party, but it is my lot to be disappointed in those in whom I trust. I shall make no answer to these messages, but will say to you that I am not to be browbeaten in my intention to divide among its rightful claimants the money now in my possession. It is not that I care for the comparatively paltry sum that will fall to myself and my daughter, but it is the principle of the matter for which I am contending. It was due to me that the amount should have been returned to me, and to no other, that I might make the proper division. I therefore rest upon my principles and my rights; and, desiring to avoid needless altercations, shall proceed to Meadowville, where, when the rest of my party arrive, I shall justly apportion the money. I suppose the man Dusante will not be foolish enough to protract his useless journey farther than Chicago. It is your duty to make him see the impropriety of so doing. Yours, etc.,

D. J. ENDERTON.

Ruth's letter was shown to all the party, and mine in private to Mr. Dusante, Mrs. Lecks, and Mrs. Aleshine. When the first moments of astonishment were over, Mrs. Lecks exclaimed:

"Well, after all, I don't know that I'm so very sorry that the old sneak has done this, for now we're rid of him for the rest of the trip; and I'm pretty certain, from the way he writes, that he hasn't dipped into that jar yet. We've skeered him from doin' that."

"'THE IMPIDENCE OF HIM!'"

"But the impidence of him!" said Mrs. Aleshine. "Think of his goin' to the very town where we live an' gittin' there fust! He'll be settin' on that tavern porch, with every loafer in the place about him, an' tellin' 'em the whole story of what happened to us from beginnin' to end, till by the time we git there it'll be all over the place an' as stale as last week's bread."

"'The man Dusante,'" quietly remarked that individual, "will not abandon the purpose of his journey. He left his island to place in the hands of Mrs. Lecks, on behalf of her party, the ginger-jar with the money inclosed. He will therefore go on with you to Meadowville, and will there make formal demand, and, if necessary, legal requisition, for the possession of that jar and that money; after which he will proceed to carry out his original intentions."

We all expressed our pleasure at having him, with his ladies, as companions for the remainder of our journey, and Mrs. Lecks immediately offered them the hospitalities of her house for as long a time as they might wish to stay with her.

"The weather there," she said, "is often splendid till past Thanksgivin' day, an' nobody could be welcomer than you."

"I'd have asked you myself," said Mrs. Aleshine, "if Mrs. Lecks hadn't done it—which of course she would, bein' alive—but I'm goin' to have Mr. Craig an' his wife, an' as our houses is near, we'll see each other all the time. An' if Mr. Enderton chooses to stay awhile at the tavern, he can come over to see his daughter whenever he likes. I'll go as fur as that, though no further can I go. I'm not the one to turn anybody from my door, be he heathen, or jus' as bad, or wuss. But tea once, or perhaps twice, is all that I can find it in my heart to offer that man after what he's done."

As the Dusantes and Ruth expressed a desire to see something of Chicago, where they had never been before, we remained in this city for two days, feeling that, as Mr. Enderton would await our coming, there was no necessity for haste.

Early in the afternoon of the second day I went into the parlor of the hotel, where I expected to find our party prepared for a sight-seeing excursion; but I found the room tenanted only by Mrs. Aleshine, who was sitting with her bonnet and wraps on, ready to start forth. I had said but a few words to her when Mrs. Lecks entered, without bonnet or shawl, and with her knitting in her hand. She took a seat in a large easy-chair, put on her spectacles, and proceeded to knit.

"Mrs. Lecks!" exclaimed her friend, in surprise, "don't you intend goin' out this afternoon?"

"No," said Mrs. Lecks. "I've seen all I want to see, an' I'm goin' to stay in the house an' keep quiet."

"Isn't Mr. Dusante goin' out this afternoon?" asked Mrs. Aleshine.

Mrs. Lecks laid her knitting in her lap; then she took off her spectacles, folded them, and placed them beside the ball of yarn, and, turning her chair around, she faced her friend. "Barb'ry Aleshine," said she, speaking very deliberately, "has any such a thing got into your mind as that I'm settin' my cap at Mr. Dusante?"

"I don't say you have, an' I don't say you haven't," answered Mrs. Aleshine, her fat hands folded on her knees, and her round face shining from under her new bonnet with an expression of hearty good will; "but this I will say—an' I don't care who hears it—that if you was to set your cap at Mr. Dusante, there needn't nobody say anythin' ag'in' it, so long as you are content. He isn't what I'd choose for you, if I had the choosin', for I'd git one with an American name an' no islands. But that's neither here nor there, for you're a grown woman an' can do your own choosin'. An' whether there's any choosin' to be done is your own business, too, for it's full eleven years sence you've been done with widder fixin's; an' if Mr. Lecks was to rise up out of his grave this minute, he couldn't put his hand on his heart an' say that you hadn't done your full duty by him, both before an' after he was laid away. An' so, if you did want to do choosin', an' made up your mind to set your cap at Mr. Dusante, there's no word to be said. Both of you is ripe-aged an' qualified to know your own minds, an' both of you is well off enough, to all intents an' purposes, to settle down together, if so inclined. An' as to his sister, I don't expect she will be on his hands for long. An' if you can put up with an adopted mother-in-law, that's your business, not mine; though I allus did say, Mrs. Lecks, that if you'd been 'Piscopalian, you'd been Low-church."

"Is that all?" said Mrs. Lecks.

"Yes," replied the other; "it's all I have to say jus' now, though more might come to me if I gave my mind to it."

"Well, then," said Mrs. Lecks, "I've somethin' to say on this p'int, and I'm very glad Mr. Craig is here to hear it. If I had a feelin' in the direction of Mr. Dusante that he was a man, though not exactly what I might wish, havin' somethin' of foreign manners, with ties in the Sandwich Islands, which I shouldn't have had so if I'd had the orderin' of it, who was still a Christian gentleman—as showed by his acts, not his words—a lovin' brother, an' a kind an' attentive son by his own adoption, and who would make me a good husband for the rest of our two lives, then I'd go and I'd set my cap at him—not bold nor flauntin' nor unbecomin' to a woman of my age, but just so much settin' of it at him that if he had any feelin's in my direction, and thought, although it was rather late in life for him to make a change, that if he was goin' to do it he'd rather make that change with a woman who had age enough, and experience enough, in downs as well as ups, and in married life as well as single, to make him feel that as he got her so he'd always find her, then I say all he'd have to do would be to come to me an' say what he thought, an' I'd say what I thought, an' the thing would be settled, an' nobody in this world need have one word to say, except to wish us joy, an' then go along and attend to their own business.

"But now I say to you, Barb'ry Aleshine, an' just the same to you, Mr. Craig, that I haven't got no such feelin's in the direction of Mr. Dusante, an' I don't intend to set my cap at him; an' if he wore such a thing, and set it at me, I'd say to him, kind, though firm, that he could put it straight again as far as I was concerned, an' that if he chose to set it at any other woman, if the nearest an' dearest friend I have on earth, I'd do what I could to make their married lives as happy as they could be under the circumstances, and no matter what happened, I wouldn't say one word, though I might think what I pleased. An' now you have it, all straight and plain: if I wanted to set caps, I'd set 'em; and if I didn't want to set 'em, I wouldn't. I don't want to, and I don't."

And, putting on her spectacles, she resumed her knitting.

Mrs. Aleshine turned upon her friend a beaming face.

"Mrs. Lecks," she said, "your words has lifted a load from off my mind. It wouldn't ha' broke me down, an' you wouldn't never have knowed I carried it; but it's gone, an' I'm mighty glad of it. An' as for me an' my cap—an' when you spoke of nearest and dearest friends you couldn't mean nobody but me—you needn't be afraid. No matter what I was, nor what he was, nor what I thought of him, nor what he thought of me, I couldn't never say to my son, when he comes to his mother's arms all the way from Japan: 'George, here's a Frenchman who I give to you for a father!'"

Here I burst out laughing; but Mrs. Lecks gravely remarked: "Now I hope this business of cap-settin' is settled an' done with."

"Which it is," said Mrs. Aleshine, as she rose to meet the rest of our party as they entered the room.

For several days I could not look upon the dignified and almost courtly Mr. Dusante without laughing internally, and wondering what he would think if he knew how, without the slightest provocation on his side, a matrimonial connection with him had been discussed by these good women, and how the matter had been finally settled. I think he would have considered this the most surprising incident in the whole series of his adventures.

On our journey from Chicago to the little country town in the interior of Pennsylvania we made a few stops at points of interest for the sake of Ruth and the Dusante ladies, Mrs. Lecks and Mrs. Aleshine generously consenting to these delays, although I knew they felt impatient to reach their homes. They were now on most social terms with Mrs. Dusante, and the three chatted together like old friends.

"I asked her if we might call her Emily," said Mrs. Aleshine in confidence to me, "an' she said yes, an' we're goin' to do it. I've all along wanted to, because it seemed to come nat'ral, considerin' we knowed 'em as Emily and Lucille before we set eyes on 'em. But as long as I had that load on my mind about Mrs. Lecks and Mr. Dusante I couldn't 'Emily' his adopted mother. My feelin's wouldn't ha' stood it. But now it's all right; an' though Emily isn't the woman I expected her to be, Lucille is the very picter of what I thought she was. And as for Emily, I never knowed a nicer-mannered lady, an' more willin' to learn from people that's had experience, than she is."

We arrived at Meadowville early in the afternoon, and when our party alighted from the train we were surprised not to see Mr. Enderton on the platform of the little station. Instead of him, there stood three persons whose appearance amazed and delighted us. They were the red-bearded coxswain and the two sailormen, all in neat new clothes, and with their hands raised in maritime salute.

There was a cry of joy. Mrs. Aleshine dropped her bag and umbrella, and rushed toward them with outstretched hands. In a moment Mrs. Lecks, Ruth, and myself joined the group, and greeted warmly our nautical companions of the island.

The Dusante party, when they were made acquainted with the mariners, were almost as much delighted as we were, and Mr. Dusante expressed in cordial words his pleasure in meeting the other members of the party to whom his island had given refuge.

"I am so glad to see you," said Mrs. Aleshine, "that I don't know my bonnet from my shoes! But how, in the name of all that's wonderful, did you get here?"

"'T ain't much of a story," said the coxswain, "an' this is just the whole of it. When you left us at 'Frisco we felt pretty downsome, an' the more that way because we couldn't find no vessel that we cared to ship on; an' then there come to town the agent of the house that owned our brig, and we was paid off for our last v'yage. Then, when we had fitted ourselves out with new togs, we began to think different about this shippin' on board a merchant-vessel, an' gettin' cussed at, an' livin' on hard-tack an' salt prog, an' jus' as like as not the ship springin' a leak an' all hands pumpin' night an' day, an' goin' to Davy Jones, after all. An' after talkin' this all over, we was struck hard on the weather-bow with a feelin' that it was a blamed sight better—beggin' your pardon, ma'am—to dig garden-beds in nice soft dirt, an' plant peas, an' ketch fish, an' all that kind of shore work, an' eatin' them good things you used to cook for us, Mrs. Aleshine, and dancin' hornpipes for ye, and tamin' birds when our watch was off. Wasn't that so, Jim an' Bill?"

"Aye, aye, sir!" said the black-bearded sailormen.

"Then says I, 'Now look here, mates; don't let's go and lark away all this money, but take it an' make a land trip to where Mrs. Aleshine lives'—which port I had the name of on a piece of paper which you gave me, ma'am."

And here Mrs. Aleshine nodded vigorously, not being willing to interrupt this entrancing story.

"'An' if she's got another garden, an' wants it dug in, an' things planted, an' fish caught, an' any other kind of shore work done, why we're the men for her; an' we'll sign the papers for as long a v'yage as she likes, and stick by her in fair weather or foul, bein' good for day work an' night work, an' allus ready to fall in when she passes the word.' Ain't that so, Jim an' Bill?"

"Aye, aye, sir!" returned the sailormen, with sonorous earnestness.

"Upon my word!" cried Mrs. Aleshine, tears of joy running down her cheeks, "them papers shall be signed, if I have to work night an' day to find somethin' for you to do. I've got a man takin' keer of my place now; but many a time have I said to myself that if I had anybody I could trust to do the work right, I'd buy them two fields of Squire Ramsey's, an' go into the onion business. An' now you sailormen has come like three sea angels, an' if it suits you we'll go into the onion business on sheers."

"That suits us tiptop, ma'am," said the coxswain; "and we'll plant inyans for ye on the shears, on the stocks, or in dry-dock. It don't make no dif'rence to us where you have 'em; just pass the word."

"Well, well," said Mrs. Lecks, "I don't know how that's going to work, but we won't talk about it now. An' so you came straight on to this place?"

"That did we, ma'am," said the coxswain. "An' when we got here we found the parson, but none of you folks. That took us aback a little at fust, but he said he didn't live here, an' you was comin' pretty soon. An' so we took lodgin's at the tavern, an' for three days we've been down here to meet every train, expectin' you might be on it."

Our baggage had been put on the platform, the train had moved on, and we had stood engrossed in the coxswain's narrative; but now I thought it necessary to make a move. There was but one small vehicle to hire at the station. This would hold but two persons, and in it I placed Mrs. Dusante and Ruth, the first being not accustomed to walking, and the latter very anxious to meet her father. I ordered the man to drive them to the inn, where we would stay until Mrs. Lecks and Mrs. Aleshine should get their houses properly aired and ready for our reception.

"Mrs. Craig will be glad to get to the tavern and see her father," said Mrs. Aleshine. "I expect he forgot all about its bein' time for the train to come."

"Bless you, ma'am!" exclaimed the coxswain, "is she gone to the tavern? The parson's not there!"

"Where is he, then?" asked Mrs. Aleshine.

"He's at your house, ma'am," replied the coxswain.

"An' what, in the name of common sense, is he doin' at my house?" exclaimed Mrs. Aleshine, her eyes sparkling with amazement and indignation.

"Well, ma'am, for one thing," said the coxswain, "he's had the front door painted."

"What!" cried Mrs. Lecks and Mrs. Aleshine, in one breath.

"Yes," continued the coxswain; "the parson said he hated to see men hangin' around doin' nothin'. An' then he looked about, an' said the paint was all wore off the front door, an' we might as well go to work an' paint that; an' he sent Jim to a shop to git the paint an' brushes—"

"An' have 'em charged to me?" cried Mrs. Aleshine.

"Yes, ma'am," continued the coxswain. "An' Jim an' Bill holy-stoned all the old paint off the door, an' I painted it, havin' done lots of that sort of thing on shipboard; an' I think it's a pretty good job, ma'am —red at top and bottom, an' white in the middle, like a steamer's smoke-stack."

Mrs. Lecks and Mrs. Aleshine looked at each other. "An' he told you to do that?" said Mrs. Lecks.

"Yes, ma'am," answered the coxswain. "The parson said he never liked to be nowhere without doin' what good he could. An' there was some other paintin' he talked of havin' done, but we ain't got at it yet. I s'posed he was actin' under your orders, an' I hope I haven't done no wrong, ma'am."

"You're not a bit to blame," said Mrs. Aleshine; "but I'll look into this thing. No fear about that! An' how did he come to go to my house? An' how did he get in, I'd like to know?"

"All I know about that," said the coxswain, "is what the gal that's livin' there told me, which she did along of askin' us if we was comin' to live there too, an' if she should rig up beds for us somewhere in the top-loft; but we told her no, not havin' no orders, an' payin' our own way at the tavern. She said, said she, that the parson come there, an' 'lowed he was a friend of Mrs. Aleshine's an' travelin' with her, an' that if she was at home she wouldn't let him stay at no tavern; an' that, knowin' her wishes, he'd come right there, an' 'spected to be took care of till she come. She said she felt oncertain about it, but she tuck him in till she could think it over, an' then we come an' certified that he was the parson who'd been along with Mrs. Aleshine an' the rest of us. Arter that she thought it was all right, an', beggin' your pardon if we was wrong, so did Jim an' Bill an' me, ma'am."

"Now," exclaimed Mrs. Aleshine, "if that isn't exactly like Elizabeth Grootenheimer! To think of Elizabeth Grootenheimer thinkin'!
The Grootenheimers always was the dumbest family in the township,
an' Elizabeth Grootenheimer is the dumbest of 'em all! I did say to
myself, when I went away: 'Now, Elizabeth Grootenheimer is so stone
dumb that she'll jus' stay here an' do the little I tell her to do, an' hasn't
sense enough to get into no mischief.' An' now, look at her!"

She waved her hand in the direction of
the invisible Elizabeth Grootenheimer.

Mrs. Lecks had said very little during this
startling communication, but her face had
assumed a stern and determined expression.
Now she spoke:

"I guess we've heard about enough, an'
we'd better be steppin' along an' see what else
Mr. Enderton an' Elizabeth Grootenheimer
is doin'."

The homes of Mrs. Lecks and Mrs. Aleshine
were not far from each other, and were
situated about midway between the station and the village inn, and
in the direction of these our party now started. Mrs. Aleshine, contrary
to her custom, took the lead, and walked away with strides of unusual
length. Mrs. Lecks was close behind her, followed by the two Dusantes
and myself, while the three mariners, who insisted upon carrying all
the hand-baggage, brought up the rear. We stepped quickly, for we
were all much interested in what might happen next; and very soon
we reached Mrs. Aleshine's house. It was a good-sized and pleasant-
looking dwelling, painted white, with green shutters, and with a long
covered piazza at the front. Between the road and the house was a neat
yard with grass and flower-beds, and from the gate of the picket-fence
in front of the yard a brick-paved path led up to the house.

Our approach had been perceived, for on the piazza, in front of the
gaily painted door, stood Mr. Enderton, erect, and with a bland and
benignant smile upon his face. One hand was stretched out as if in
welcome, and with the other he gracefully held the ginger-jar, now
divested of its wrappings.

At this sight Mrs. Lecks and Mrs. Aleshine made a simultaneous
dash at the gate; but it was locked. The two women stamped their feet
in fury.

"Put down that jar!" shouted Mrs. Lecks.

"Elizabeth Grootenheimer! Elizabeth Grootenheimer!" screamed
Mrs. Aleshine. "Come here and open this gate."

"Break it down!" said Mrs. Lecks, turning to the sailors.

"Don't you do it!" exclaimed Mrs. Aleshine, throwing herself in front of it. "Don't you break my gate! Elizabeth Grootenheimer!"

"My friends," said Mr. Enderton, in clear, distinct tones, "be calm. I have the key of that gate in my pocket. I locked it because I feared that on your first arrival you would hurry up to the house in a promiscuous way, and give heed to irrelevant matters. I wished to address you in a body, and in a position where your attention would not be diverted from me. I hold here, my friends, the receptacle containing the money which, under a misapprehension was paid for our board while on a desert island. This money I have taken care of, and have carefully guarded for the benefit of us all. Unfortunately, objections have arisen to this guardianship, which were forwarded to me by telegraph; but I have not heeded them. If you cannot see for yourselves the propriety of my assumption of this trust, I will not now undertake to enlighten you. But I hope there is no necessity for this, for, having had time to give the matter your fullest attention, I doubt not that you entirely agree with me. I will merely add, for I see you are impatient, that the sum which will fall to the share of each of us is comparatively insignificant and in itself not worth striving for; but what I have done has been for the sake of principle. For the sake of principle I have insisted that this money should be received by its rightful owners; for the sake of principle I assumed the custody of it; and for the sake of principle I shall now empty the contents of this jar—which by me has not been examined or touched—upon the floor of this piazza, and I shall then proceed to divide said contents into five suitable portions—the three mariners, as I understand, having paid no board. The gate can then be opened, and each one can come forward and take the portion which belongs to him or to her. The portion of my daughter, whom I saw pass here in a carriage, going, doubtless, to the inn, will be taken charge of by myself."

"You man!" shrieked Mrs. Lecks, shaking her fist over the fence "if you as much as lift that paper of fish-hooks from out the top of that ginger-jar, I'll—"

Here she was interrupted by the loud, clear voice of Mr. Dusante, who called out: "Sir, I require you to put down that jar, which is my property."

"I'll let you know," said Mrs. Lecks, "that other people have principles!"

But what more she said was drowned by the voice of Mrs. Aleshine, who screamed for Elizabeth Grootenheimer, and who was now so much excited that she was actually trying to break open her own gate.

I called out to Mr. Enderton not to make trouble by disturbing the contents of the jar; and even Miss Lucille, who was intensely amused at the scene, could be heard joining her voice to the general clamor.

But the threats and demands of our united party had no effect upon Mr. Enderton. He stood up, serene and bland, fully appreciating the advantage of having the key of the gate's padlock in his pocket and the ginger-jar in his hand.

"'YOU MAN!' SHRIEKED MRS. LECKS."

"I will now proceed," said he. But at that moment his attention was attracted by the three mariners, who had clambered over the pointed pales of the fence, and who now appeared on the piazza, Bill to the right hand of Mr. Enderton, Jim to the left, and the red-bearded coxswain at his back. They all seemed to speak at once, though what they said we could not hear, nothing but a few hoarse mutterings coming down to us.

But in consequence of what Bill said, Mr. Enderton handed him the key of the gate; and in consequence of what Jim said, Mr. Enderton delivered to him the ginger-jar; and in consequence of what the coxswain said, he and Mr. Enderton walked off the piazza; and the two proceeded to a distant corner of the yard, where they stood out of the way, as it were, while the gate was opened. Bill bungled a little, but the padlock was soon removed, and we all hurried through the gate and up to the piazza, where Jim still stood, the ginger-jar held reverently in his hands.

The coxswain now left Mr. Enderton, and that gentleman proceeded to the open gate, through which he passed into the road, and then turned, and in a loud and severe tone addressed Mrs. Aleshine:

"I leave your inhospitable house, and go to join my daughter at the inn, where I request you to send my valise and umbrella as soon as possible."

Mrs. Aleshine's indignation at this invasion of her home and this trampling on her right to open her own gate had entirely driven away her accustomed geniality, and in angry tones she cried:

"Jus' you stop at that paint-shop, when you git to the village, an' pay for the paint you had charged to me; an' when you've done that you can send for your things."

"Come, now, Barb'ry," said Mrs. Lecks, "don't let your feelin's run away with you. You ought to be thankful that he's let you off so easy, an' that he's gone."

"I'm all that," said Mrs. Aleshine; "an', on second thoughts, every whip-stitch of his bag and baggage shall be trundled after him as soon as I kin git it away."

We all now stood upon the piazza, and Mrs. Aleshine, in calmer tones, but with her face still flushed from her recent excitement, turned to us and said: "Now, isn't this a pretty comin' home? My front gate fastened in my very face; my front door painted red and white; the inside of the house, as like as not, turned upside down by that man jus' as much as the outside; an' where in the world, I'd like to know, is Elizabeth Grootenheimer?"

"Now don't you be too hard on her," said Mrs. Lecks, "after havin' been away from her so long. I haven't a doubt she's feedin' the pigs; and you know very well she never would leave them as long as she felt they needed her. You needn't mind if your house is upset, for none of us is comin' in, havin' only intended to see you to your door, which I must say is a pretty blazin' one."

"And now, Mrs. Lecks," said Mr. Dusante, taking, as he spoke, the ginger-jar from the hand of Jim, "I think this is a suitable opportunity for me to accomplish the object for which my present journey was undertaken, and to return to you the contents of this jar."

"Which," said Mrs. Lecks, in a very decided tone, "I don't take now no more 'n I did before."

Mr. Dusante looked surprised and troubled. After all the dangers and adventures through which that ginger-jar had gone, I believe that he expected Mrs. Lecks would at last relent and consent to accept it from him.

"Now, look here," said Mrs. Aleshine, "don't let us have any more fuss about the ginger-jar, or anything else. Let's put off talkin' about that till we're all settled and fixed. It won't do for you to take the jar to the tavern with you, Mr. Dusante, for like as not Mr. Enderton will git hold of it ag'in, an' I know Mrs. Lecks won't let it come into her house; so, if you like, you may jus' leave it here for the present, and you may make up your minds nobody 'll touch it while I'm about. An' about I intend to be."

This arrangement was gladly agreed upon, and the jar being delivered to Mrs. Aleshine, we took our leave of her.

Mrs. Lecks found no difficulty in entering her gate, where she was duly welcomed by a man and his wife she had left in charge, while the Dusantes and myself walked on to the inn, or "Hotel," as its sign imported, about which the greater part of the little town clustered. The three mariners remained behind to await further orders from Mrs. Aleshine.

By the afternoon of the next day the abodes of those two most energetic and capable housewives, Mrs. Lecks and Mrs. Aleshine, were fully prepared for the reception of their visitors, and the Dusante family were ensconced beneath the roof of the one, while my wife and I were most warmly welcomed at the gaily adorned door of the other.

Mr. Enderton remained at the inn, where he found very comfortable quarters, an arrangement satisfactory to all parties.

In Mrs. Aleshine's dwelling, where, from the very first, Lucille took her position as a most constant visitor, being equally welcomed by Ruth and the mistress of the house, all was satisfaction and high good humor. The ceaseless activity and cheerful spirits of our hostess seemed to animate us all. At Mrs. Lecks's home the case was different. There, I could plainly see, there was a certain uneasiness amounting almost to stiffness between Mrs. Lecks and Mr. Dusante. The latter had not accomplished the purpose for which he had made this long journey; and though, if things had turned out as he wished, he would have been very glad to be the guest of Mrs. Lecks, still, under the present circumstances, the situation did not suit him. Mrs. Lecks, too, possessed an unsettled mind. She did not know when Mr. Dusante would again endeavor to force back upon her the board money in the ginger-jar, and in this state of uneasy expectancy she was not at her best.

"He's not satisfied," said she to me, on the morning after the Dusantes had come to her; "he wants to do somethin', or else to go away. I wish that ginger-jar had dropped into the bottom of the sea while he was bringin' it, or else had smashed itself into a thousand bits while he was slidin' down the mountain, and the money had melted itself into the snow. S'posin' at the end of the week he was to come to me and offer to pay me board for himself and his family, sayin' that was no more than I'd done to him! Of course the two cases are not a bit alike; for we went to his house strangers, without leave or license, while he comes to mine as a friend, bein' fully invited and pressed. But I don't suppose I could make him see it in that light, and it worries me."

I was convinced that something ought to be done to end this unpleasant state of affairs, and I took my wife and Miss Lucille into council on the subject. After we had deliberated a little while an idea came to Ruth.

"In my opinion," said she, "the best thing we can do with that board money is to give it to those three sailors. They are poor and will be glad to get it; Mr. Dusante and Mrs. Lecks ought to be fully satisfied, for the one doesn't keep it and the other doesn't take it back; and I'm sure that this plan will please all the rest of us."

This proposition was agreed to by the council, and I was appointed to go immediately and lay it before the parties interested.

Mr. Dusante gave his ready consent to this proposal. "It is not what I intended to do," said he, "but it amounts to almost the same thing. The money is in fact restored to its owners, and they agree to make a certain disposition of it. I am satisfied."

Mrs. Lecks hesitated a little. "All right," said she. "He takes the money and gives it to who he chooses. I've nothin' to say against it."

Of course no opposition to the plan was to be expected from anybody else, except Mr. Enderton. But when I mentioned it to him, I found, to my surprise, that he was not unwilling to agree to it. Half closing the book he had been reading, he said: "What I have done was on behalf of principle. I did not believe, and do not believe, that upon an entirely deserted island money should be paid for board. I paid it under protest, and I do not withdraw that protest. According to all the laws of justice and hospitality, the man who owned that island should not retain that money, and Mrs. Lecks had no right to insist upon such retention. But if it is proposed to give the sum total to three mariners who paid no board, and to whom the gift is an absolute charity, I am content. To be sure, they interfered with me at a moment when I was about to make a suitable settlement of the matter, but I have no doubt they were told to do so; and I must admit that while they carried out their orders with a certain firmness, characteristic of persons accustomed to unreasoning obedience, they treated me with entire respect. If equal respect had been shown to me at the beginning of these disputes, it would have been much better for all concerned."

And opening his book, he recommenced his reading.

That afternoon all of us, except Mr. Enderton, assembled on Mrs. Aleshine's piazza to witness the presentation of the board money. The three sailors, who had been informed of the nature of the proceedings, stood in line on the second step of the piazza, clad in their best toggery, and with their new tarpaulin hats in their hands. Mrs. Aleshine went into the house, and soon reappeared carrying the ginger-jar, which she presented to Mr. Dusante. That gentleman took it, and stood holding it for a moment as if he were about to speak; but even if he had intended to say anything, he had no further opportunity, for Mrs. Lecks now stepped forward and addressed him.

"Mr. Dusante," said she, "from what I have seen of you myself and heard tell of you from others, I believe you are a man who tries to do his duty, as he sees it, with a single heart and no turnin' from one side to the other. You made up your mind that you'd travel over the whole world, if it had to be done, with that ginger-jar and the board money inside of it, till you'd found the people who'd been livin' in your house; and then that you'd give back that jar, jus' as you'd found it, to the person who took upon herself the overseein' of the reg'lar payin' of the money and the puttin' of it therein. With that purpose in your mind you carried that jar over the ocean; you wandered with it up and down California; and holdin' it tight fast in your arms, you slid down the slipperiest mountain that was ever made yet, I believe, and if it had been your only infant child, you couldn't have held it firmer, nor regarded it more careful. Through ups and downs, and thicks and smooths, you carried that jar or followed it, and for the sake of doin' what you'd set your mind on you came all the way to this place; to which, if it hadn't been for that one idea, it isn't likely you'd ever dreamed of comin'. Now, Mr. Dusante, we've all agreed on what we think is the right thing to do, and you agreed with us, but I can see by your face that you're disapp'inted. The thing you set out to do you haven't done; and I'm not goin' to have it to say to myself that you was the only one of all of us that wasn't satisfied, and that I was the stumblin'-block that stood in your way. So I'll back down from sayin' that I'd never touch that jar again, and you can put it into my hands, as you set out to do."

Mr. Dusante made no answer, but stepped forward, and taking Mrs. Lecks's large brown and work-worn hand, he respectfully touched it with his lips. It is not probable that Mrs. Lecks's hand had ever before been kissed. It is not probable that she had ever seen any one kiss the hand of another. But the hard sense and keen insight of that independent countrywoman made her instantly aware of what was meant by that old-fashioned act of courteous homage. Her tall form grew more erect; she slightly bowed her head, and received the salute with a quiet dignity which would have become a duchess.

This little scene touched us all, and Mrs. Aleshine afterward informed me that for a moment she hadn't a dry eye in her head.

Mr. Dusante now handed the ginger-jar to Mrs. Lecks, who immediately stepped toward Ruth and Lucille.

"You two young ones," she said, "can jus' take this jar, an' your hands can be the first to lift off that paper of fish-hooks and take out the money, which you will then divide among our good friends, these sailormen."

Ruth and Lucille immediately sat down on the floor of the piazza, and the one emptied the board money into the lap of the other, where it was speedily divided into three equal portions, one of which was placed in the hands of each mariner.

"HE RESPECTFULLY TOUCHED IT WITH HIS LIPS."

The men stood motionless, each holding his money in his open right hand, and then the red-bearded coxswain spoke.

"It ain't for me, nor for Bill, nor for Jim nuther, to say a word ag'in what you all think is right and square. We've stood by ye an' obeyed orders since we first shipped on that island, an' we intend to do so straight along. Don't we, Jim an' Bill?"

"Aye, aye, sir!" said Jim and Bill, in hearty hoarse response.

"There's some of ye, specially Mrs. Aleshine, though meanin' no dis-respec' to anybody else, that we'd follow to the crosstrees of the top-gallantmast of the tallest ship that ever floated in the middle of the ragin'est typhoon that ever blowed. Wouldn't we, Jim an' Bill?"

"Aye, aye, sir!" sang out Jim and Bill.

"But though we stand ready to obey orders," said the coxswain, "we made up our minds, when we heard what was goin' to be done, that we'd listen keerful fer one thing, an' we have listened keerful, an' we haven't heard that one thing, an' that thing was what we should do with this money. An' not havin' heard it, an' so bein' under no orders as to the spendin' of it, we take the money, an' thank you kindly, one an' all. Don't we, Jim an' Bill?"

"Aye, aye, sir!" said Jim and Bill.

And into the pocket of each mariner clinked the money.

Mr. Dusante now took up the ginger-jar, and approached Mrs. Lecks. "I hope, madam," he said, "that as the subject of our little differences has now been removed from this jar, you will consent to accept it from me as a memento of the somewhat remarkable experiences through which it has accompanied us."

"Take it, sir?" said she. "To be sure I will. An' very glad am I to get it. As long as I live it shall stand on the mantelpiece in my parlor; an' when I die it shall be left to my heirs, to be taken care of as long as it holds together."

Every reason for dissatisfaction having now been banished from our little company, we all settled down for a season of enjoyment. Even Mr. Enderton, who had found on the top shelf of a closet in his room at the inn a lot of old books, appeared to be in a state of perfect content. To the Dusantes a residence in this absolutely rural portion of our Middle States in the autumnal season was an entirely novel experience. The crisp and invigorating air, the mists and the glowing hues of the Indian-summer time, the softness of the sunshine, and even those masses of limbs and twigs which had already dropped their leaves and spread themselves in a delicate network against the clear blue sky, were all full of a novel beauty for these people who had lived so long in tropical lands and among perennial foliage, and had never known the delights of an American country life out of season. Having enjoyed Mrs. Lecks's hospitality for a suitable period, they proposed to that sensible woman that she should receive them as boarders until the winter should set in; and to this practical proposition she gave a ready assent, hoping that the really cold weather would long defer its coming.

Ruth and I established ourselves on the same terms with Mrs. Aleshine. A prolonged holiday from the labors of my business had been the object of my attempted journey to Japan, and I could think of no place where it would better please my young wife and myself to rest for a time than here among these good friends.

A continual source of amusement to us were the acts and doings of Mrs. Aleshine and her three sailormen. These bold mariners had enlisted, soul and body, into the service of the thrifty housewife; and as it was impossible to do anything in connection with the growing of the onions until the desired fields should be acquired and the spring should open, many and diverse were the labors at which the coxswain and those two able-bodied seamen Bill and Jim set themselves, or were set by Mrs. Aleshine.

The brilliantly painted front door, which at first had excited the good woman's ire, gradually came to command her admiration; and when her sailormen had done everything else that they could in the barns, the fields, or at the woodpile, she gave them the privilege to paint various portions of her property, leaving designs and colors to their own taste and fancy. Whether they milked the cows, cut the wood, or painted the sides of the house, they always worked like good fellows, and in nautical costume. They holystoned the front deck, as they called the floor of the piazza, until it seemed sacrilegious to set foot upon it; and when the house and the pale-fence had been suitably painted, they allowed their fancies lofty flights in the decoration of the smaller outbuildings and various objects in the grounds. One of the men had a pocket-chart of the colors adopted by the different steamship companies all over the world, and now smoke-houses, corn-cribs, chicken-houses, and so on, down to pumps and hitching-posts, were painted in great bands of blue and red and white and black, arranged in alternating orders, until an observer might have supposed that a commercial navy had been sunk beneath Mrs. Aleshine's house grounds, leaving nothing but its smoke-stacks visible.

The greatest work of decoration, however, was reserved by the red-bearded coxswain for himself, designed by his own brain, and executed by his own hands. This was the tattooing of the barn. Around this building, the sides of which were already of a color sufficiently resembling a well-tanned human skin, the coxswain painted in blue spots resembling tattooing, an immense cable passing several times about the structure, a sea-serpent almost as long as the cable, eight anchors, two ships under full sail, with a variety of cannons and flags which filled up all the remaining spaces. This great work was a long time in execution, and before it was half finished its fame had spread over the surrounding country.

The decoration of her premises was greatly enjoyed by Mrs. Aleshine. "It gives 'em somethin' to do," said she, "till the onion season comes on; it makes 'em happy; an' the leaves an' flowers bein' pretty nigh gone, I like to see the place blossoming' out as if it was a cold-weather garden."

In the evenings, in the large kitchen, the sailormen danced their hornpipes, and around the great fireplace they spun long yarns of haps

"THE GREATEST WORK OF DECORATION WAS RESERVED BY THE
RED-BEARDED COXSWAIN FOR HIMSELF."

and mishaps on distant seas. Mrs. Aleshine always, and the rest of us often, sat by the fire and enjoyed these nautical recreations.

"Havin' myself done housekeepin' in the torrid zone," she once said, "a lot of the things they tell come home to me quite nat'ral. An' I'd do anything in the world to make 'em content to live on dry land like common Christians, instead of cavortin' about on the pitchin' ocean, runnin' into each other, an' springin' leaks, with no likelihood of findin' a furnished island at every p'int where their ship happened to go down."

On one subject only did any trouble now come into the mind of Mrs. Aleshine, and she once had a little talk with me in regard to it.

"I've been afeard from the very beginnin'," she said, "an, after a while I more 'n half believed it, that Elizabeth Grootenheimer was settin' her cap at the coxswain; so I just went to him an' I spoke to him plain. 'This sort o' thing won't do at all,' says I; 'an' although I haven't a doubt you see it for yourself, I thought it my dooty to speak my mind about it. There's plenty of young women in this township that would make you sailormen fust-rate wives, an' glad enough I'd be to see you all married an' settled an' gone to farmin' right here amongst us; but Elizabeth Grootenheimer won't do. Settin' aside everythin' else, if there was to be any children, they might be little coxswains, but they'd be Grootenheimers too, stone-dumb Grootenheimers; an' I tell you plain that this county can't stand no more Grootenheimers!' To which he says, says he, 'I want you to understan', ma'am. that if ever me or Jim or Bill makes up our mind to set sail for any sort of a weddin' port, we won't weigh anchor till we've got our clearance papers from you.' By which he meant that he'd ask my advice about courtin'. An' now my mind is easy, an' I can look ahead with comfort to onion-time."

I found it necessary to go to Philadelphia for a day or two to attend to some business matters; and, the evening before I started, the coxswain came to me and asked a favor for himself and his mates.

"It mayn't have passed out of your mind, sir," said he, "that when me an' Jim an' Bill took that money that you all gave us, which wasn't 'zackly like prize-money, because the rest of the crew, to put it that way, didn't get any, we listened keerful to see if anything was said as to what we was to do with the money; an' nothin' bein' said, we took it, and we wasn't long makin' up our minds as to what we was goin' to do with it. What we wanted to do was to put up some sort of signal what couldn't get blowed away, or, more like, a kind of reg'lar moniment as would make them that looked at it remember the rough squalls and the jolly larks we've gone through with together; an' it was when we was talkin' about Mrs. Lecks bein' give' the ginger-jar to put on her mantel-piece an' keep forever that me an' Jim and Bill we said, says we, that Mrs. Aleshine should have a ginger-jar too, havin' as much right to one as her mate, an' that that would be the signal-flag or the moniment that we'd put up. Now, sir, as you're goin' to town, we ask you to take this money, which is the whole lot that was give' us, an' have a ginger-jar built, jus' the size an' shape an' gen'ral trim of that other one, but of no pottery-stuff, for you kin buy 'em jus' like that, an' that ain't what we want. We want her built of good oak, stout an' strong, with live-oak knees inside to keep her stiff an' save her from bein' stove in, in case of a collision. We want her bottom coppered up above the water-line with real silver, an' we want a turtle-back deck with a round hatchway, with a tight-fittin' hatch, jus' like common jars. We want her sides calked with oakum, an' well scraped an' painted, so that with water inside of her or outside of her she won't leak. An' on the bottom of her, so they kin be seen if she keels over, we wants the names of me an' Jim an' Bill, which we've wrote on this piece of paper. An' on her sides, below the water-line, on the silver copperin', we want the names of all the rest of you, an' the latitood an' longitood of that island, an' anything out of the logs that might 'a' been kep' by any of you, as might help to be remembered the thing what happened. An' then, if there's any room left on the copperin', an any money lef' to pay for 'em, you might have cut on as many anchors, an' hearts, an' bits of cable, an' such like suitable things as would fill up. An' that jar we're goin' to give to Mrs. Aleshine to put on her mantelpiece, to stay there as long as she lives, or anybody that belongs to her. An', by George, sir!" he added behind his hand, although there was nobody to hear, "if ever them two jars run into each other, it won't be Mrs. Aleshine's that'll go down!"

I undertook this commission, and in due course of time there came to the village the most astonishing ginger-jar that was ever built, and which satisfied the three mariners in every particular. When it was presented to Mrs. Aleshine, her admiration of this work of art, her delight in its ownership, and her gratitude to the donors were alike boundless.

"However could I have had the idee," said she privately to me, "that any one of them noble sailormen could have brought himself down to marry Elizabeth Grootenheimer!"

It was not long after this happy event that another great joy came to Mrs. Aleshine. Her son returned from Japan. He had heard of the loss of the steamer in which his mother and Mrs. Lecks had set sail, and was in great trouble of mind until he received a letter from his mother which brought him speedily home. He had no intention of settling in Meadowville, but it had been a long time since he had seen his mother.

He was a fine young man, handsome and well educated, and we were all delighted with him; and in a very short time he and Lucille Dusante, being the only young bachelor and maiden of the company, became super-friendly that it was easy to see that to Mrs. Aleshine might come the unexpected rapture of eventually being the mother of Lucille.

We stayed much later at Meadowville than we had expected. Even after the little hills and vales had been well covered with snow, sleighing and coasting parties, led by the lively new-comer, offered attractions, especially to Lucille, which bound us to the cheery homes of Mrs. Lecks and Mrs. Aleshine. But, after a time, the Dusantes considered it prudent to go to Florida for the rest of the winter; Mr. Enderton had long since read all the books on his closet shelf and departed for New York; and Ruth and I determined that we, too, must move eastward.

But, before our little company separated, Mrs. Aleshine's son and Lucille Dusante had settled it between them that when the springtime came they would set sail for a wedding port. This match was a highly satisfactory one to all concerned, for Mr. Dusante could scarcely have found a young brother-in-law who would make his sister so happy, and who was, at the same time, so well fitted by disposition and previous occupation to assist in his increasing business cares.

In the spring the Dusante family came North again, and Lucille and her lover were married; and then all of us, except Mr. Enderton, who had obtained a most congenial position as assistant librarian in a public institution seldom visited, gathered at Meadowville to spend a week or two together, after which Ruth and I would repair to the New England town which was to be our home, and the Dusante family, the young husband included, would set out on a tour, partly of business and partly of pleasure, through Canada and the far Northwest.

It was arranged that, whenever it should be possible, Lucille and Mrs. Dusante should spend their summers at Meadowville; and as this would also give her much of the society of her son, the heart of Mrs. Aleshine could ask no more.

This visit to Meadowville was in the onion season; and one morning Ruth and I sat upon a fence and watched the three sailormen busily at work. The soil looked so fine and smooth that one might almost have supposed that it had been holystoned; and the three nautical farmers, in their tight-waisted, loose-bottomed trousers, their tarpaulin hats, and their wide-collared shirts, were seated on the ground at different points, engrossed in the absorbing task of setting out young onions as onions had never been set out before. All the careful attention to patient minutiae which nautical handiwork had taught them was now displayed in their new vocation. In a portion of the field which had been first planted the onions had sprouted, and we could see evidences of astonishing designs. Here were anchors in onions; hearts in onions; brigs, barks, and schooners in onions; and more things pertaining to ships, the heart's affections, and the raging main outlined in onions than Ruth and I could give names to.

"It seems to me," said I, "that there must have been some sort of enchantment in that little island in the Pacific, for in one way or another it has made us all very happy."

"That is true," answered Ruth, "and, do you know, I believe the cause of a great part of that happiness was the board money in the ginger-jar!"

Catalog
of
DOVER BOOKS

BOOKS EXPLAINING SCIENCE

(Note: The books listed under this category are general introductions, surveys, reviews, and non-technical expositions of science for the interested layman or scientist who wishes to brush up. Dover also publishes the largest list of inexpensive reprints of books on intermediate and higher mathematics, mathematical physics, engineering, chemistry, astronomy, etc., for the professional mathematician or scientist. For our complete Science Catalog, write Dept. catrr., Dover Publications, Inc., 180 Varick Street, New York 14, N. Y.)

CONCERNING THE NATURE OF THINGS, Sir William· Bragg. Royal Institute Christmas Lectures by Nobel Laureate. Excellent plain-language introduction to gases, molecules, crystal structure, etc. explains "building blocks" of universe, basic properties of matter, with simplest, clearest examples, demonstrations. 32pp. of photos; 57ᵗ figures. 244pp. 5⅜ x 8.
T31 Paperbound **$1.35**

MATTER AND LIGHT, THE NEW PHYSICS, Louis de Broglie. Non-technical explanations by a Nobel Laureate of electro-magnetic theory, relativity, wave mechanics, quantum physics, philosophies of science, etc. Simple, yet accurate introduction to work of Planck, Bohr, Einstein, other modern physicists. Only 2 of 12 chapters require mathematics. 300pp. 5⅜ x 8.
T35 Paperbound **$1.60**

THE COMMON ·SENSE OF THE EXACT SCIENCES, W. K. Clifford. For 70 years, Clifford's work has been acclaimed as one of the clearest, yet most precise introductions to mathematical symbolism, measurement, surface boundaries, position, space, motion, mass and force, etc. Prefaces by Bertrand Russell and Karl Pearson. Introduction by James Newman. 130 figures. 249pp. 5⅜ x 8.
T61 Paperbound **$1.60**

THE NATURE OF LIGHT AND COLOUR IN THE OPEN AIR, M. Minnaert. What causes mirages? haloes? "multiple" suns and moons? Professor Minnaert explains these and hundreds of other fascinating natural optical phenomena in simple terms, tells how to observe them, suggests hundreds of experiments. 200 illus; 42 photos. xvi + 362pp.
T196 Paperbound **$1:95**

SPINNING TOPS AND GYROSCOPIC MOTION, John Perry. Classic elementary text on dynamics of rotation treats gyroscopes, tops, how quasi-rigidity is induced in paper disks, smoke rings, chains, etc, by rapid motion, precession, earth's motion, etc. Contains many easy-to-perform experiments. Appendix on practical uses of gyroscopes. 62 figures. 128pp.
T416 Paperbound **$1.00**

A CONCISE HISTORY OF MATHEMATICS, D. Struik. This lucid, easily followed history of mathematics from the Ancient Near East to modern times requires no mathematical background itself, yet introduces both mathematicians and laymen to basic concepts and discoveries and the men who made them. Contains a collection of 31 portraits of eminent mathematicians. Bibliography. xix + 299pp. 5⅜ x 8.
T255 Paperbound **$1.75**

THE RESTLESS UNIVERSE, Max Born. A remarkably clear, thorough exposition of gases, electrons, ions, waves and particles, electronic structure of the atom, nuclear physics, written for the layman by a Nobel Laureate. "Much ·more thorough and deep than most attempts . . . easy and delightful," CHEMICAL AND ENGINEERING NEWS. Includes 7 animated sequences showing motion of molecules, alpha particles, etc. 11 full-page plates of photographs. Total of nearly 600 illus. 315pp. 6⅛ x 9¼.
T412 Paperbound **$2.00**

WHAT IS SCIENCE?, N. Campbell. The role of experiment, the function of mathematics, the nature of scientific laws, the limitations of science, and many other provocative topics are explored without technicalities by an eminent scientist. "Still an excellent introduction to scientific philosophy," H. Margenau in PHYSICS TODAY. 192pp. 5⅜ x 8.
S43 Paperbound **$1.25**

FADS AND FALLACIES IN THE NAME OF SCIENCE, Martin Gardner. The standard account of the various cults, quack systems and delusions which have recently masqueraded as science: hollow earth theory, Atlantis, dianetics, Reich's orgone theory, flying saucers, Bridey Murphy, psionics, irridiagnosis, many other fascinating fallacies that deluded tens of thousands. "Should be read by everyone, scientist and non-scientist alike," R. T. Birge, Prof. Emeritus, Univ. of California; Former President, American Physical Society. Formerly titled, "In the Name of Science." Revised and enlarged edition. x + 365pp. 5⅜ x 8.
T394 Paperbound **$1.50**

THE STUDY OF THE HISTORY OF MATHEMATICS, THE STUDY OF THE HISTORY OF SCIENCE, G. Sarton. Two books bound as one. Both volumes are standard introductions to their fields by an eminent science historian. They discuss problems of historical research, teaching, pitfalls, other matters of interest to the historically oriented writer, teacher, or student. Both have extensive bibliographies. 10 illustrations. 188pp. 5⅜ x 8.   T240 Paperbound **$1.25**

THE PRINCIPLES OF SCIENCE, W. S. Jevons. Unabridged reprinting of a milestone in the development of symbolic logic and other subjects concerning scientific methodology, probability, inferential validity, etc. Also describes Jevons' "logic machine," an early precursor of modern electronic calculators. Preface by E. Nagel. 839pp. 5⅜ x 8.   S446 Paperbound **$2.98**

SCIENCE THEORY AND MAN, Erwin Schroedinger. Complete, unabridged reprinting of "Science and the Human Temperament" plus an additional essay "What is an Elementary Particle?" Nobel Laureate Schroedinger discusses many aspects of modern physics from novel points of view which provide unusual insights for both laymen and physicists. 192 pp. 5⅜ x 8.
T428 Paperbound **$1.35**

BRIDGES AND THEIR BUILDERS, D. B. Steinman & S. R. Watson. Information about ancient, medieval, modern bridges; how they were built; who built them; the structural principles employed; the materials they are built of; etc. Written by one of the world's leading authorities on bridge design and construction. New, revised, expanded edition. 23 photos; 26 line drawings, xvii + 401pp. 5⅜ x 8.   T431 Paperbound **$1.95**

HISTORY OF MATHEMATICS, D. E. Smith. Most comprehensive non-technical history of math in English. In two volumes. Vol. I: A chronological examination of the growth of mathematics from primitive concepts up to 1900. Vol. II: The development of ideas in specific fields and areas, up through elementary calculus. The lives and works of over a thousand mathematicians are covered; thousands of specific historical problems and their solutions are clearly explained. Total of 510 illustrations, 1355pp. 5⅜ x 8. Set boxed in attractive container.   T429, T430 Paperbound, the set **$5.00**

PHILOSOPHY AND THE PHYSICISTS, L. S. Stebbing. A philosopher examines the philosophical implications of modern science by posing a lively critical attack on the popular science expositions of Sir James Jeans and Arthur Eddington. xvi + 295pp. 5⅜ x 8.
T480 Paperbound **$1.65**

ON MATHEMATICS AND MATHEMATICIANS, R. E. Moritz. The first collection of quotations by and about mathematicians in English. 1140 anecdotes, aphorisms, definitions, speculations, etc. give both mathematicians and layman stimulating new insights into what mathematics is, and into the personalities of the great mathematicians from Archimedes to Euler, Gauss, Klein, Weierstrass. Invaluable to teachers, writers. Extensive cross index. 410pp. 5⅜ x 8.
T489 Paperbound **$1.95**

NATURAL SCIENCE, BIOLOGY, GEOLOGY, TRAVEL

A SHORT HISTORY OF ANATOMY AND PHYSIOLOGY FROM THE GREEKS TO HARVEY, C. Singer. A great medical historian's fascinating intermediate account of the slow advance of anatomical and physiological knowledge from pre-scientific times to Vesalius, Harvey. 139 unusually interesting illustrations. 221pp. 5⅜ x 8.   T389 Paperbound **$1.75**

THE BEHAVIOUR AND SOCIAL LIFE OF HONEYBEES, Ronald Ribbands. The most comprehensive, lucid and authoritative book on bee habits, communication, duties, cell life, motivations, etc. "A MUST for every scientist, experimenter, and educator, and a happy and valuable selection for all interested in the honeybee," AMERICAN BEE JOURNAL. 690-item bibliography. 127 illus.; 11 photographic plates. 352pp. 5⅜ x 8⅜.   S410 Clothbound **$4.50**

TRAVELS OF WILLIAM BARTRAM, edited by Mark Van Doren. One of the 18th century's most delightful books, and one of the few first-hand sources of information about American geography, natural history, and anthropology of American Indian tribes of the time. "The mind of a scientist with the soul of a poet," John Livingston Lowes. 13 original illustrations, maps. Introduction by Mark Van Doren. 448pp. 5⅜ x 8.   T326 Paperbound **$2.00**

STUDIES ON THE STRUCTURE AND DEVELOPMENT OF VERTEBRATES, Edwin Goodrich. The definitive study of the skeleton, fins and limbs, head region, divisions of the body cavity, vascular, respiratory, excretory systems, etc., of vertebrates from fish to higher mammals, by the greatest comparative anatomist of recent times. "The standard textbook," JOURNAL OF ANATOMY. 754 illus. 69-page biographical study. 1186-item bibliography. 2 vols. Total of 906pp. 5⅜ x 8.
Vol. I: S449 Paperbound **$2.50**
Vol. II: S450 Paperbound **$2.50**

THE BIRTH AND DEVELOPMENT OF THE GEOLOGICAL SCIENCES, F. D. Adams. The most complete and thorough history of the earth sciences in print. Covers over 300 geological thinkers and systems; treats fossils, theories of stone growth, paleontology, earthquakes, vulcanists vs. neptunists, odd theories, etc. 91 illustrations, including medieval, Renaissance wood cuts, etc. 632 footnotes and bibliographic notes. 511pp. 308pp. 5⅜ x 8.   T5 Paperbound **$2.00**

FROM MAGIC TO SCIENCE, Charles Singer. A close study of aspects of medical science from the Roman Empire through the Renaissance. The sections on early herbals, and "The Visions of Hildegarde of Bingen," are probably the best studies of these subjects available. 158 unusual classic and medieval illustrations. xxvii + 365pp. 5⅜ x 8.   T390 Paperbound **$2.00**

SAILING ALONE AROUND THE WORLD, Captain Joshua Slocum. Captain Slocum's personal account of his single-handed voyage around the world in a 34-foot boat he rebuilt himself. A classic of both seamanship and descriptive writing. "A nautical equivalent of Thoreau's account," Van Wyck Brooks. 67 illus. 308pp. 5⅜ x 8.   T326 Paperbound **$1.00**

TREES OF THE EASTERN AND CENTRAL UNITED STATES AND CANADA, W. M. Harlow. Standard middle-level guide designed to help you know the characteristics of Eastern trees and identify them at sight by means of an 8-page synoptic key. More than 600 drawings and photographs of twigs, leaves, fruit, other features. xiii + 288pp. 4⅝ x 6½.
                                                                          T395 Paperbound **$1.35**

FRUIT KEY AND TWIG KEY ("Fruit Key to Northeastern Trees," "Twig Key to Deciduous Woody Plants of Eastern North America"), **W. M. Harlow.** Identify trees in fall, winter, spring. Easy-to-use, synoptic keys, with photographs of every twig and fruit identified. Covers 120 different fruits, 160 different twigs. Over 350 photos. Bibliographies. Glossaries. Total of 143pp. 5⅝ x 8⅜.   T511 Paperbound **$1.25**

INTRODUCTION TO THE STUDY OF EXPERIMENTAL MEDICINE, Claude Bernard. This classic records Bernard's far-reaching efforts to transform physiology into an exact science. It covers problems of vivisection, the limits of physiological experiment, hypotheses in medical experimentation, hundreds of others. Many of his own famous experiments on the liver, the pancreas, etc., are used as examples. Foreword by I. B. Cohen. xxv + 266pp. 5⅜ x 8.
                                                                          T400 Paperbound **$1.50**

THE ORIGIN OF LIFE, A. I. Oparin. The first modern statement that life evolved from complex nitro-carbon compounds, carefully presented according to modern biochemical knowledge of primary colloids, organic molecules, etc. Begins with historical introduction to the problem of the origin of life. Bibliography. xxv + 270pp. 5⅜ x 8.   S213 Paperbound **$1.75**

A HISTORY OF ASTRONOMY FROM THALES TO KEPLER, J. L. E. Dreyer. The only work in English which provides a detailed picture of man's cosmological views from Egypt, Babylonia, Greece, and Alexandria to Copernicus, Tycho Brahe and Kepler. "Standard reference on Greek astronomy and the Copernican revolution," SKY AND TELESCOPE. Formerly called "A History of Planetary Systems From Thales to Kepler." Bibliography. 21 diagrams. xvii + 430pp. 5⅜ x 8.
                                                                          S79 Paperbound **$1.98**

URANIUM PROSPECTING, H. L. Barnes. A professional geologist tells you what you need to know. Hundreds of facts about minerals, tests, detectors, sampling, assays, claiming, developing, government regulations, etc. Glossary of technical terms. Annotated bibliography. x + 117pp. 5⅜ x 8.   T309 Paperbound **$1.00**

DE RE METALLICA, Georgius Agricola. All 12 books of this 400 year old classic on metals and metal production, fully annotated, and containing all 289 of the 16th century woodcuts which made the original an artistic masterpiece. A superb gift for geologists, engineers, libraries, artists, historians. Translated by Herbert Hoover & L. H. Hoover. Bibliography, survey of ancient authors. 289 illustrations of the excavating, assaying, smelting, refining, and countless other metal production operations described in the text. 672pp. 6¾ x 10¾. Deluxe library edition.   S6 Clothbound **$10.00**

DE MAGNETE, William Gilbert. A landmark of science by the man who first used the word "electricity," distinguished between static electricity and magnetism, and founded a new science. P. F. Mottelay translation. 90 figures. lix + 368pp. 5⅜ x 8.   S470 Paperbound **$2.00**

THE AUTOBIOGRAPHY OF CHARLES DARWIN AND SELECTED LETTERS, Francis Darwin, ed. Fascinating documents on Darwin's early life, the voyage of the "Beagle," the discovery of evolution, Darwin's thought on mimicry, plant development, vivisection, evolution, many other subjects Letters to Henslow, Lyell, Hooker, Wallace, Kingsley, etc. Appendix. 365pp. 5⅜ x 8.   T479 Paperbound **$1.65**

A WAY OF LIFE AND OTHER SELECTED WRITINGS OF SIR WILLIAM OSLER. 16 of the great physician, teacher and humanist's most inspiring writings on a practical philosophy of life, science and the humanities, and the history of medicine. 5 photographs. Introduction by G. L. Keynes, M.D., F.R.C.S. xx + 278pp. 5⅜ x 8.   T488 Paperbound **$1.50**

WORLD DRAMA, B. H. Clark. 46 plays from Ancient Greece, Rome, to India, China, Japan. Plays by Aeschylus, Sophocles, Euripides, Aristophanes, Plautus, Marlowe, Jonson, Farquhar, Goldsmith, Cervantes, Molière, Dumas, Goethe, Schiller, Ibsen, many others. One of the most comprehensive collections of important plays from all literature available in English. Over ⅓ of this material is unavailable in any other current edition. Reading lists. 2 volumes. Total of 1364pp. 5⅜ x 8.

Vol. I, T57 Paperbound **$2.00**
Vol. II, T59 Paperbound **$2.00**

MASTERS OF THE DRAMA, John Gassner. The most comprehensive history of the drama in print. Covers more than 800 dramatists and over 2000 plays from the Greeks to modern Western, Near Eastern, Oriental drama. Plot summaries, theatre history, etc. "Best of its kind in English," NEW REPUBLIC. 35 pages of bibliography. 77 photos and drawings. Deluxe edition. xxii + 890pp. 5⅜ x 8.
T100 Clothbound **$5.95**

THE DRAMA OF LUIGI PIRANDELLO, D. Vittorini. All 38 of Pirandello's plays (to 1935) summarized and analyzed in terms of symbolic techniques, plot structure, etc. The only authorized work. Foreword by Pirandello. Biography. Bibliography. xiii + 350pp. 5⅜ x 8.
T435 Paperbound **$1.98**

ARISTOTLE'S THEORY OF POETRY AND THE FINE ARTS, S. H. Butcher, ed. The celebrated "Butcher translation" faced page by page with the Greek text; Butcher's 300-page introduction to Greek poetic, dramatic thought. Modern Aristotelian criticism discussed by John Gassner. lxxvi + 421pp. 5⅜ x 8.
T42 Paperbound **$2.00**

EUGENE O'NEILL: THE MAN AND HIS PLAYS, B. H. Clark. The first published source-book on O'Neill's life and work. Analyzes each play from the early THE WEB up to THE ICEMAN COMETH. Supplies much information about environmental and dramatic influences. ix + 182pp. 5⅜ x 8.
T379 Paperbound **$1.25**

INTRODUCTION TO ENGLISH LITERATURE, B. Dobrée, ed. Most compendious literary aid in its price range. Extensive, categorized bibliography (with entries up to 1949) of more than 5,000 poets, dramatists, novelists, as well as historians, philosophers, economists, religious writers, travellers, and scientists of literary stature. Information about manuscripts, important biographical data. Critical, historical, background works not simply listed, but evaluated. Each volume also contains a long introduction to the period it covers.

Vol. I: **THE BEGINNINGS OF ENGLISH LITERATURE TO SKELTON, 1509, W. L. Renwick. H. Orton.** 450pp. 5⅛ x 7⅛.
T75 Clothbound **$3.50**

Vol. II: **THE ENGLISH RENAISSANCE, 1510-1688, V. de Sola Pinto.** 381pp. 5⅛ x 7⅛.
T76 Clothbound **$3.50**

Vol. III: **THE AUGUSTANS AND ROMANTICS, 1689-1830, H. Dyson, J. Butt.** 320pp. 5⅛ x·7⅛.
T77 Clothbound **$3.50**

Vol. IV: **THE VICTORIANS AND AFTER, 1830-1914, E. Batho, B. Dobrée.** 360pp. 5⅛ x 7⅛.
T78 Clothbound **$3.50**

EPIC AND ROMANCE, W. P. Ker. The standard survey of Medieval epic and romance by a foremost authority on Medieval literature. Covers historical background, plot, literary analysis, significance of Teutonic epics, Icelandic sagas, Beowulf, French chansons de geste, the Niebelungenlied, Arthurian romances, much more. 422pp. 5⅜ x 8. T355 Paperbound **$1.95**

THE HEART OF EMERSON'S JOURNALS, Bliss Perry, ed. Emerson's most intimate thoughts, impressions, records of conversations with Channing, Hawthorne, Thoreau, etc., carefully chosen from the 10 volumes of The Journals. "The essays do not reveal the power of Emerson's mind . . .as do these hasty and informal writings," N. Y. TIMES. Preface by B. Perry. 370pp. 5⅜ x 8. T447 Paperbound **$1.85**

A SOURCE BOOK IN THEATRICAL HISTORY, A. M. Nagler. (Formerly, "Sources of Theatrical History.") Over 300 selected passages by contemporary observers tell about styles of acting, direction, make-up, scene designing, etc., in the theatre's great periods from ancient Greece to the Théâtre Libre. "Indispensable complement to the study of drama," EDUCATIONAL THEATRE JOURNAL. Prof. Nagler, Yale Univ. School of Drama, also supplies notes, references. 85 illustrations. 611pp. 5⅜ x 8. T515 Paperbound **$2.75**

THE ART OF THE STORY-TELLER, M. L. Shedlock. Regarded as the finest, most helpful book on telling stories to children, by a great story-teller. How to catch, hold, recapture attention; how to choose material; many other aspects. Also includes: a 99-page selection of Miss Shedlock's most successful stories; extensive bibliography of other stories. xxi + 320pp. 5⅜ x 8. T245 Clothbound **$3.50**

THE DEVIL'S DICTIONARY, Ambrose Bierce. Over 1000 short, ironic definitions in alphabetical order, by America's greatest satirist in the classical tradition. "Some of the most gorgeous witticisms in the English language," H. L. Mencken. 144pp. 5⅜ x 8. T487 Paperbound **$1.00**

MUSIC

A DICTIONARY OF HYMNOLOGY, John Julian. More than 30,000 entries on individual hymns, their authorship, textual variations, location of texts, dates and circumstances of composition, denominational and ritual usages, the biographies of more than 9,000 hymn writers, essays on important topics such as children's hymns and Christmas carols, and hundreds of thousands of other important facts about hymns which are virtually impossible to find anywhere else. Convenient alphabetical listing, and a 200-page double-columned index of first lines enable you to track down virtually any hymn ever written. Total of 1786pp. 6¼ x 9¼. 2 volumes.   T133. The Set, Clothbound **$15.00**

STRUCTURAL HEARING, TONAL COHERENCE IN MUSIC, Felix Salzer. Extends the well-known Schenker approach to include modern music, music of the middle ages, and Renaissance music. Explores the phenomenon of tonal organization by discussing more than 500 compositions, and offers unusual new insights into the theory of composition and musical relationships. "The foundation on which all teaching in music theory has been based at this college," Leopold Mannes, President, The Mannes College of Music. Total of 658pp. 6½ x 9¼. 2 volumes.   S418 The set, Clothbound **$8.00**

A GENERAL HISTORY OF MUSIC, Charles Burney. The complete history of music from the Greeks up to 1789 by the 18th century musical historian who personally knew the great Baroque composers. Covers sacred and secular, vocal and instrumental, operatic and symphonic music; treats theory, notation, forms, instruments; discusses composers, performers, important works. Invaluable as a source of information on the period for students, historians, musicians. "Surprisingly few of Burney's statements have been invalidated by modern research . . . still of great value," NEW YORK TIMES. Edited and corrected by Frank Mercer. 35 figures. 1915pp. 5½ x 8½. 2 volumes.   T36 The set, Clothbound **$12.50**

JOHANN SEBASTIAN BACH, Phillip Spitta. Recognized as one of the greatest accomplishments of musical scholarship and far and away the definitive coverage of Bach's works. Hundreds of individual pieces are analyzed. Major works, such as the B Minor Mass and the St. Matthew Passion are examined in minute detail. Spitta also deals with the works of Buxtehude, Pachelbel, and others of the period. Can be read with profit even by those without a knowledge of the technicalities of musical composition. "Unchallenged as the last word on one of the supreme geniuses of music," John Barkham, SATURDAY REVIEW SYNDICATE. Total of 1819pp. 5⅜ x 8. 2 volumes.   T252 The set, Clothbound **$10.00**

HISTORY

THE IDEA OF PROGRESS, J. B. Bury. Prof. Bury traces the evolution of a central concept of Western civilization in Greek, Roman, Medieval, and Renaissance thought to its flowering in the 17th and 18th centuries. Introduction by Charles Beard. xl + 357pp. 5⅜ x 8.
T39 Clothbound **$3.95**
T40 Paperbound **$1.95**

THE ANCIENT GREEK HISTORIANS, J. B. Bury. Greek historians such as Herodotus, Thucydides, Xenophon; Roman historians such as Tacitus, Caesar, Livy; scores of others fully analyzed in terms of sources, concepts, influences, etc., by a great scholar and historian. 291pp. 5⅜ x 8.   T397 Paperbound **$1.50**

HISTORY OF THE LATER ROMAN EMPIRE, J. B. Bury. The standard work on the Byzantine Empire from 395 A.D. to the death of Justinian in 565 A.D., by the leading Byzantine scholar of our time. Covers political, social, cultural, theological, military history. Quotes contemporary documents extensively. "Most unlikely that it will ever be superseded," Glanville Downey, Dumbarton Oaks Research Library. Genealogical tables. 5 maps. Bibliography. 2 vols. Total of 965pp. 5⅜ x 8.   T398, T399 Paperbound, the set **$4.00**

GARDNER'S PHOTOGRAPHIC SKETCH BOOK OF THE CIVIL WAR, Alexander Gardner. One of the rarest and most valuable Civil War photographic collections exactly reproduced for the first time since 1866. Scenes of Manassas, Bull Run, Harper's Ferry, Appomattox, Mechanicsville, Fredericksburg, Gettysburg, etc.; battle ruins, prisons, arsenals, a slave pen, fortifications; Lincoln on the field, officers, men, corpses. By one of the most famous pioneers in documentary photography. Original copies of the "Sketch Book" sold for $425 in 1952. Introduction by E. Bleiler. 100 full-page 7 x 10 photographs (original size). 244pp. 10¾ x 8½.
T476 Clothbound **$6.00**

THE WORLD'S GREAT SPEECHES, L. Copeland and L. Lamm, eds. 255 speeches from Pericles to Churchill, Dylan Thomas. Invaluable as a guide to speakers; fascinating as history past and present; a source of much difficult-to-find material. Includes an extensive section of informal and humorous speeches. 3 indices: Topic, Author, Nation. xx + 745pp. 5⅜ x 8.
T468 Paperbound **$2.49**

FOUNDERS OF THE MIDDLE AGES, E. K. Rand. The best non-technical discussion of the transformation of Latin paganism into medieval civilization. Tertullian, Gregory, Jerome, Boethius, Augustine, the Neoplatonists, other crucial figures, philosophies examined. Excellent for the intelligent non-specialist. "Extraordinarily accurate," Richard McKeon, THE NATION. ix + 365pp. 5⅜ x 8.   T369 Paperbound **$1.85**

THE POLITICAL THOUGHT OF PLATO AND ARISTOTLE, Ernest Barker. The standard, comprehensive exposition of Greek political thought. Covers every aspect of the "Republic" and the "Politics" as well as minor writings, other philosophers, theorists of the period, and the later history of Greek political thought. Unabridged edition. 584pp. 5⅜ x 8.
T521 Paperbound **$1.85**

PHILOSOPHY

THE GIFT OF LANGUAGE, M. Schlauch. (Formerly, "The Gift of Tongues.") A sound, middle-level treatment of linguistic families, word histories, grammatical processes, semantics, language taboos, word-coining of Joyce, Cummings, Stein, etc. 232 bibliographical notes. 350pp. 5⅜ x 8.
T243 Paperbound **$1.85**

THE PHILOSOPHY OF HEGEL, W. T. Stace. The first work in English to give a complete and connected view of Hegel's entire system. Especially valuable to those who do not have time to study the highly complicated original texts, yet want an accurate presentation by a most reputable scholar of one of the most influential 19th century thinkers. Includes a 14 x 20 fold-out chart of Hegelian system. 536pp. 5⅜ x 8.
T254 Paperbound **$2.00**

ARISTOTLE, A. E. Taylor. A lucid, non-technical account of Aristotle written by a foremost Platonist. Covers life and works; thought on matter, form, causes, logic, God, physics, metaphysics, etc. Bibliography. New index compiled for this edition. 128pp. 5⅜ x 8.
T280 Paperbound **$1.00**

GUIDE TO PHILOSOPHY, C. E. M. Joad. This basic work describes the major philosophic problems and evaluates the answers propounded by great philosophers from the Greeks to Whitehead, Russell. "The finest introduction," BOSTON TRANSCRIPT. Bibliography, 592pp. 5⅜ x 8.
T297 Paperbound **$2.00**

LANGUAGE AND MYTH, E. Cassirer. Cassirer's brilliant demonstration that beneath both language and myth lies an unconscious "grammar" of experience whose categories and canons are not those of logical thought. Introduction and translation by Susanne Langer. Index. x + 103pp. 5⅜ x 8.
T51 Paperbound **$1.25**

SUBSTANCE AND FUNCTION, EINSTEIN'S THEORY OF RELATIVITY, E. Cassirer. This double volume contains the German philosopher's profound philosophical formulation of the differences between traditional logic and the new logic of science. Number, space, energy, relativity, many other topics are treated in detail. Authorized translation by W. C. and M. C. Swabey. xii + 465pp. 5⅜ x 8.
T50 Paperbound **$2.00**

THE PHILOSOPHICAL WORKS OF DESCARTES. The definitive English edition, in two volumes, of all major philosophical works and letters of René Descartes, father of modern philosophy of knowledge and science. Translated by E. S. Haldane and G. Ross. Introductory notes. Total of 842pp. 5⅜ x 8.
T71 Vol. 1, Paperbound **$2.00**
T72 Vol. 2, Paperbound **$2.00**

ESSAYS IN EXPERIMENTAL LOGIC, J. Dewey. Based upon Dewey's theory that knowledge implies a judgment which in turn implies an inquiry, these papers consider such topics as the thought of Bertrand Russell, pragmatism, the logic of values, antecedents of thought, data and meanings. 452pp. 5⅜ x 8.
T73 Paperbound **$1.95**

THE PHILOSOPHY OF HISTORY, G. W. F. Hegel. This classic of Western thought is Hegel's detailed formulation of the thesis that history is not chance but a rational process, the realization of the Spirit of Freedom. Translated and introduced by J. Sibree. Introduction by C. Hegel. Special introduction for this edition by Prof. Carl Friedrich, Harvard University. xxxix + 447pp. 5⅜ x 8.
T112 Paperbound **$1.85**

THE WILL TO BELIEVE and HUMAN IMMORTALITY, W. James. Two of James's most profound investigations of human belief in God and immortality, bound as one volume. Both are powerful expressions of James's views on chance vs. determinism, pluralism vs. monism, will and intellect, arguments for survival after death, etc. Two prefaces. 429pp. 5⅜ x 8.
T294 Clothbound **$3.75**
T291 Paperbound **$1.65**

INTRODUCTION TO SYMBOLIC LOGIC, S. Langer. A lucid, general introduction to modern logic, covering forms, classes, the use of symbols, the calculus of propositions, the Boole-Schroeder and the Russell-Whitehead systems, etc. "One of the clearest and simplest introductions," MATHEMATICS GAZETTE. Second, enlarged, revised edition. 368pp. 5⅜ x 8.
S164 Paperbound **$1.75**

MIND AND THE WORLD-ORDER, C. I. Lewis. Building upon the work of Peirce, James, and Dewey, Professor Lewis outlines a theory of knowledge in terms of "conceptual pragmatism," and demonstrates why the traditional understanding of the a priori must be abandoned. Appendices. xiv + 446pp. 5⅜ x 8.
T359 Paperbound **$1.95**

THE GUIDE FOR THE PERPLEXED, M. Maimonides One of the great philosophical works of all time, Maimonides' formulation of the meeting-ground between Old Testament and Aristotelian thought is essential to anyone interested in Jewish, Christian, and Moslem thought in the Middle Ages. 2nd revised edition of the Friedlander translation. Extensive introduction. lix + 414pp. 5⅜ x 8.
T351 Paperbound **$1.85**

DOVER BOOKS

THE PHILOSOPHICAL WRITINGS OF PEIRCE, J. Buchler, ed. (Formerly, "The Philosophy of Peirce.") This carefully integrated selection of Peirce's papers is considered the best coverage of the complete thought of one of the greatest philosophers of modern times. Covers Peirce's work on the theory of signs, pragmatism, epistemology, symbolic logic, the scientific method, chance, etc. xvi + 386pp. 5 3/8 x 8.   T216 Clothbound **$5.00**
    T217 Paperbound **$1.95**

HISTORY OF ANCIENT PHILOSOPHY, W. Windelband. Considered the clearest survey of Greek and Roman philosophy. Examines Thales, Anaximander, Anaximenes, Heraclitus, the Eleatics, Empedocles, the Pythagoreans, the Sophists, Socrates, Democritus, Stoics, Epicureans, Sceptics, Neo-platonists, etc. 50 pages on Plato; 70 on Aristotle. 2nd German edition tr. by H. E. Cushman. xv + 393pp. 5 3/8 x 8.   T357 Paperbound **$1.75**

INTRODUCTION TO SYMBOLIC LOGIC AND ITS APPLICATIONS, R. Carnap. A comprehensive, rigorous introduction to modern logic by perhaps its greatest living master. Includes demonstrations of applications in mathematics, physics, biology. "Of the rank of a masterpiece," Z. für Mathematik und ihre Grenzgebiete. Over 300 exercises. xvi + 241pp. 5 3/8 x 8.   Clothbound **$4.00**
    S453 Paperbound **$1.85**

SCEPTICISM AND ANIMAL FAITH, G. Santayana. Santayana's unusually lucid exposition of the difference between the independent existence of objects and the essence our mind attributes to them, and of the necessity of scepticism as a form of belief and animal faith as a necessary condition of knowledge. Discusses belief, memory, intuition, symbols, etc. xii + 314pp. 5 3/8 x 8.   T235 Clothbound **$3.50**
    T236 Paperbound **$1.50**

THE ANALYSIS OF MATTER, B. Russell. With his usual brilliance, Russell analyzes physics, causality, scientific inference, Weyl's theory, tensors, invariants, periodicity, etc. in order to discover the basic concepts of scientific thought about matter. "Most thorough treatment of the subject," THE NATION. Introduction. 8 figures. viii + 408pp. 5 3/8 x 8.
    T231 Paperbound **$1.95**

THE SENSE OF BEAUTY, G. Santayana. This important philosophical study of why, when, and how beauty appears, and what conditions must be fulfilled, is in itself a revelation of the beauty of language. "It is doubtful if a better treatment of the subject has since appeared," PEABODY JOURNAL. ix + 275pp. 5 3/8 x 8.   T238 Paperbound **$1.00**

THE CHIEF WORKS OF SPINOZA. In two volumes. Vol. I: The Theologico-Political Treatise and the Political Treatise. Vol. II: On the Improvement of Understanding, The Ethics, and Selected Letters. The permanent and enduring ideas in these works on God, the universe, religion, society, etc., have had tremendous impact on later philosophical works. Introduction. Total of 862pp. 5 3/8 x 8.   T249 Vol. I, Paperbound **$1.50**
    T250 Vol. II, Paperbound **$1.50**

TRAGIC SENSE OF LIFE, M. de Unamuno. The acknowledged masterpiece of one of Spain's most influential thinkers. Between the despair at the inevitable death of man and all his works, and the desire for immortality, Unamuno finds a "saving incertitude." Called "a masterpiece," by the ENCYCLOPAEDIA BRITANNICA. xxx + 332pp. 5 3/8 x 8.
    T257 Paperbound **$1.95**

EXPERIENCE AND NATURE, John Dewey. The enlarged, revised edition of the Paul Carus lectures (1925). One of Dewey's clearest presentations of the philosophy of empirical naturalism which reestablishes the continuity between "inner" experience and "outer" nature. These lectures are among the most significant ever delivered by an American philosopher. 457pp. 5 3/8 x 8.   T471 Paperbound **$1.85**

PHILOSOPHY AND CIVILIZATION IN THE MIDDLE AGES, M. de Wulf. A semi-popular survey of medieval intellectual life, religion, philosophy, science, the arts, etc. that covers feudalism vs. Catholicism, rise of the universities, mendicant orders, and similar topics. Bibliography. viii + 320pp. 5 3/8 x 8.   T284 Paperbound **$1.75**

AN INTRODUCTION TO SCHOLASTIC PHILOSOPHY, M. de Wulf. (Formerly, "Scholasticism Old and New.") Prof. de Wulf covers the central scholastic tradition from St. Anselm, Albertus Magnus, Thomas Aquinas, up to Suarez in the 17th century; and then treats the modern revival of. scholasticism, the Louvain position, relations with Kantianism and positivism, etc. xvi + 271pp. 5 3/8 x 8.   T296 Clothbound **$3.50**
    T283 Paperbound **$1.75**

A HISTORY OF MODERN PHILOSOPHY, H. Höffding. An exceptionally clear and detailed coverage of Western philosophy from the Renaissance to the end of the 19th century. Both major and minor figures are examined in terms of theory of knowledge, logic, cosmology, psychology. Covers Pomponazzi, Bodin, Boehme, Telesius, Bruno, Copernicus, Descartes, Spinoza, Hobbes, Locke, Hume, Kant, Fichte, Schopenhauer, Mill, Spencer, Langer, scores of others. A standard reference work. 2 volumes. Total of 1159pp. 5 3/8 x 8.   T117 Vol. 1, Paperbound **$2.00**
    T118 Vol. 2, Paperbound **$2.00**

LANGUAGE, TRUTH AND LOGIC, A. J. Ayer. The first full-length development of Logical Positivism in English. Building on the work of Schlick, Russell, Carnap, and the Vienna school, Ayer presents the tenets of one of the most important systems of modern philosophical thought. 160pp. 5 3/8 x 8.   T10 Paperbound **$1.25**

ORIENTALIA AND RELIGION

THE MYSTERIES OF MITHRA, F. Cumont. The great Belgian scholar's definitive study of the Persian mystery religion that almost vanquished Christianity in the ideological struggle for the Roman Empire. A masterpiece of scholarly detection that reconstructs secret doctrines, organization, rites. Mithraic art is discussed and analyzed. 70 illus. 239pp. 5⅜ x 8.
T323 Paperbound **$1.85**

CHRISTIAN AND ORIENTAL PHILOSOPHY OF ART. A. K. Coomaraswamy. The late art historian and orientalist discusses artistic symbolism, the role of traditional culture in enriching art, medieval art, folklore, philosophy of art, other similar topics. Bibliography. 148pp. 5⅜ x 8.
T378 Paperbound **$1.25**

TRANSFORMATION OF NATURE IN ART, A. K. Coomaraswamy. A basic work on Asiatic religious art. Includes discussions of religious art in Asia and Medieval Europe (exemplified by Meister Eckhart), the origin and use of images in Indian art, Indian Medieval aesthetic manuals, and other fascinating, little known topics. Glossaries of Sanskrit and Chinese terms. Bibliography. 41pp. of notes. 245pp. 5⅜ x 8.
T368 Paperbound **$1.75**

ORIENTAL RELIGIONS IN ROMAN PAGANISM, F. Cumont. This well-known study treats the ecstatic cults of Syria and Phrygia (Cybele, Attis, Adonis, their orgies and mutilatory rites); the mysteries of Egypt (Serapis, Isis, Osiris); Persian dualism; Mithraic cults; Hermes Trismegistus, Ishtar, Astarte, etc. and their influence on the religious thought of the Roman Empire. Introduction. 55pp. of notes; extensive bibliography. xxiv + 298pp. 5⅜ x 8.
T321 Paperbound **$1.75**

ANTHROPOLOGY, SOCIOLOGY, AND PSYCHOLOGY

PRIMITIVE MAN AS PHILOSOPHER, P. Radin. A standard anthropological work based on Radin's investigations of the Winnebago, Maori, Batak, Zuni, other primitive tribes. Describes primitive thought on the purpose of life, marital relations, death, personality, gods, etc. Extensive selections of original primitive documents. Bibliography. xviii + 420pp. 5⅜ x 8.
T392 Paperbound **$2.00**

PRIMITIVE RELIGION, P. Radin. Radin's thoroughgoing treatment of supernatural beliefs, shamanism, initiations, religious expression, etc. in primitive societies. Arunta, Ashanti, Aztec, Bushman, Crow, Fijian, many other tribes examined. "Excellent," NATURE. New preface by the author. Bibliographic notes. x + 322pp. 5⅜ x 8.   T393 Paperbound **$1.85**

SEX IN PSYCHO-ANALYSIS, S. Ferenczi. (Formerly, "Contributions to Psycho-analysis.") 14 selected papers on impotence, transference, analysis and children, dreams, obscene words, homosexuality, paranoia, etc. by an associate of Freud. Also included: THE DEVELOPMENT OF PSYCHO-ANALYSIS, by Ferenczi and Otto Rank. Two books bound as one. Total of 406pp. 5⅜ x 8.   T324 Paperbound **$1.85**

THE PRINCIPLES OF PSYCHOLOGY, William James. The complete text of the famous "long course," one of the great books of Western thought. An almost incredible amount of information about psychological processes, the stream of consciousness, habit, time perception, memory, emotions, reason, consciousness of self, abnormal phenomena, and similar topics. Based on James's own discoveries integrated with the work of Descartes, Locke, Hume, Royce, Wundt, Berkeley, Lotse, Herbart, scores of others. "A classic of interpretation," PSYCHIATRIC QUARTERLY. 94 illus. 1408pp. 2 volumes. 5⅜ x 8.
T381 Vol. 1, Paperbound **$2.50**
T382 Vol. 2, Paperbound **$2.50**

THE POLISH PEASANT IN EUROPE AND AMERICA, W. I. Thomas, F. Znaniecki. Monumental sociological study of peasant primary groups (family and community) and the disruptions produced by a new industrial system and emigration to America, by two of the foremost sociologists of recent times. One of the most important works in sociological thought. Includes hundreds of pages of primary documentation; point by point analysis of causes of social decay, breakdown of morality, crime, drunkenness, prostitution, etc. 2nd revised edition. 2 volumes. Total of 2250pp. 6 x 9.   T478 2 volume set, Clothbound **$12.50**

FOLKWAYS, W. G. Sumner. The great Yale sociologist's detailed exposition of thousands of social, sexual, and religious customs in hundreds of cultures from ancient Greece to Modern Western societies. Preface by A. G. Keller. Introduction by William Lyon Phelps. 705pp. 5⅜ x 8.   S508 Paperbound **$2.49**

BEYOND PSYCHOLOGY, Otto Rank. The author, an early associate of Freud, uses psychoanalytic techniques of myth-analysis to explore ultimates of human existence. Treats love, immortality, the soul, sexual identity, kingship, sources of state power, many other topics which illuminate the irrational basis of human existence. 291pp. 5⅜ x 8.   T485 Paperbound **$1.75**

ILLUSIONS AND DELUSIONS OF THE SUPERNATURAL AND THE OCCULT, D. H. Rawcliffe. A rational, scientific examination of crystal gazing, automatic writing, table turning, stigmata, the Indian rope trick, dowsing, telepathy, clairvoyance, ghosts, ESP, PK, thousands of other supposedly occult phenomena. Originally titled "The Psychology of the Occult." 14 illustrations. 551pp. 5⅜ x 8.   T503 Paperbound **$2.00**

YOGA: A SCIENTIFIC EVALUATION, Kovoor T. Behanan. A scientific study of the physiological and psychological effects of Yoga discipline, written under the auspices of the Yale University Institute of Human Relations. Foreword by W. A. Miles, Yale Univ. 17 photographs. 290pp. 5⅜ x 8.   **T505 Paperbound $1.65**

HOAXES, C. D. MacDougall. Delightful, entertaining, yet scholarly exposition of how hoaxes start, why they succeed, documented with stories of hundreds of the most famous hoaxes. "A stupendous collection . . . and shrewd analysis," NEW YORKER. New, revised edition. 54 photographs. 320pp. 5⅜ x 8.   **T465 Paperbound $1.75**

CREATIVE POWER: THE EDUCATION OF YOUTH IN THE CREATIVE ARTS, Hughes Mearns. Named by the National Education Association as one of the 20 foremost books on education in recent times. Tells how to help children express themselves in drama, poetry, music, art, develop latent creative power. Should be read by every parent, teacher. New, enlarged, revised edition. Introduction. 272pp. 5⅜ x 8.   **T490 Paperbound $1.50**

LANGUAGES

NEW RUSSIAN-ENGLISH, ENGLISH-RUSSIAN DICTIONARY, M. A. O'Brien. Over 70,000 entries in new orthography! Idiomatic usages, colloquialisms. One of the few dictionaries that indicate accent changes in conjugation and declension. "One of the best," Prof. E. J. Simmons, Cornell. First names, geographical terms, bibliography, many other features. 738pp. 4½ x 6¼.
T208 Paperbound $2.00

MONEY CONVERTER AND TIPPING GUIDE FOR EUROPEAN TRAVEL, C. Vomacka. Invaluable, handy source of currency regulations, conversion tables, tipping rules, postal rates, much other travel information for every European country plus Israel, Egypt and Turkey. 128pp. 3½ x 5¼.
T260 Paperbound 60¢

MONEY CONVERTER AND TIPPING GUIDE FOR TRAVEL IN THE AMERICAS (including the United States and Canada), **C. Vomacka.** The information you need for informed and confident travel in the Americas: money conversion tables, tipping guide, postal, telephone rates, etc. 128pp. 3½ x 5¼.
T261 Paperbound 65¢

DUTCH-ENGLISH, ENGLISH-DUTCH DICTIONARY, F. G. Renier. The most convenient, practical Dutch-English dictionary on the market. New orthography. More than 60,000 entries: idioms, compounds, technical terms, etc. Gender of nouns indicated. xviii + 571pp. 5½ x 6¼.
T224 Clothbound $2.50

LEARN DUTCH!, F. G. Renier. The most satisfactory and easily-used grammar of modern Dutch. Used and recommended by the Fulbright Committee in the Netherlands. Over 1200 simple exercises lead to mastery of spoken and written Dutch. Dutch-English, English-Dutch vocabularies. 181pp. 4¼ x 7¼.
T441 Clothbound $1.75

PHRASE AND SENTENCE DICTIONARY OF SPOKEN RUSSIAN, English-Russian, Russian-English. Based on phrases and complete sentences, rather than isolated words; recognized as one of the best methods of learning the idiomatic speech of a country. Over 11,500 entries, indexed by single words, with more than 32,000 English and Russian sentences and phrases, in immediately usable form. Probably the largest list ever published. Shows accent changes in conjugation and declension; irregular forms listed in both alphabetical place and under main form of word. 15,000 word introduction covering Russian sounds, writing, grammar, syntax. 15-page appendix of geographical names, money, important signs, given names, foods, special Soviet terms, etc. Travellers, businessmen, students, government employees have found this their best source for Russian expressions. Originally published as U.S. Government Technical Manual TM 30-944. iv + 573pp. 5⅝ x 8⅜.   **T496 Paperbound $2.75**

PHRASE AND SENTENCE DICTIONARY OF SPOKEN SPANISH, Spanish-English, English-Spanish. Compiled from spoken Spanish, emphasizing idiom and colloquial usage in both Castilian and Latin-American. More than 16,000 entries containing over 25,000 idioms—the largest list of idiomatic constructions ever published. Complete sentences given, indexed under single words —language in immediately usable form, for travellers, businessmen, students, etc. 25-page introduction provides rapid survey of sounds, grammar, syntax, with full consideration of irregular verbs. Especially apt in modern treatment of phrases and structure. 17-page glossary gives translations of geographical names, money values, numbers, national holidays, important street signs, useful expressions of high frequency, plus unique 7-page glossary of Spanish and Spanish-American foods and dishes. Originally published as U.S. Government Technical Manual TM 30-900. iv + 513pp. 5⅝ x 8⅜.   **T495 Paperbound $1.75**

SAY IT language phrase books

"SAY IT" in the foreign language of your choice! We have sold over ½ million copies of these popular, useful language books. They will not make you an expert linguist overnight, but they do cover most practical matters of everyday life abroad.

Over 1000 useful phrases, expressions, with additional variants, substitutions.

Modern! Useful! Hundreds of phrases not available in other texts: "Nylon," "air-conditioned," etc.

The ONLY inexpensive phrase book **completely indexed.** Everything is available at a flip of your finger, ready for use.

Prepared by native linguists, travel experts.

Based on years of travel experience abroad.

This handy phrase book may be used by itself, or it may supplement any other text or course; it provides a living element. Used by many colleges and institutions: Hunter College; Barnard College; Army Ordnance School, Aberdeen; and many others.

Available, 1 book per language:

Danish (T818) 75¢	**Italian** (T806) 60¢
Dutch T(817) 75¢	**Japanese** (T807) 60¢
English (for German-speaking people) (T801) 60¢	**Norwegian** (T814) 75¢
English (for Italian-speaking people) (T816) 60¢	**Russian** (T810) 75¢
English (for Spanish-speaking people) (T802) 60¢	**Spanish** (T811) 60¢
Esperanto (T820) 75¢	**Turkish** (T821) 75¢
French (T803) 60¢	**Yiddish** (T815) 75¢
German (T804) 60¢	**Swedish** (T812) 75¢
Modern Greek (T813) 75¢	**Polish** (T808) 75¢
Hebrew (T805) 60¢	**Portuguese** (T809) 75¢

LISTEN & LEARN language record sets

LISTEN & LEARN is the only language record course designed especially to meet your travel needs, or help you learn essential foreign language quickly by yourself, or in conjunction with any school course, by means of the automatic association method. Each set contains three 33⅓ rpm long-playing records — 1½ hours of recorded speech by eminent native speakers who are professors at Columbia, N.Y.U., Queens College and other leading universities. The sets are priced far below other sets of similar quality, yet they contain many special features not found in other record sets:

* Over 800 selected phrases and sentences, a basic vocabulary of over 3200 words.
* Both English and foreign language recorded; with a pause for your repetition.
* Designed for persons with limited time; no time wasted on material you cannot use immediately.
* Living, modern expressions that answer modern needs: drugstore items, "air-conditioned," etc.
* 128-196 page manuals contain everything on the records, plus simple pronunciation guides.
* Manual is fully indexed; find the phrase you want instantly.
* High fidelity recording—equal to any records costing up to $6 each.

The phrases on these records cover 41 different categories useful to the traveller or student interested in learning the living, spoken language: greetings, introductions, making yourself understood, passing customs, planes, trains, boats, buses, taxis, nightclubs, restaurants, menu items, sports, concerts, cameras, automobile travel, repairs, drugstores, doctors, dentists, medicines, barber shops, beauty parlors, laundries, many, many more.

"Excellent . . . among the very best on the market," Prof. Mario Pei, Dept. of Romance Languages, Columbia University. "Inexpensive and well-done . . . an ideal present," CHICAGO SUNDAY TRIBUNE. "More genuinely helpful than anything of its kind which I have previously encountered," Sidney Clark, well-known author of "ALL THE BEST" travel books. Each set contains 3   33⅓ rpm pure vinyl records, 128- 196 page   with full record text, and album. One language per set. LISTEN & LEARN record sets are now available in—

FRENCH	the set $4.95		**GERMAN**	the set $4.95
ITALIAN	the set $4.95		**SPANISH**	the set $4.95
RUSSIAN	the set $5.95		**JAPANESE** *	the set $5.95

* Available Sept. 1, 1959

UNCONDITIONAL GUARANTEE: Dover Publications stands behind every Listen and Learn record set. If you are dissatisfied with these sets for any reason whatever, return them within 10 days and your money will be refunded in full.

ART HISTORY

STICKS AND STONES, Lewis Mumford. An examination of forces influencing American architecture: the medieval tradition in early New England, the classical influence in Jefferson's time, the Brown Decades, the imperial facade, the machine age, etc. "A truly remarkable book," SAT. REV. OF LITERATURE. 2nd revised edition. 21 illus. xvii + 228pp. 5⅜ x 8.
T202 Paperbound **$1.60**

THE AUTOBIOGRAPHY OF AN IDEA, Louis Sullivan. The architect whom Frank Lloyd Wright called "the master," records the development of the theories that revolutionized America's skyline. 34 full-page plates of Sullivan's finest work. New introduction by R. M. Line. xiv + 335pp. 5⅜ x 8.
T281 Paperbound **$1.85**

THE MATERIALS AND TECHNIQUES OF MEDIEVAL PAINTING, D. V. Thompson. An invaluable study of carriers and grounds, binding media, pigments, metals used in painting, al fresco and al secco techniques, burnishing, etc. used by the medieval masters. Preface by Bernard Berenson. 239pp. 5⅜ x 8.
T327 Paperbound **$1.85**

PRINCIPLES OF ART HISTORY, H. Wölfflin. This remarkably instructive work demonstrates the tremendous change in artistic conception from the 14th to the 18th centuries, by analyzing 164 works by Botticelli, Dürer, Hobbema, Holbein, Hals, Titian, Rembrandt, Vermeer, etc., and pointing out exactly what is meant by "baroque," "classic," "primitive," "picturesque," and other basic terms of art history and criticism. "A remarkable lesson in the art of seeing," SAT. REV. OF LITERATURE. Translated from the 7th German edition. 150 illus. 254pp. 6⅛ x 9¼.
T276 Paperbound **$2.00**

FOUNDATIONS OF MODERN ART, A. Ozenfant. Stimulating discussion of human creativity from paleolithic cave painting to modern painting, architecture, decorative arts. Fully illustrated with works of Gris, Lipchitz, Léger, Picasso, primitive, modern artifacts, architecture, industrial art, much more. 226 illustrations. 368pp. 6⅛ x 9¼.
T215 Paperbound **$1.95**

HANDICRAFTS, APPLIED ART, ART SOURCES, ETC.

WILD FOWL DECOYS, J. Barber. The standard work on this fascinating branch of folk art, ranging from Indian mud and grass devices to realistic wooden decoys. Discusses styles, types, periods; gives full information on how to make decoys. 140 illustrations (including 14 new plates) show decoys and provide full sets of plans for handicrafters, artists, hunters, and students of folk art. 281pp. 7⅞ x 10¾. Deluxe edition.
T11 Clothbound **$8.50**

METALWORK AND ENAMELLING, H. Maryon. Probably the best book ever written on the subject. Tells everything necessary for the home manufacture of jewelry, rings, ear pendants, bowls, etc. Covers materials, tools, soldering, filigree, setting stones, raising patterns, repoussé work, damascening, niello, cloisonné, polishing, assaying, casting, and dozens of other techniques. The best substitute for apprenticeship to a master metalworker. 363 photos and figures. 374pp. 5½ x 8½.
T183 Clothbound **$7.50**

SHAKER FURNITURE, E. D. and F. Andrews. The most illuminating study of Shaker furniture ever written. Covers chronology, craftsmanship, houses, shops, etc. Includes over 200 photographs of chairs, tables, clocks, beds, benches, etc. "Mr. & Mrs. Andrews know all there is to know about Shaker furniture," Mark Van Doren, NATION. 48 full-page plates. 192pp. Deluxe cloth binding. 7⅞ x 10¾.
T7 Clothbound **$6.00**

PRIMITIVE ART, Franz Boas. A great American anthropologist covers theory, technical virtuosity, styles, symbolism, patterns, etc. of primitive art. The more than 900 illustrations will interest artists, designers, craftworkers. Over 900 illustrations. 376pp. 5⅜ x 8.
T25 Paperbound **$1.95**

ON THE LAWS OF JAPANESE PAINTING, H. Bowie. The best possible substitute for lessons from an oriental master. Treats both spirit and technique; exercises for control of the brush; inks, brushes, colors; use of dots, lines to express whole moods, etc. 220 illus. 132pp. 6⅛ x 9¼.
T30 Paperbound **$1.95**

HANDBOOK OF ORNAMENT, F. S. Meyer. One of the largest collections of copyright-free traditional art: over 3300 line cuts of Greek, Roman, Medieval, Renaissance, Baroque, 18th and 19th century art motifs (tracery, geometric elements, flower and animal motifs, etc.) and decorated objects (chairs, thrones, weapons, vases, jewelry, armor, etc.). Full text. 3300 illustrations. 562pp. 5⅜ x 8.
T302 Paperbound **$2.00**

THREE CLASSICS OF ITALIAN CALLIGRAPHY. Oscar Ogg, ed. Exact reproductions of three famous Renaissance calligraphic works: Arrighi's OPERINA and IL MODO, Tagliente's LO PRESENTE LIBRO, and Palatino's LIBRO NUOVO. More than 200 complete alphabets, thousands of lettered specimens, in Papal Chancery and other beautiful, ornate handwriting. Introduction. 245 plates. 282pp. 6⅛ x 9¼.
T212 Paperbound **$1.95**

THE HISTORY AND TECHNIQUES OF LETTERING, A. Nesbitt. A thorough history of lettering from the ancient Egyptians to the present, and a 65-page course in lettering for artists. Every major development in lettering history is illustrated by a complete alphabet. Fully analyzes such masters as Caslon, Koch, Garamont, Jenson, and many more. 89 alphabets, 165 other specimens. 317pp. 5⅜ x 8.
T427 Paperbound **$2.00**

LETTERING AND ALPHABETS, J. A. Cavanagh. An unabridged reissue of "Lettering," containing the full discussion, analysis, illustration of 89 basic hand lettering tyles based on Caslon, Bodoni, Gothic, many other types. Hundreds of technical hints on construction, strokes, pens, brushes, etc. 89 alphabets, 72 lettered specimens, which may be reproduced permission-free. 121pp. 9¾ x 8.　　　　　　　　　　　　　　　　　　　　　**T53 Paperbound $1.25**

THE HUMAN FIGURÉ IN MOTION, Eadweard Muybridge. The largest collection in print of Muybridge's famous high-speed action photos. 4789 photographs in more than 500 action-strip-sequences (at shutter speeds up to 1/6000th of a second) illustrate men, women, children—mostly undraped—performing such actions as walking, running, getting up, lying down, carrying objects, throwing, etc. "An unparalleled dictionary of action for all artists," AMERICAN ARTIST. 390 full-page plates, with 4789 photographs. Heavy glossy stock, reinforced binding with headbands. 7⅞ x 10¾.　　　　　　　　　　　　　**T204 Clothbound $10.00**

ANIMALS IN MOTION, Eadweard Muybridge. The largest collection of animal action photos in print. 34 different animals (horses, mules, oxen, goats, camels, pigs, cats, lions, gnus, deer, monkeys, eagles—and 22 others) in 132 characteristic actions. All 3919 photographs are taken in series at speeds up to 1/1600th of a second, offering artists, biologists, cartoonists a remarkable opportunity to see exactly how an ostrich's head bobs when running, how a lion puts his foot down, how an elephant's knee bends, how a bird flaps his wings, thousands of other hard-to-catch details. "A really marvelous series of plates," NATURE. 380 full-pages of plates. Heavy glossy stock, reinforced binding with headbands. 7⅞ x10¾.　　　　　　　　　　　　　　　　　　　　　　**T203 Clothbound $10.00**

THE BOOK OF SIGNS, R. Koch. 493 symbols—crosses, monograms, astrological, biological symbols, runes, etc.—from ancient manuscripts, cathedrals, coins, catacombs, pottery. May be reproduced permission-free. 493 illustrations by Fritz Kredel. 104pp. 6⅛ x 9¼.　　　　　　　　　　　　　　　　　　　　　　　　　　　**T162 Paperbound $1.00**

A HANDBOOK OF EARLY ADVERTISING ART, C. P. Hornung. The largest collection of copyright-free early advertising art ever compiled. Vol. I: 2,000 illustrations of animals, old automobiles, buildings, allegorical figures, fire engines, Indians, ships, trains, more than 33 other categories! Vol II: Over 4,000 typographical specimens; 600 Roman, Gothic, Barnum, Old English faces; 630 ornamental type faces; hundreds of scrolls, initials, flourishes, etc. "A remarkable collection," PRINTERS' INK.

Vol. I: Pictorial Volume. Over 2000 illustrations. 256pp. 9 x 12.　　**T122 Clothbound $10.00**
Vol. II: Typographical Volume. Over 4000 speciments. 319pp. 9 x 12.　**T123 Clothbound $10.00**
　　　　　　　　　　　　　　　　　Two volume set, Clothbound, only **$18.50**

DESIGN FOR ARTISTS AND CRAFTSMEN, L. Wolchonok. The most thorough course on the creation of art motifs and designs. Shows you step-by-step, with hundreds of examples and 113 detailed exercises, how to create original designs from geometric patterns, plants, birds, animals, humans, and man-made objects. "A great contribution to the field of design and crafts," N. Y. SOCIETY OF CRAFTSMEN. More than 1300 entirely new illustrations. xv + 207pp. 7⅞ x 10¾.　　　　　　　　　　　　　　　　　**T274 Clothbound $4.95**

HANDBOOK OF DESIGNS AND DEVICES, C. P. Hornung. A remarkable working collection of 1836 basic designs and variations, all copyright-free. Variations of circle, line, cross, diamond, swastika, star, scroll, shield, many more. Notes on symbolism. "A necessity to every 'designer who would be original without having to labor heavily," ARTIST and ADVERTISER. 204 plates. 240pp. 5⅜ x 8.
　　　　　　　　　　　　　　　　　　　　　　　　　　T125 Paperbound $1.90

THE UNIVERSAL PENMAN, George Bickham. Exact reproduction of beautiful 18th century book of handwriting. 22 complete alphabets in finest English roundhand, other scripts, over 2000 elaborate flourishes, 122 calligraphic illustrations, etc. Material is copyright-free. "An essential part of any art library, and a book of permanent value," AMERICAN ARTIST. 212 plates. 224pp. 9 x 13¾.　　　　　　　　　　　　　　　　　**T20 Clothbound $10.00**

AN ATLAS OF ANATOMY FOR ARTISTS, F. Schider. This standard work contains 189 full-page plates, more than 647 illustrations of all aspects of the human skeleton, musculature, cutaway portions of the body, each part of the anatomy, hand forms, eyelids, breasts, location of muscles under the flesh, etc. 59 plates illustrate how Michelangelo, da Vinci, Goya, 15 others, drew human anatomy. New 3rd edition enlarged by 52 new illustrations by Cloquet, Barcsay. "The standard reference tool," AMERICAN LIBRARY ASSOCIATION. "Excellent," AMERICAN ARTIST. 189 plates, 647 illustrations. xxvi + 192pp. 7⅞ x 10⅝.　　**T241 Clothbound $6.00**

AN ATLAS OF ANIMAL ANATOMY FOR ARTISTS, W. Ellenberger, H. Baum, H. Dittrich. The largest, richest animal anatomy for artists in English. Form, musculature, tendons, bone structure, expression, detailed cross sections of head, other features, of the horse, lion, dog, cat, deer, seal, kangaroo, cow, bull, goat, monkey, hare, many other animals. "Highly recommended," DESIGN. Second, revised, enlarged edition with new plates from Cuvier, Stubbs, etc. 288 illustrations. 153pp. 11⅜ x 9.　　　　　　　　　　　　　　　　　**T82 Clothbound $6.00**

ANIMAL DRAWING: ANATOMY AND ACTION FOR ARTISTS, C. R. Knight. 158 studies, with full accompanying text, of such animals as the gorilla, bear, bison, dromedary, camel, vulture, pelican, iguana, shark, etc., by one of the greatest modern masters of animal drawing. Innumerable tips on how to get life expression into your work. "An excellent reference work,' SAN FRANCISCO CHRONICLE. 158 illustrations. 156pp. 10½ x 8½.
　　　　　　　　　　　　　　　　　　　　　　　　　　T426 Paperbound $2.00

DOVER BOOKS

THE CRAFTSMAN'S HANDBOOK, Cennino Cennini. The finest English translation of IL LIBRO DELL' ARTE, the 15th century introduction to art technique that is both a mirror of Quatrocento life and a source of many useful but nearly forgotten facets of the painter's art. 4 illustrations. xxvii + 142pp. D. V. Thompson, translator. 6⅛ x 9¼.   T54 Paperbound **$1.50**

THE BROWN DECADES, Lewis Mumford. A picture of the "buried renaissance" of the post-Civil War period, and the founding of modern architecture (Sullivan, Richardson, Root, Roebling), landscape development (Marsh, Olmstead, Eliot), and the graphic arts (Homer, Eakins, Ryder). 2nd revised, enlarged edition. Bibliography. 12 illustrations. xiv + 266 pp. 5⅜ x 8.   T200 Paperbound **$1.65**

STIEGEL GLASS, F. W. Hunter. The story of the most highly esteemed early American glassware, fully illustrated. How a German adventurer, "Baron" Stiegel, founded a glass empire; detailed accounts of individual glasswork. "This pioneer work is reprinted in an edition even more beautiful than the original," ANTIQUES DEALER. New introduction by Helen McKearin. 171 illustrations, 12 in full color. xxii + 338pp. 7⅞ x 10¾.
     T128 Clothbound **$10.00**

THE HUMAN FIGURE, J. H. Vanderpoel. Not just a picture book, but a complete course by a famous figure artist. Extensive text, illustrated by 430 pencil and charcoal drawings of both male and female anatomy. 2nd enlarged edition. Foreword. 430 illus. 143pp. 6⅛ x 9¼.
     T432 Paperbound **$1.45**

PINE FURNITURE OF EARLY NEW ENGLAND, R. H. Kettell. Over 400 illustrations, over 50 working drawings of early New England chairs, benches, beds cupboards, mirrors, shelves, tables, other furniture esteemed for simple beauty and character. "Rich store of illustrations . . . emphasizes the individuality and varied design," ANTIQUES. 413 illustrations, 55 working drawings. 475pp. 8 x 10¾.   T145 Clothbound **$10.00**

BASIC BOOKBINDING, A. W. Lewis. Enables both beginners and experts to rebind old books or bind paperbacks in hard covers. Treats materials, tools; gives step-by-step instruction in how to collate a book, sew it, back it, make boards, etc. 261 illus. Appendices. 155pp. 5⅜ x 8.   T169 Paperbound **$1.35**

DESIGN MOTIFS OF ANCIENT MEXICO, J. Enciso. Nearly 90% of these 766 superb designs from Aztec, Olmec, Totonac, Maya, and Toltec origins are unobtainable elsewhere! Contains plumed serpents, wind gods, animals, demons, dancers, monsters, etc. Excellent applied design source. Originally $17.50. 766 illustrations, thousands of motifs. 192pp. 6⅛ x 9¼.
     T84 Paperbound **$1.85**

AFRICAN SCULPTURE, Ladislas Segy. 163 full-page plates illustrating masks, fertility figures, ceremonial objects, etc., of 50 West and Central African tribes—95% never before illustrated. 34-page introduction to African sculpture. "Mr. Segy is one of its top authorities," NEW YORKER. 164 full-page photographic plates. Introduction. Bibliography. 244pp. 6⅛ x 9¼.
     T396 Paperbound **$2.00**

THE PROCESSES OF GRAPHIC REPRODUCTION IN PRINTING, H. Curwen. A thorough and practical survey of wood, linoleum, and rubber engraving; copper engraving; drypoint, mezzotint, etching, aquatint, steel engraving, die sinking, stencilling, lithography (extensively); photographic reproduction utilizing line, continuous tone, photoengravure, collotype; every other process in general use. Note on color reproduction. Section on bookbinding. Over 200 illustrations, 25 in color. 143pp. 5½ x 8½.   T512 Clothbound **$4.00**

CALLIGRAPHY, J. G. Schwandner. First reprinting in 200 years of this legendary book of beautiful handwriting. Over 300 ornamental initials, 12 complete calligraphic alphabets, over 150 ornate frames and panels, 75 calligraphic pictures of cherubs, stags, lions, etc., thousands of flourishes, scrolls, etc., by the greatest 18th century masters. All material can be copied or adapted without permission. Historical introduction. 158 full-page plates. 368pp. 9 x 13.   T475 Clothbound **$10.00**

* * *

A DIDEROT PICTORIAL ENCYCLOPEDIA OF TRADES AND INDUSTRY, Manufacturing and the Technical Arts in Plates Selected from "L'Encyclopédie ou Dictionnaire Raisonné des Sciences, des Arts, et des Métiers," of Denis Diderot, edited with text by C. Gillispie. Over 2000 illustrations on 485 full-page plates. Magnificent 18th century engravings of men, women, and children working at such trades as milling flour, cheesemaking, charcoal burning, mining, silverplating, shoeing horses, making fine glass, printing, hundreds more, showing details of machinery, different steps in sequence, etc. A remarkable art work, but also the largest collection of working figures in print, copyright-free, for art directors, designers, etc. Two vols. 920pp. 9 x 12. Heavy library cloth.   T421 Two volume set **$18.50**

* * *

SILK SCREEN TECHNIQUES, J. Biegeleisen, M. Cohn. A practical step-by-step home course in one of the most versatile, least expensive graphic arts processes. How to build an inexpensive silk screen, prepare stencils, print, achieve special textures, use color, etc. Every step explained, diagrammed. 149 illustrations, 8 in color. 201pp. 6⅛ x 9¼.
     T433 Paperbound **$1.45**

PUZZLES, GAMES, AND ENTERTAINMENTS

MATHEMATICS, MAGIC AND MYSTERY, Martin Gardner. Astonishing feats of mind reading, mystifying "magic" tricks, are often based on mathematical principles anyone can learn. This book shows you how to perform scores of tricks with cards, dice, coins, knots, numbers, etc., by using simple principles from set theory, theory of numbers, topology, other areas of mathematics, fascinating in themselves. No special knowledge required. 135 illus. 186pp. 5⅜ x 8.   T335 Paperbound **$1.00**

MATHEMATICAL PUZZLES FOR BEGINNERS AND ENTHUSIASTS, G. Mott-Smith. Test your problem-solving techniques and powers of inference on 188 challenging, amusing puzzles based on algebra, dissection of plane figures, permutations, probabilities, etc. Appendix of primes, square roots, etc. 135 illus. 2nd revised edition. 248pp. 5⅜ x 8.
T198 Paperbound **$1.00**

LEARN CHESS FROM THE MASTERS, F. Reinfeld. Play 10 games against Marshall, Bronstein, Najdorf, other masters, and grade yourself on each move. Detailed annotations reveal principles of play, strategy, etc. as you proceed. An excellent way to get a real insight into the game. Formerly titled, "Chess by Yourself." 91 diagrams. vii + 144pp. 5⅜ x 8.
T362 Paperbound **$1.00**

REINFELD ON THE END GAME IN CHESS, F. Reinfeld. 62 end games of Alekhine, Tarrasch, Morphy, other masters, are carefully analyzed with emphasis on transition from middle game to end play. Tempo moves, queen endings, weak squares, other basic principles clearly illustrated. Excellent for understanding why some moves are weak or incorrect, how to avoid errors. Formerly titled, "Practical End-game Play." 62 diagrams. vi + 177pp. 5⅜ x 8.
T417 Paperbound **$1.25**

101 PUZZLES IN THOUGHT AND LOGIC, C. R. Wylie, Jr. Brand new puzzles you need no special knowledge to solve! Each one is a gem of ingenuity that will really challenge your problem-solving technique. Introduction with simplified explanation of scientic puzzle solving. 128pp. 5⅜ x 8.   T167 Paperbound **$1.00**

THE COMPLETE NONSENSE OF EDWARD LEAR. The only complete edition of this master of gentle madness at a popular price. The Dong with the Luminous Nose, The Jumblies, The Owl and the Pussycat, hundreds of other bits of wonderful nonsense. 214 limericks, 3 sets of Nonsense Botany, 5 Nonsense Alphabets, 546 fantastic drawings, much more. 320pp. 5⅜ x 8.   T167 Paperbound **$1.00**

28 SCIENCE FICTION STORIES OF H. G. WELLS. Two complete novels, "Men Like Gods" and "Star Begotten," plus 26 short stories by the master science-fiction writer of all time. Stories of space, time, future adventure that are among the all-time classics of science fiction. 928pp. 5⅜ x 8.   T265 Clothbound **$3.95**

SEVEN SCIENCE FICTION NOVELS, H. G. Wells. Unabridged texts of "The Time Machine," "The Island of Dr. Moreau," "First Men in the Moon," "The Invisible Man," "The War of the Worlds," "The Food of the Gods," "In the Days of the Comet." "One will have to go so far to match this for entertainment, excitement, and sheer pleasure," N. Y. TIMES. 1015pp. 5⅜ x 8.   T264 Clothbound **$3.95**

MATHEMAGIC, MAGIC PUZZLES, AND GAMES WITH NUMBERS, R. V. Heath. More than 60 new puzzles and stunts based on number properties: multiplying large numbers mentally, finding the date of any day in the year, etc. Edited by J. S. Meyer. 76 illus. 129pp. 5⅜ x 8.
T110 Paperbound **$1.00**

FIVE ADVENTURE NOVELS OF H. RIDER HAGGARD. The master story-teller's five best tales of mystery and adventure set against authentic African backgrounds: "She," "King Solomon's Mines," "Allan Quatermain," "Allan's Wife," "Maiwa's Revenge." 821pp. 5⅜ x 8.
T108 Clothbound **$3.95**

WIN AT CHECKERS, M. Hopper. (Formerly "Checkers.") The former World's Unrestricted Checker Champion gives you valuable lessons in openings, traps, end games, ways to draw when you are behind, etc. More than 100 questions and answers anticipate your problems. Appendix. 75 problems diagrammed, solved. 79 figures. xi + 107pp. 5⅜ x 8.
T363 Paperbound **$1.00**

CRYPTOGRAPHY, L. D. Smith. Excellent introductory work on ciphers and their solution, history of secret writing, techniques, etc. Appendices on Japanese methods, the Baconian cipher, frequency tables. Bibliography. Over 150 problems, solutions. 160pp. 5⅜ x 8.
T247 Paperbound **$1.00**

CRYPTANALYSIS, H. F. Gaines. (Formerly, "Elementary Cryptanalysis.") The best book available on cryptograms and how to solve them. Contains all major techniques: substitution, transposition, mixed alphabets, multafid, Kasiski and Vignere methods, etc. Word frequency appendix. 167 problems, solutions. 173 figures. 236pp. 5⅜ x 8.   T97 Paperbound **$1.95**

FLATLAND, E. A. Abbot. The science-fiction classic of life in a 2-dimensional world that is considered a first-rate introduction to relativity and hyperspace, as well as a scathing satire on society, politics and religion. 7th edition. 16 illus. 128pp. 5⅜ x 8.
T1 Paperbound **$1.00**

DOVER BOOKS

HOW TO FORCE CHECKMATE, F. Reinfeld. (Formerly "Challenge to Chessplayers.") No board needed to sharpen your checkmate skill on 300 checkmate situations. Learn to plan up to 3 moves ahead and play a superior end game. 300 situations diagrammed; notes and full solutions. 111pp. 5⅜ x 8.
T439 Paperbound **$1.25**

MORPHY'S GAMES OF CHESS, P. W. Sergeant, ed. Play forcefully by following the techniques used by one of the greatest chess champions. 300 of Morphy's games carefully annotated to reveal principles. Bibliography. New introduction by F. Reinfeld. 235 diagrams. x + 352pp. 5⅜ x 8.
T386 Paperbound **$1.75**

MATHEMATICAL RECREATIONS, M. Kraitchik. Hundreds of unusual mathematical puzzlers and odd bypaths of math, elementary and advanced. Greek, Medieval, Arabic, Hindu problems; figurate numbers, Fermat numbers, primes; magic, Euler, Latin squares; fairy chess, latruncles, reversi, jinx, ruma, tetrachrome other positional and permutational games. Rigorous solutions. Revised second edition. 181 illus. 330pp. 5⅜ x 8.
T163 Paperbound **$1.75**

MATHEMATICAL EXCURSIONS, H. A. Merrill. Revealing stimulating insights into elementary math, not usually taught in school. 90 problems demonstrate Russian peasant multiplication, memory systems for pi, magic squares, dyadic systems, division by inspection, many more. Solutions to difficult problems. 50 illus. 5⅜ x 8.
T350 Paperbound **$1.00**

MAGIC TRICKS & CARD TRICKS, W. Jonson. Best introduction to tricks with coins, bills, eggs, ribbons, slates, cards, easily performed without elaborate equipment. Professional routines, tips on presentation, misdirection, etc. Two books bound as one: 52 tricks with cards, 37 tricks with common objects. 106 figures. 224pp. 5⅜ x 8.
T909 Paperbound **$1.00**

MATHEMATICAL PUZZLES OF SAM LOYD, selected and edited by **M. Gardner.** 177 most ingenious mathematical puzzles of America's greatest puzzle originator, based on arithmetic, algebra, game theory, dissection, route tracing, operations research, probability, etc. 120 drawings, diagrams. Solutions. 187pp. 5⅜ x 8.
T498 Paperbound **$1.00**

THE ART OF CHESS, J. Mason. The most famous general study of chess ever written. More than 90 openings, middle game, end game, how to attack, sacrifice, defend, exchange, form general strategy. Supplement on "How Do You Play Chess?" by F. Reinfeld. 448 diagrams. 356pp. 5⅜ x 8.
T463 Paperbound **$1.85**

HYPERMODERN CHESS as Developed in the Games of its Greatest Exponent, ARON NIMZOVICH, F. Reinfeld, ed. Learn how the game's greatest innovator defeated Alekhine, Lasker, and many others; and use these methods in your own game. 180 diagrams. 228pp. 5⅜ x 8.
T448 Paperbound **$1.35**

A TREASURY OF CHESS LORE, F. Reinfeld, ed. Hundreds of fascinating stories by and about the masters, accounts of tournaments and famous games, aphorisms, word portraits, little known incidents, photographs, etc., that will delight the chess enthusiast captivate the beginner. 49 photographs (14 full-page plates), 12 diagrams. 315pp. 5⅜ x 8.
T458 Paperbound **$1.75**

A NONSENSE ANTHOLOGY, collected by **Carolyn Wells.** 245 of the best nonsense verses ever written: nonsense puns, absurd arguments, mock epics, nonsense ballads, "sick" verses, dog-Latin verses, French nonsense verses, limericks. Lear, Carroll, Belloc, Burgess, nearly 100 other writers. Introduction by Carolyn Wells. 3 indices: Title, Author, First Lines. xxxiii + 279pp. 5⅜ x 8.
T499 Paperbound **$1.25**

SYMBOLIC LOGIC and THE GAME OF LOGIC, Lewis Carroll. Two delightful puzzle books by the author of "Alice," bound as one. Both works concern the symbolic representation of traditional logic and together contain more than 500 ingenious, amusing and instructive syllogistic puzzlers. Total of 326pp. 5⅜ x 8.
T492 Paperbound **$1.50**

PILLOW PROBLEMS and A TANGLED TALE, Lewis Carroll. Two of Carroll's rare puzzle works bound as one. "Pillow Problems" contain 72 original math puzzles. The puzzles in "A Tangled Tale" are given in delightful story form. Total of 291pp. 5⅜ x 8.
T493 Paperbound **$1.50**

PECK'S BAD BOY AND HIS PA, G. W. Peck. Both volumes of one of the most widely read of all American humor books. A classic of American folk humor, also invaluable as a portrait of an age. 100 original illustrations. Introduction by E. Bleiler. 347pp. 5⅜ x 8.
T497 Paperbound **$1.35**

Dover publishes books on art, music, philosophy, literature, languages, history, social sciences, psychology, handcrafts, orientalia, puzzles and entertainments, chess, pets and gardens, books explaining science, intermediate and higher mathematics mathematical physics, engineering, biological sciences, earth sciences, classics of science, etc. Write to:

Dept. catrr.
Dover Publications, Inc.
180 Varick Street, N. Y. 14, N. Y.